"You could kiss me."

She'd said it without thinking. But deep down she knew it was because she wanted him to. It had nothing to do with putting on a show for Mia.

He raised his eyebrows. "Now? Here?"

She tilted her head up just a fraction, her lips inches from his. "Mia is just a few feet away. I think this is the perfect time for some handsy-ness. Unless you want to wait until—"

"Sometimes you talk too much."

Tomás whispered the last few words against her mouth. When she didn't protest, he pushed in for a kiss.

The
Cowboy
Whisperer

Other Books by Sabrina Sol

Second Chance at Rancho Lindo

The
Cowboy
Whisperer

Cowboys of Rancho Lindo

Sabrina Sol

FOREVER

New York   Boston

Forever
Hachette Book Group
1290 Avenue of the Americas, New York, NY 10104
read-forever.com
twitter.com/readforeverpub

First Mass Market Edition: November 2023

Forever is an imprint of Grand Central Publishing. The Forever name and logo are trademarks of Hachette Book Group, Inc.

The publisher is not responsible for websites (or their content) that are not owned by the publisher.

The Hachette Speakers Bureau provides a wide range of authors for speaking events. To find out more, go to hachettespeakersbureau.com or email HachetteSpeakers@hbgusa.com.

Forever books may be purchased in bulk for business, educational, or promotional use. For information, please contact your local bookseller or the Hachette Book Group Special Markets Department at special.markets@hbgusa.com.

ISBNs: 978-1-5387-2232-9 (Mass Market); 978-1-5387-2233-6 (ebook)

Printed in the United States of America

OPM

10 9 8 7 6 5 4 3 2 1

For those who got back in the saddle and rode again.

The
Cowboy
Whisperer

Chapter One

If he didn't know any better, Tomás could've sworn he'd stepped into the Twilight Zone instead of a cottage on the grounds of Rancho Lindo.

It would be the only explanation why he was currently listening to his brother Gabe have an intense discussion over throw pillows.

"It's too many, Nora," Gabe said, clutching one of them like a football. This offender was gray and rectangle-shaped and boasted the word *Blessed* in a script font. "Where the hell is the poor woman going to sit?"

Nora was the ranch's horticulturist and Gabe's girlfriend. Tomás wondered if she was just as flabbergasted at his brother's impassioned argument over the subject. He had never known Gabe, a retired soldier, to care about room décor so much.

If Nora was taken aback, though, she didn't show it.

"She can move them when she needs to sit," she said. "I think the pillows make the room more homey, more welcoming."

"Well, I think it looks like we grabbed all the pillows from Target and threw them in here."

Tomás walked farther into the small living room. "Do you want to know what I think?"

"No," Gabe said.

"Of course," Nora answered at the same time.

He shot an annoyed look at his older brother and opened his mouth anyway. "I think the pillows are the least of our problems. The cottage still needs a lot of work. The water temp is wonky, some of the drawers in the kitchen still get stuck if you open them too fast, and don't get me started on that front porch. This place has been vacant for over a year and you think someone is actually going to want to sleep here after a quick patch-and-paint job? You and Cruz never should've said yes to this."

This was an agreement to let a woman and her horse stay at Rancho Lindo for the next three months while she trained for some sort of equestrian competition. He had no idea how she knew about the ranch, especially since he'd only started accepting stable boarders at the end of last year. He'd had a total of three clients since. And even though Rancho Lindo was one of the biggest properties in Esperanza, California, it was not, nor had it ever been, known as a professional equestrian training facility. They also had never let anyone, outside of family members or employees, live on the ranch.

This woman's seemingly out-of-the-blue proposal demanded a lot of firsts for them. Tomás would bet good money that this was not going to be the smooth experience his brothers were expecting.

"You know exactly why we said yes." Gabe threw the pillow back onto the small love seat with its friends.

Tomás did. The ranch had been in their family for

four generations. Their father had been running the ranch until he got sick last year. His oldest brother, Cruz, who had always been second in charge, took over managing the business full-time while their dad was undergoing treatment for prostate cancer. And when an injury forced Gabe to leave the army, he came home to Rancho Lindo and began helping Cruz. His other brothers, Nico and Daniel, also worked on the ranch and were in charge of the cattle. He was the horse guy.

But Cruz and Gabe were the ones who knew the most about the ranch's overall finances, and they'd made it clear that they were falling behind on some bills. Tomás and his brothers didn't aways see eye-to-eye, but they all agreed that they weren't about to be the generation that lost Rancho Lindo. That meant making some hard choices. The reason this particular cottage had been empty for so long was because they hadn't had the money to fill it with a new full-time live-in ranch hand. There were five one-bedroom cottages on the property and only two of them were currently occupied—Nora lived in one of them.

While Tomás admitted the new boarder would help their finances in the short term, he prayed the whole thing wouldn't backfire.

"Well, you guys should've told her to come next week or next month," he grumbled.

"We tried, but the lawyer insisted it had to be this weekend," Gabe explained.

"And what's up with all the secrecy anyway?" he asked.

The name of the woman and the fact that she was training at Rancho Lindo were not to be shared with anyone outside the family. At least that's what Cruz had instructed after reading the contract the woman's lawyer had sent over a few days ago. If that wasn't a red flag, then Tomás didn't know what was.

Gabe stuck his hands into the front pockets of his blue jeans. "I don't know anything more than you do, Tomás. Maybe the lady just wants her privacy? But she's paying us a lot of money to stay here, so we're going to give her whatever she wants, okay?"

When Tomás didn't answer, Gabe repeated, "*Okay*, Tomás?"

"Okay," he finally said.

"Good. You're probably going to be the one who deals with her the most, so we need you to be on board."

He figured the same thing, which was why he was more anxious about it than the rest of his family.

Gabe walked into the kitchen muttering something about "checking those drawers," leaving Nora to continue rearranging pillows.

"I'm sorry," he said to her. "I didn't mean for it to sound like I don't think you did a good job getting this place ready for her."

His friend looked at him over her shoulder. "No need to apologize. I understood what you meant."

When she finally seemed satisfied with what she saw, Nora turned around and faced him and continued the conversation. "I also know that having someone else around your stable every day is going to get some getting used to. That's your space, Tomás. It's normal to feel uneasy about letting a stranger in there."

"What do you mean?" he scoffed. "The guys are in and out of the stable all the time. That doesn't bother me. And you're in there at least once a week when you need to ride to the orchard."

Nora gave him a kind smile. "That's different and we both know it."

"Fine," he admitted. "I don't like the idea. But not for the reason you think."

"Then what is it?" she asked.

"The lady's horse arrived this morning. He's beautiful...and expensive. What if something happens to him while she's here? Rancho Lindo can't afford that. So now it's all on me to make sure nothing does."

She walked closer to him and touched his shoulder. "It's not all on you. Rancho Lindo is a family business. Everyone does their part to make it run. This isn't going to be any different."

As usual, Nora was the calm and reasonable voice he needed to hear. Tomás knew her words were coming from her heart. Despite not officially being an Ortega—well, not yet anyway—Nora loved Rancho Lindo as much as any of them. She'd basically grown up on the ranch too, spending several summers visiting her tío and tía, who'd both worked for his family for many years. After her tío Chucho passed away two years ago, her tía Luz moved to Texas. He knew Nora talked to her every week and was planning to go visit her over the summer.

If Nora was confident that this plan would work, then he decided he would try to believe it.

"I guess," he said with a shrug.

A few seconds passed before Nora spoke again. "So, I was talking to your abuelita earlier. Doña Alma showed me the invitation for the Riveras' thirty-fifth anniversary party next month. I think it's special that Lina and Carlos are going to renew their vows."

Tomás had walked over to check a lock on one of

the living room windows that had been stuck a few days ago. "Yeah," he said without looking back at her. "They eloped when they were eighteen, so Lina told Mom that this is her chance to have a real wedding."

He heard Nora chuckle and continued moving the lock to make sure it wasn't sticking anymore.

"Good for her. Sounds like it's going to be a big event with lots of their family and friends. I'm looking forward to finally meeting Omar and Mia."

The mention of the Riveras' adult children—especially Mia—made him still. He understood now why Nora had brought up the subject of the anniversary party. He turned around and met her eyes.

"Is there something you want to ask me, Nora?" he said softly. Judging by the pinched expression on her face, Tomás could tell there was, but it was obvious that she was worried about bringing it up. "It's fine," he assured her. "Out with it."

She let out a relieved sigh. "Well, we—me and Gabe… and also Daniel and your mom. All right, all of us were wondering how you were feeling about seeing Mia again."

He shrugged again. "Fine, I guess. I saw her last year when she came to visit her parents for Christmas, remember?"

Nora waved her finger. "No, you told me you ran into her. This is going to be different. You're both going to be in the same place for a few hours. It's probably inevitable that you're going to have to talk."

Tomás hadn't thought about it like that. Because the last time they had talked—really, truly had a conversation—was eight years ago when he'd flown to New York for her college graduation prepared to propose at her celebration dinner in front of her parents and brother. Instead, Mia had told him before her commencement ceremony that she'd accepted a job and was going to stay in New York. And that they should break up...for good.

Since then they'd crossed each other's paths only a handful of times when Mia had come back to Esperanza to see her mom and dad. Their parents were best friends, so he was regularly updated on her life in between visits as well.

Still, he'd managed to avoid any social situations where he would be forced to say more than ten words to her. But Nora was right. The Riveras' anniversary party was going to be different.

He wasn't about to admit anything, though. "You can report back to everyone that I will be perfectly fine seeing Mia at the party," Tomás said. "It's not going to be a big deal."

Nora offered him a smile. "Good. I'm glad."

Tomás smiled back, hoping she couldn't see the slight irritation behind his expression. While he knew that his family had good intentions, it did bother him that they couldn't believe he was over Mia. So what if they had dated all through high school and continued a long-distance relationship when she moved away? And so what if he hadn't had a serious girlfriend since Mia? It didn't mean that he was still in love with her or that he couldn't handle being around her. It might be awkward, but only because it had been so long.

He was about to tell Nora all of that when Gabe appeared and announced, "She's about ten minutes away. Tomás, Dad wants you at the house to meet her."

They both nodded and then followed Gabe out the front door of the little cottage. As his brother and

Nora walked ahead of him on the dirt path, Tomás couldn't help but turn around and take one last look at its weathered white wooden panels and roof made of mismatched shingles.

He wasn't sure why, but he felt like they were both about to be tested.

"Good luck to us both," he said.

Chapter Two

Veronica looked out the back passenger-side window of the SUV and sighed.

"There's absolutely nothing here," she said into the phone as the car passed one empty field after another.

"That's the point," her father explained on the other end.

She sighed again.

Her father must have heard it. "Vero, it's only for three months," he answered as if her exhale had been another complaint. "You need this time."

Veronica shook her head to disagree even though she knew he couldn't see it. "What I need is to be in familiar surroundings and around other riders. You know how I thrive in competitive situations. That would help my mental training just as much as my physical training."

It was his turn to sigh into the phone. "The Kentucky center has already had some of the usual reporters poking their noses around. You can't afford to be the target of their chisme."

"Apa, I'm old chisme. They have new riders to gossip about. They couldn't care less about me."

"Is that so? Then why did the manager of the center's stables already get an email from one of those reporters asking why Takuache was moved yesterday?"

Veronica froze at the news. They'd taken so many precautions to make sure her prized stallion was transported safely and quietly to his new temporary home. How had the news spread so swiftly? It was the last thing she had wanted to hear. "Are you serious?"

"You know I wouldn't lie to you about this, Vero."

She hung her head. "Yes, I know."

Her dad was quiet for a few seconds before speaking again. "This is for the best. The ranch is run by one family, and they have a very good reputation for being honest and fair. They don't have a big staff either. It's the perfect place for you to train without having to worry about being bothered by anyone. It's almost as good as being home."

Although her father was right about most things, he was wrong about that. A small ranch in the middle of nowhere was a long, long way from home. Literally and figuratively. It had been difficult to leave what had become her safe haven. She'd spent the past three years at her family's estate in Guadalajara healing her body and her mind after a devastating fall during her last equestrian jumping competition. It had been so bad that she had nearly retired from the sport altogether. Her father knew better than anyone just how close she'd come to breaking the promise she'd made to her mother years ago.

So when Veronica had made the decision late last year to attempt to qualify for the Olympics one more time, he'd been elated and promised he'd spare no expense to get her there. And when he told her that he'd found a place for her to train in the United States for the next three months, she'd expected a facility similar to the one she'd used before in Kentucky. But a family-run ranch in a tiny town called Esperanza? She'd nearly called their family doctor to have her father checked out.

"Fine," Veronica finally said, with a hint of dejection in her voice. She knew there would be no point in arguing. Once she had gotten on the plane earlier that day, the argument was over. He'd won as usual.

"Good girl. I knew you would see it my way."

It would be hard not to.

"When does Charles arrive?" she asked, changing the subject.

"Tomorrow. You can start your training then."

"Is he staying on the property too?"

Her father cleared his throat. "No. I thought it would be for the best if you each, uh, had your own space in between sessions. I rented him a condo in Santa Barbara."

Veronica ignored the implication about them needing space away from each other and said, "Lucky guy."

Charles Wright was her new trainer. She had only ever talked to him on a Zoom call and then had promptly told her dad afterward that she didn't think he was the right person. The man had lots of experience, but he'd admitted that he hadn't been on a horse in nearly twenty years and hadn't trained anyone in over ten. But of course her dad had convinced her to give him a shot. Time was running out and she needed to focus on her training instead of shopping around for trainers.

"Trust me, Vero. This is going to be what you need. I can feel it. This is going to be your year."

She wasn't sure if her father actually believed his own words. Mainly because she'd heard them before. Many times. It didn't matter, though. Everything was already in motion. She couldn't stop it if she wanted.

"I trust you, Apa," she told him. "And we just got here. I'll call you after I get settled, okay?"

"Okay. Te amo."

"Te amo."

Veronica watched through the window as the SUV made its way through the open doors of a wrought-iron gate. She noticed the large *R* and *L* on the emblem atop the archway and assumed the letters stood for "Rancho Lindo"—her home for the next ninety days.

Within a few minutes, the dirt road they were on turned into a cobblestone driveway that ended at a turnabout with a fountain in the middle. Veronica took off her sunglasses and moved closer to the window. Her eyes grew big at the view before her. A beautiful two-story house modeled after the large haciendas back in Mexico stood behind three tall men wearing boots and cowboy hats.

She hadn't expected a welcoming party. It was a nice gesture and she told herself to think more positively about the whole experience. Her dad believed that this was the year she would finally make it to the Olympics. She was going to try to believe it too.

The oldest man was the first to greet her when she stepped out of the car. "Hola, Señorita del Valle. Welcome to Rancho Lindo. I'm Santiago Ortega, the owner."

Veronica shook his hand and gave him one of her camera-ready smiles. "Hola, Señor Ortega. Thank you so much for allowing me to stay here. Your hospitality is much appreciated."

Señor Ortega motioned to one of the younger men standing next to him. "This is Cruz, the ranch manager. And Tomás, the stable manager. If you need anything during your stay, please feel free to go directly to them and they will give you whatever you need."

Cruz's handshake was firm but friendly. Tomás, on the other hand, barely held on to hers. He also didn't smile at her like the others had.

Well, okay then, she thought as she studied his emotionless face.

She dismissed any more thoughts of the man and turned her attention back to Señor Ortega.

"I believe my horse has already arrived?" she asked.

But it was Tomás who answered. "Yes, he's been here for a few hours already. If you'd like, I can escort you to the stables after you've settled in so you check on him."

She waved her hand. "That's okay. I trust he's in good hands. I'm a little tired after all my traveling today. I'd like to go to my room and rest."

"Of course, of course," Señor Ortega said. "Tomás will take your bags and show you to the cottage."

Veronica raised her eyebrows and pointed behind them. "Wait. I'm not staying in this house?"

"Oh no, Señorita del Valle. That's my family's home. We thought you'd be more comfortable in your own private cottage. It has a living room and a kitchen stocked with groceries in case you're hungry. But if you're feeling up to it, you are also more than welcome to join us for dinner at five thirty."

A private cottage? Veronica decided that was indeed a better idea.

"Wonderful," she told him. "Thank you so much."

Tomás walked over to the six suitcases the driver had just unloaded from the back of the SUV. She thought she saw him roll his eyes.

"Everything okay?" she asked.

He cleared his throat as he grabbed the handle of the largest piece of luggage and picked up two smaller bags. "No problem, Miss del Valle. I'll just come back for the rest."

She said her goodbyes to Señor Ortega and Cruz and followed Tomás to the side of the house. He loaded the bags into the back of what looked like some sort of hybrid ATV and golf cart.

"What's this?" she asked.

He jumped into the seat behind the steering wheel and motioned for her to get inside. "It's called a Mule. We use them to get around the ranch, along with golf carts."

"How far is the cottage exactly from the main house?"

"Only about half a mile, but I figured you'd have luggage so I thought the Mule would be better than the golf cart."

The drive to the cottage took less than five minutes. But part of her almost told him to keep driving once she saw it. To her, the word *cottage* evoked warmth and a shabby chic vibe. This was more like shabby shack.

"This is where I'm staying?" she said incredulously when Tomás turned off the ignition. The place looked smaller than her bedroom back home.

"Yes. I know it doesn't look like much from the outside. But the inside is very, uh, cozy."

He got out of the vehicle and went to grab her luggage.

Veronica didn't move for a few seconds. She needed to compose herself before she said something she shouldn't. After taking a long, deep breath, she joined Tomás, who was now inside.

It was true that the inside wasn't like the outside. But that wasn't necessarily a good thing.

Tomás disappeared with the luggage and then reappeared. "I put your bags in the bedroom back there. The bathroom is the only door on the right just before the bedroom. There are a few dishes, pots and pans, and some cutlery in the kitchen. Oh, and the fireplace does work. There are extra logs sitting out there on the porch, and the matches are on the mantel."

"Of course there are," she mumbled. This place looked like it was built in the 1800s and never brought into the twenty-first century. She hoped it at least had running water and electricity.

"Excuse me?" Tomás asked.

Veronica coughed. She hadn't meant to say that out loud. "Of course, because that makes sense to leave them there."

"Okay, well, I'm going to go get the rest of your luggage," he said quickly, and then he was gone.

She dropped her purse onto a green velvet armchair and looked around the small, nearly bare living room and plain kitchen that sat off to the left.

Her dad had been dead wrong. This place was so not like their home in Guadalajara. In fact, the entire cottage could fit inside her bedroom alone. Not to mention the fact that it looked like all the furniture had seen better days.

It wasn't that Veronica was a snob. It was just that for the amount of money she knew her dad was paying the owner, she had expected her accommodations to be more... well, more.

She pulled out her phone from her purse and took a picture of the living room. Then she sent the photo to her sister, Valeria, along with the text: *My home for the next 3 months.*

Valeria immediately texted back: *Where's the rest of it?*

That made Veronica laugh. She could always count on Val to think just like her. There was a ten-year age difference, but they could've been twins based on how much alike they were. Well, in most things, anyway. While Veronica had dedicated her life to equestrian jumping, Val had decided she wanted to be a doctor. She was in her first year at the university in Mexico City, and it had been the longest they'd ever been apart. After losing their mom when Val was only six, Veronica had tried to step up and fill that role. But it had been hard when she was competing and training to always be there for her sister. While her accident had almost destroyed her professional career, it had also been a blessing in some ways. Their dad had moved them both out of Colorado to Guadalajara, and the two leaned on each other even more. She would always be grateful for the three years when she didn't have to worry about the next competition and instead could focus on just living a normal life and being a big sister.

But when Valeria had announced her college and future career plans, Veronica had a choice to make. What on earth was she going to do with her own life? She could either continue hiding behind the tall gates of their family estate or face the music and try one more time to achieve her Olympic dreams.

Her answer had landed here in this very small cottage on a ranch in a very small town.

Veronica put her face in her hands and for the millionth time that day, she wondered if she had made the wrong decision.

Chapter Three

The gray skies and chilly morning air weren't exactly what Tomás was hoping for when Abuelita wished him a good day as he left the house after breakfast.

If rain was coming then that would add extra chores to his already long To Do list, and he had no time for anything else. Not today.

As it was, he'd been out in the stable an hour earlier than normal getting things situated in preparation for Veronica's first day. Judging by her tone and body language the day before, she was already disappointed in what Rancho Lindo was offering her.

He didn't want to add his stables to that opinion.

Tomás didn't know the first thing about what exactly Veronica was going to be doing in the corral, but he did know it had something to do with jumping. He'd ordered six poles that fit onto X-shaped structures. The poles, once arranged, sat only a few inches above the ground. But Tomás wasn't sure if that was what Veronica needed for her first training. So instead he'd left the poles and their riser blocks near the corral entrance. He'd bought them used from his usual supplier and although he'd been told he was getting them at a bargain price, it still hurt to fork over that much money. Some of the other items on the equipment list were expected to arrive in a few more days—including more poles with different fence-like holders. He hoped they weren't things she'd worry about during her first week on the ranch.

Veronica had mentioned that she would begin her training at nine in the morning, so Tomás made sure he was in his office at that time. But at 9:01, it wasn't Veronica who walked in to meet him.

Instead he lifted his head from the paperwork he'd been signing to see his brother Daniel and a man he'd never met before.

"Mr. Wright, this is my brother Tomás. He runs the stable and can help with whatever you or Miss del Valle need," Daniel said. "Tomás, this is Miss del Valle's coach, Charles Wright."

Tomás stood up and shook the man's hand. He was shorter than Tomás and had close-cropped white hair, pale skin, and bright blue eyes. He looked about the same age as his father, if not a few years older.

"Good to meet you," the man said. Tomás noticed his British accent.

He nodded and replied, "Good to meet you too, Mr. Wright."

Daniel left and Tomás motioned for Mr. Wright to take the seat in front of his desk.

"This is an impressive ranch," he told Tomás. "I'd love to get a tour when you have the time."

"Yes, of course," Tomás said after sitting back down in his own chair. "Although I'm sure it's not exactly what you're used to in terms of a training facility."

The man chuckled. "No, but I can train anywhere. All I need is my athlete and a horse. Speaking of, where can I find Veronica? I'm anxious to meet her."

Tomás didn't even try to hide his surprise. "You two have never met?"

"Not exactly. We've talked over Zoom, but this will be the first time we meet in person. I'm Veronica's latest trainer."

"Latest?" Tomás thought it was an odd word choice.

Charles shifted in the chair. "Well, she's been out of the circuit for a few years, and let's just say she has been sort of auditioning new coaches."

Tomás was really curious now. "And what circuit would that be?"

"Equestrian jumping," Charles said as though it was the only sport that existed. "Veronica is training for the upcoming National Equestrian Championships in Kentucky. It's a qualifying event for the Olympics."

"The Olympics? Wow." Tomás was actually impressed. He'd never met an Olympic athlete before. His anxiety level began to rise. He didn't know one thing about equestrian jumping. But he knew that Olympic athletes needed the best equipment to train. And although he took great pride in his stables, they were far from Olympian.

"Just a minute here," Charles said. "Are you telling me that you don't really know anything about Veronica?"

Tomás shrugged. "I'd never heard her name until two weeks ago when her lawyer reached out to my brother to ask if she could train here."

"So you don't know what happened?"

"What are you talking about?"

Before Charles could answer, a female's voice interrupted their conversation.

"Good morning."

Tomás looked over at the doorway and saw his new boarding client standing in the middle of it. He had to consciously restrain his mouth from dropping open. Yesterday, she'd worn her dark wavy hair down and it had fallen past her shoulders. Now it was tied up in a slick, tight bun just above her neck. She was dressed in a crisp white long-sleeved fitted shirt, tan-colored breeches, and black riding boots. She held her helmet and gloves in her hands. The outfit enhanced the curves that had been camouflaged yesterday underneath her long baggy sweater and loose flowy pants. Tomás ignored the hint of attraction stirring up emotions he had no business feeling about this particular woman.

Charles stood up and introduced himself. Veronica didn't bother with any chitchat and told the man that she was ready to get to work.

"Takuache is in the third stall," Tomás announced before they left.

Veronica nodded and then walked over to his desk and put a piece of paper on it.

"What's this?" he asked as he picked it up.

"It's a list of all the things that need fixing in the cottage, along with some items I need someone to order or buy today," she said as she put on her right glove. "I saw some stores on the drive over. Hopefully you can find everything there?"

Immediately annoyance flared deep in his gut, and

whatever wisp of attraction he'd felt moments earlier completely dissipated.

"I'll get right on it, Miss del Valle," he replied, a little testily.

"Oh, and what about laundry service? Is there a designated pickup day or do I just let you know when I need it?"

He had to stop himself from laughing out loud. "Uh, we don't provide laundry service."

Veronica's eyes flared in surprise. "What am I supposed to do with my dirty clothes? Does the town's dry cleaner offer pickup or delivery at least?"

"No, he doesn't. I guess we could make some type of arrangement to take you into town for stuff like that. In the meantime, you're welcome to use the washer and dryer up at the house."

He may not have known the woman very long, but Tomás could see the wheels spinning in her head. And he braced himself for whatever tirade it was about to spit out.

But then she actually surprised him. Because instead of complaining, Veronica simply nodded. "Gracias," she said tightly. And then she was gone.

Tomás looked at her list and couldn't help but laugh. Sure, there were some things that seemed reasonable. But there were a lot that were ridiculous.

Espresso maker?

White-noise machine?

Wardrobe, rack, or some other additional clothing storage option?

Who did this woman think she was? Yes, they'd agreed to make sure her stay at Rancho Lindo was as comfortable as possible. But that didn't mean they were going to spend what seemed like his entire stable budget on her. He pushed the paper away in frustration.

Then his phone rang. He answered as soon as he saw the contact name.

"Hello, this is Tomás Ortega," he said.

"Hello, Mr. Ortega. This is Collin Martin. We spoke a few days ago?" the man on the other line said.

"Yes, hello. How are you?" Tomás's chest tightened with anticipation.

"Good, thank you. Listen, I was calling to let you know that we decided to go with a different boarding stable over in Santa Ynez."

Tomás's heart sank. Mr. Martin had inquired about boarding two horses at Rancho Lindo longterm since he and his wife were downsizing and their new home didn't have a stable on the property. He had seemed very interested at the time, but mentioned he was going to check with another stable as well.

Although Mr. Martin had made no promises, Tomás had still expected to get the business based on his gut feeling. Well, his gut had lied.

"I'm sorry to hear that," he told Mr. Martin. "Can I ask the reason why you decided to go with someone else? I thought our pricing was pretty fair."

The man cleared his throat. "Oh, it was. It had nothing to do with money and more to do with the fact the other stable had more staff and that made me feel a little more comfortable with the arrangements."

And there it was. Tomás couldn't compete with the bigger stables that had the budget to hire employees. The stable at Rancho Lindo was basically a one-man show. Sure, his brothers and other ranch hands could help out in a pinch or on bigger projects. But the day-to-day upkeep and operations all fell solely on him. Usually he preferred it that way. But not if it was going to cost him potential customers. He had to talk to Gabe and Cruz about hiring more help.

After the call with Mr. Martin ended, Tomás picked up Veronica's list again. That's when he noticed there was a different list on the other side of the paper. This list had things she expected Tomás's "staff" to take care of when it came to her horse. Well, she was in for a rude awakening. Although he was willing to do most of the tasks listed, there were a few she was going to have to handle on her own. He decided he'd let Cruz worry about the items for the cottage while he figured out the rest. He had to focus on bringing in more income to the stable to help Rancho Lindo, and getting an espresso maker wasn't going to do it.

Maybe Rancho Lindo wasn't up to her standards. But Veronica del Valle was going to find out soon that not everything in this world was about her.

Chapter Four

Although the temperature was mild, in the mid-seventies, clouds cast a gray gloom over Rancho Lindo. Fitting for Veronica's overall mood, which at first was anxious and hopeful but then quickly turned to frustration.

It had only taken ten minutes for her openness to Charles's training techniques to disappear.

"I think it's important that we set up some ground rules before we get started," he said as they reached the corral where six cavalletti poles and their X-shaped riser blocks had been left near the entrance.

She was a little irked that Tomás had not set them up, although admittedly she hadn't told him that she needed it.

"Of course," Veronica replied. "I do have a few rules I'd like—"

Charles cut her off. "I meant my rules. And actually, I only have one. This is only going to work if you give me your complete attention and respect. You might not agree with my methods at first, but all I ask is that you try them. And if we both agree that they aren't working, then we can try something else. But I can't train someone who won't listen to me."

Veronica couldn't help but raise her eyebrows. She didn't like his tone. However, she tried not to let it bother her. It was clear that Charles was old-school. She'd had trainers like him before; they just liked to assert their dominance, as if that proved they were competent. Since it was their first training session, Veronica was willing to let the attitude slide. For now.

"Understood," she said.

"Very good. All right, why don't you take the horse for a walk around the corral to loosen up his joints."

"Takuache," Veronica told him.

Charles scrunched his expression in confusion. "Excuse me?"

"He is not *the horse*," she said tightly. "He is Takuache."

"Fine. Fine," he said, waving a hand as if to dismiss her. "Take Takuache around the corral and practice proper lead changes while keeping a nice, steady rhythm."

Veronica took Takuache by his lead and slowly walked away from Charles. Part of her wanted to run. An uneasy feeling was growing by the second in the pit of her stomach. They hadn't even started the real training and Veronica was already sensing that there could be issues between her and Charles. She breathed in and out a few times, hoping to shrug off the worry and unexpected sadness. She'd had such high hopes for the morning.

Veronica prayed that things would improve.

"Let's get started with some basic exercises with the cavalletti poles," he said after Veronica and Takuache returned from their ten-minute walk around the corral. Veronica noticed that Charles had set up the poles on the ground about four feet apart.

"Aren't you going to set the poles on their riser blocks?" she asked.

"Not yet. I want Takuache to do some trotting exercises first," Charles explained.

"Believe me," Veronica said, trying to contain her irritation. "Takuache knows how to trot."

Charles met her eyes in a challenge. "I want to see the horse trot."

She opened her mouth to argue, but remembered the promise she'd made to herself and to her father that she would do whatever it took to do well in the competition. Part of that was trusting that her trainer knew what was best—even if she didn't see it.

"Okay then," Veronica told Charles.

A few minutes later, she and Takuache did a few laps along the perimeter of the corral to get their rhythm in sync. As soon as she felt comfortable, Veronica directed him back to the center to line up with the poles. As expected, he trotted over the poles several times with no problem.

"Very good," Charles called out as he brought out the *X*-shaped blocks. He set up a short course with two poles on the ground and one pole on a riser, followed by another two poles on the ground and then one more on a second riser.

Veronica guided Takuache around the perimeter a few more times in order to pick up his trotting speed. Instinctively, she took her weight off the saddle to give him space to move his back. But this time their rhythm seemed off. Sensing that he seemed a little anxious, she let go of the reins with her left hand to give his neck a little rub. "You got this, Takuache," she told him as they made the last turn and headed for the first pole.

He passed over the first three poles clumsily and then totally bypassed the last three.

"What's wrong?" Charles yelled out from his position on the corral entrance.

She ignored him and guided Takuache back to the beginning of the course so they could run it again. But this time, he stopped short of the first raised pole.

"What's going on, boy?" she said. Veronica tried to tamp down her own anxiety and surprise. Takuache was an experienced jumper. He was flying over poles higher than these back home. She honestly had no idea what was happening.

Veronica dismounted to check Takuache's legs for cuts or any other type of injury. But he was fine.

Charles eventually walked over and did the same. "There's nothing wrong with his legs and he was trotting fine just a few minutes ago. Why is he being so stubborn?"

Veronica glared at the man. "Takuache isn't a stubborn horse."

"Maybe you need to be using a crop?"

"I don't use crops on Takuache," she said sternly. "Ever."

"Fine. Then what about a more severe bit?"

"I'm not going to punish him because he missed one jump."

"Technically, he missed two. And none of those things are punishment. They will help with his discipline."

Veronica put her hands on her hips. "It's the first day. It's too early to talk about any of those things."

She half expected him to remind her about his rule. Instead he told her that they should call it a day. Normally, the perfectionist in her would've argued that barely one hour of training wasn't enough. But based on Takuache's performance, she figured it was probably a good idea.

"All right, let's try it again tomorrow," she said.

Charles nodded. "I know it wasn't a smooth first day, but I see a lot of potential," he said.

Veronica didn't know if she felt the same way, so she kept quiet and took off her helmet.

"Obviously you're very experienced," Charles continued. "And I realize we might have different styles when it comes to training objectives."

That was an understatement. Charles had a been a equestrian jumping trainer for almost twenty years. Usually, that long a tenure meant his methods must be successful.

Usually.

Because as far as Veronica was concerned, Charles Wright had no idea what it meant to prepare for the Olympics.

She wanted to be challenged. She needed the thrill of seeking perfection.

Charles, on the other hand, treated her like she'd only started riding a few days ago, insisting on going over basic mechanics like trotting. Takuache, like her, was probably offended. No wonder he had refused to jump. Even though it was technically their first day of training, Veronica had expected to pick up where she'd left off three years ago at the height of her career. Instead, Charles had acted like she was some beginner.

It didn't help that she had felt like one.

"Don't worry," Charles continued. "My plan is going to get you to the Olympics this time."

Veronica didn't think Charles's plan would fix anything, but she didn't have the energy to tell him otherwise. All she wanted was to get Takuache cooled down and to go back to the cottage, take a shower, and eat some lunch. Her stomach growled at the thought of food, and she decided it was time to get away from the stables.

"That's all I want," she told him. "I'll see you tomorrow."

Charles nodded. "Wonderful. Glad to hear it. I'll be headed back to my flat then."

When she didn't say anything, he seemed to take the hint and walked away. Once he was out of her sight she exhaled and leaned her forehead against Takuache.

"I'm sorry it was such a rough morning for you too," she said. "And I promise that I will never ever force you to do anything. I swear."

As she led Takuache over to the water trough inside the corral, she tried to shake off the last dregs of the anxiety that had been roiling in her stomach since she'd woken up that morning. But only a wave of disappointment in herself replaced them.

Training with Charles had been her own personal deadline. It was supposed to be the official start to her comeback. Sure, she'd been riding and practicing on her own back in Mexico—but she'd had some missteps and setbacks. Veronica had convinced herself that once she'd started working with a trainer, everything would come back to her, especially her confidence. It wasn't real until she worked with a trainer. So she'd dismissed those waves of doubt and failed attempts. Deep down, though, she knew the disastrous morning wasn't only Charles's fault.

No trainer would ever be good enough for her, because the only trainer Veronica wanted wasn't here anymore.

Veronica realized then that the cloud that seemed to be hanging over that morning had nothing to do with the weather and everything to do with the fact that she was missing her mom. Her mom would know exactly what to say to get Veronica out of whatever headspace she was in that was preventing her from performing the way she used to.

After Takuache seemed to be done drinking, Veronica looked around for Tomás. She wanted him to cool Takuache down with a walk around the perimeter. But the stable manager was nowhere in sight.

Of course he wasn't. So far, she was not impressed with the man. She made a note to tell Señor Ortega that his employee didn't seem like he was capable of the kind of service she expected.

"Where is he?" she asked as if she expected the horse to answer. Her stomach grumbled again. Veronica decided she wasn't going to wait for Tomás any longer and led Takuache away from the trough so she could walk him around the corral.

After about fifteen minutes, she led Takuache back to his stall. That's when she spotted Tomás entering the stable.

"There you are," she said once he was closer.

"Hello, Veronica," he replied and continued on his way.

She patted Takuache on his side and then headed after Tomás. She thought it was rude of him not to even ask if she needed something.

When she caught up to him, she stood behind him and said to his back, "I need you to be available after my training sessions so you can take Takuache and cool him down."

Tomás didn't even glance at her. Instead he unlocked his office and walked inside. "No can do. This is more of a self-service stable."

She followed right behind him. "What's that supposed to mean?"

"It means except for taking care of Takuache while he's in the stall, you're going to have to cool him down," he said, tossing some papers onto his desk before taking a seat behind it. "I might be able to grab a ranch hand for you once a week for some of the other things, like cleaning your saddle and bridles. But this is a busy working ranch, and everyone else has their own work that needs to get done."

She couldn't help but bristle at his tone. Maybe it was all of the stress of that morning, but irritation flared inside her and her cheeks heated.

"I don't think that's what my father and I agreed to," she said through gritted teeth.

"Actually, it is," he said. "Didn't you read the contract your lawyer sent over?"

Veronica crossed her arms against her chest. She didn't like the implication that she was someone who didn't take responsibility for such things. She was an experienced professional and she had read that contract not just once, but several times. "Of course I read it," she told him. Her exasperation was quickly escalating into irritation. "And it clearly lists all the amenities and equipment we required."

"Not required," Tomás corrected her. "Suggested."

"It does not say suggested," she said, moving her hands to her hips.

"It most certainly does. Do you need me to pull up a copy on my laptop?"

Veronica's blood began to boil. He was so stubborn. Even though she knew he was wrong, she decided to move on. "And what about the list of things for the cottage?"

"I gave it to Cruz. He'll take care of your living accommodations; I only handle the stable."

Her shoulders sagged in relief. "Good. Can I expect to have everything on that list by tomorrow then?"

He swiveled in his chair to look through the filing cabinet behind him. "You can expect whatever you want. Doesn't mean it's going to happen, though."

She bristled at his flippant remark. "Then when?"

"You need to ask Cruz that."

His six words were short ones, but they spoke volumes about what kind of attitude she was dealing with. Veronica usually hated confrontation, but she wasn't the type of woman to keep her mouth shut if she thought she was being wronged.

"Do I need talk to Señor Ortega?"

"I don't know. Do you?"

"If I can't get the services or supplies I need, then yes, I'll have to voice my doubts about whether this arrangement is going to work out."

He finally turned around to face her. "Look, I'm not

trying to be difficult. We are going to do whatever we can to make sure you have what you need, but it's going to take a little time. I don't have some of the equipment on hand and it's not like there's a Stables R Us down the street. Some things will need to be ordered."

Veronica crossed her arms against her chest again. "And how long is that going to take?"

"Who knows? Just depends on whether my suppliers have them on hand. In case you hadn't noticed, Esperanza is a small town."

"I may have only been here for a day, but believe me, I've noticed."

"Great! I'm glad we're finally on the same page," he said and stood up.

Tomás's chipper tone and wide smile made her dig her nails into the sides of her arms. She was about to list all the things she absolutely did not agree with, but Tomás didn't give her the chance. Instead he told her he had to do his rounds, tipped his hat in her direction, and walked out of the office.

Veronica began to stomp after him, but then she heard her sister's ringtone coming from her jacket, hanging on a hook outside Takuache's stall. She debated for a few seconds whether to try to catch up to Tomás or answer her phone. It was probably better for her blood pressure if she took the call. She pulled the phone from the jacket's pocket and greeted her sister.

"Oh, you actually picked up," Val said right away.

Veronica held the phone between her ear and her shoulder while she grabbed her jacket. "If you didn't think I would, then why did you call?"

"I was just going to leave you a voicemail to remind you to call me later. Are you on a break or something?"

"No, I'm done for the day." She walked out of the stable and headed in the direction of her cottage. Her stomach rolled with hunger as if it could see where she was going.

"So how's it going?" Val asked.

Part of Veronica wanted to vent every frustration and annoyance that had been building inside her for the past couple of hours. But she knew her sister hadn't called to hear her whine about her practice.

She rolled her shoulders and hoped some of the stress from earlier would fall onto the dirt beneath her boots. Talking to her sister was the best part of her day, and Veronica was determined not to let Charles or that awful stable manager ruin it.

"Oh, you know, it was just practice. What about you? How did you do on that biology exam?"

The half-mile walk to the cottage seemed shorter than usual. Valeria was super chatty, and it helped distract Veronica from everything that had happened that morning.

"Sounds like you have some pretty amazing professors this semester," she told her sister after collapsing onto the small couch. "I'm so excited for you. Which class is your favorite so far?"

"History, I guess."

"Really? I thought for sure you were going to say biology."

"Oh, I love that class too," Val said. "Let's just say they both have their attractive qualities."

Her sister's obvious giddiness let Veronica know exactly what kind of attractiveness they were talking about.

She sighed into the phone. "All right. Spill it, Val. What's his name?"

"Alonzo," she answered right away. Veronica had expected a few attempts at denial. That sent different alarm bells off in her brain. Ever since she'd become a teenager, Valeria had fallen hard and fast for any boy who flashed a smile in her direction. But usually Veronica had to pry details from her sister about her latest crush. So the fact that she'd immediately given up his name told her that this boy—this man—was different.

"And I'm assuming he's in your history class?" she asked her.

"Yeah. It's assigned seating and so our desks are right next to each other. The first day of class he let me borrow some notebook paper."

"How romantic," Veronica said.

"It was. He gave me everything he had."

Veronica laughed. "Smooth move."

She heard her sister sigh. "Right? But now I don't know if he's still interested. He hasn't even asked for my Insta."

"Did you ask for his?"

"Why would I do that?" Val questioned her question.

Veronica couldn't help but laugh. "Oh, I don't know," she said with a hint of good-natured sarcasm.

"I need help, Vero," her sister said with a sigh. "What do you think? Should I say something to him or just pretend like I don't care?"

Veronica studied the floral pattern of the cushion next to her. "I don't know, sweetie. I mean, playing games doesn't seem like the best move here. But at the same time, if you say something then you risk being humiliated."

"Gee. Thanks. I hadn't thought about that."

Val's frustrated tone cut through her. Veronica hated it when she didn't know how to help her sister.

"I'm sorry, Val. I wish was I better with the advice today."

"Whoa. What's with the negative vibes? What's going on with you, Vero?"

A heaviness in her heart made her sink into the couch even more. Although it had been thirteen years since their mom died in a car accident, she sometimes found herself wondering how she was expected to just go on with her life. When it first happened, Veronica didn't think a day would go by when she didn't sob. Then days turned into weeks and those weeks turned into months. Eventually, the days when she didn't cry were more than the days when she did. But just when she thought she was almost okay again, a memory or regret would sneak its way into her heart and it was like that first day all over again.

Her mom had been Veronica's first trainer. And it wasn't fair that she wasn't here to help Veronica get ready for one of the most important competitions of her life. Instead, she had to settle for Charles. And Val deserved to have a mother to talk to about boys and get advice about life in general. Instead, she had to settle for Veronica. And that made Veronica angry and sad for them both.

"I'm okay," Veronica said softly. "I guess I'm just missing her. I wish Mamá was here. She would know what to say. I'm definitely no relationship expert."

Her sister sighed. "I wish she was here too. But that

doesn't mean I don't appreciate your advice. I didn't mean to burden you with my silly boy problems."

"They're not silly, Val. I love that you feel you can talk to me about this kind of stuff. Don't ever stop, okay?"

"Okay. But you have to promise me the same thing. You can talk to me, Vero. About anything."

Veronica's heart warmed and emotions tightened her throat. "Thanks, sweetie. I appreciate that."

"So spill it then."

"Spill what?" Veronica asked, knowing exactly what her sister meant.

"Spill whatever has been bothering you. And don't even deny it, because you know I know you like the back of my hand."

It was true. Valeria had always been able to detect her mood by the tone of her voice.

She moved the throw pillows to one end of the couch and then lay down. "All right. You might as well go get a snack because it has been a day."

Chapter Five

I still don't understand why I need to be here."

Tomás let out a long, loud sigh to emphasize his frustration.

Cruz, who had been helping him set the dinner table, looked over at him and rolled his eyes. "Why are you throwing a tantrum about it? It's just dinner."

He put down the last water glass and then plopped into the chair closest to him. "Exactly. It's just dinner. I don't know why you and Dad are making such a big deal about all of us coming tonight. It's not like she's going to care if I'm here anyway."

"It's Veronica's first dinner with the entire family," Cruz explained as he continued to place plates in front of the other chairs. "Dad wants to make a good impression. Why can't you understand that?"

Cruz had been the one to offer the dinner invitation to Veronica that morning. He'd wanted Tomás to do it, but after their interaction the day before over her lists, he told Cruz she was more likely to say yes if the invitation came from him.

Tomás wanted to tell Cruz all the reasons why he

didn't understand. Veronica had made it perfectly clear that she did not like him or the way he ran the stable. To be honest, he was kind of surprised that she hadn't packed up her horse and left the ranch yesterday. It wasn't that he didn't want to give her what she had asked for—within reason. He just needed time. That was probably the main reason he didn't want to be around her at dinner. He had a feeling she'd use the chance to complain about him to his dad and Cruz.

Nora walked into the dining room carrying two crystal vases of colorful flowers. "Your mom wants to put these in the middle of the table," she said.

"Are those from Jerry's shop?" Tomás asked as he watched her place them in the center of the place settings.

"Absolutely not. They're from my garden," Nora said, obviously offended. Nora was responsible for the abundant vegetable garden located on the property. Although she'd only been working at Rancho Lindo for about two years, he and his brothers had always considered her part of the family, and he'd bet good money it would be official pretty soon. Nora and Gabe had been dating for several months and it was obvious to everyone how much they loved each other.

Tomás got up from the table and walked over to Nora. "They're beautiful, Nora. Of course I knew they were from your garden."

She playfully slapped him on his arm. "You're such a brat. Why do you Ortega boys like teasing me so much?"

Cruz answered. "Because it's easy?"

"And fun," he added.

That earned him a soft punch this time. "Okay,

be serious for a moment. Do you really think they're good enough?"

Her question confused him. "Good enough for what?"

"Not what. Who. Veronica. I actually had asked your mom if I should go buy some roses or hydrangeas from Jerry, but she was adamant that she wanted me to pick some wildflowers. I'm sure Veronica is used to more expensive arrangements, so I hope she doesn't think they look cheap."

Now Tomás was the one who was offended on Nora's behalf. The fact that she was worried about impressing Veronica left a bad taste in his mouth. Why on earth was everyone bending over backward for this woman?

"Nora, trust me, your flowers are as beautiful as anything Jerry sells. I wish you wouldn't worry so much about what Veronica thinks. If you ask me, she doesn't deserve all of this fuss. If she doesn't like the way we do things here on Rancho Lindo, then that's her problem, not ours."

"Of course it's our problem," Cruz said from across the table. "That's what they're paying us for."

"Who's *they*?" Tomás asked.

"Veronica and her father. Well, her father mostly," Cruz replied.

"Right," Nora agreed. "And we can't afford to get on that man's bad side."

Tomás didn't understand Nora's concern. "Why?"

Cruz cleared his throat and shot Nora a pointed glare, which in turn made Nora suddenly decide to rearrange the flowers. He could tell she didn't want to look at him.

"Nora? Who's Veronica's father?" he asked. He hated pressing her, but he knew his brother wouldn't fess up. Nora, however, couldn't keep a secret to save her life.

"He's, uh, he's Enrique del Valle."

"Okay? And?"

"He's Enrique del Valle," she repeated. "He's like the Rupert Murdoch of Mexico."

Tomás had figured that Veronica must have come from a wealthy family based on her horse and what her dad was paying them for her to train and live at Rancho Lindo. But this news was surprising—and worrisome. He may not have known who Veronica's dad was, but if he was as rich as Nora was insinuating, that meant he was also powerful. And powerful usually meant demanding.

It explained Veronica's attitude. She was probably used to getting whatever she wanted. Tomás's original irritation at having to be here for this dinner returned. He was just about to tell Cruz that he was leaving when excited voices carried from the kitchen and he knew it was too late.

"She's here," Nora said, voicing his own assumption, and walked out of the dining room. Cruz followed but turned around to see Tomás not moving. He raised his eyebrow and tilted his head in the direction of the kitchen. "It's just dinner. Stop being such a grump," his brother told him.

Tomás let out a long sigh and eventually joined Cruz and the rest of the family in the kitchen.

Veronica was already surrounded by his mom and abuelita, and all of them were engaged in a very animated conversation in Spanish regarding what they were about to eat for dinner. Apparently, they were both very excited for her to taste what they had made.

"Trust me," his dad was telling Veronica, "Margarita and her mother are the best cooks in all of the Central Valley."

Tomás watched as Veronica smiled widely at his mother and abuelita. "Thank you again for having me, Señora Ortega and Doña Alma. I'm so honored that you all have gone to so much trouble. I'm very touched," Veronica said.

"Well, we are very honored to have you in our home," his dad told her. "Let me introduce you now to everyone else in my family. I don't think you've met my sons Gabe, Daniel, and Nico. And this is Nora, who is in charge of our beautiful garden. And you know my other two sons, Tomás and Cruz."

He might have imagined it, but it seemed like Veronica raised her eyebrows at him in a question. But then almost immediately, her eyebrows relaxed and she smiled at the two panting border collies standing next to his dad.

"And who are these cuties?" she cooed before petting them both on their heads.

"That's Oreo and Shadow. They take care of Rancho Lindo too," his dad said proudly.

"We also have a manic shih tzu named Princesa," Gabe added. "But she's been banished to the laundry room because she doesn't do well with visitors...or me."

That made everyone laugh—even their dad. He took that as a good sign that dinner might not be that uncomfortable after all.

His mom then instructed everyone to go into the

dining room. But Veronica raised her hand and asked if she could use the bathroom before they sat down to eat. "The water pressure in the cottage wasn't cooperating tonight and I'd just like to freshen up," she explained.

"Of course, Miss del Valle. I'll show you where it is," his mom said and motioned for Veronica to follow her.

"I'll go check the pipes after dinner," Cruz called out after them.

When his dad, Abuelita, and Nora disappeared into the dining room, Tomás told his brother, "I'm sure the water pressure is fine."

"Why do you say that?" Nico asked.

Tomás threw up both hands. "Because the woman is high-maintenance. She is used to certain accommodations and can't quite grasp the fact that we're a ranch and not a five-star hotel. I honestly don't understand why she agreed to stay here in the first place."

"Because we can offer her something those fancy hotels in Santa Barbara can't?" Cruz replied.

"What? The smell of cow manure in the morning?" he scoffed.

Cruz pointed at him. "Privacy."

Daniel put his hand on Tomás's shoulder. "It's only been a few days. She just needs some time to acclimate."

"We'll see," Tomás answered.

"Come on, let's go sit down. I'm starving," Gabe said.

"You guys go ahead. I need to go grab something from Dad's desk."

Tomás didn't wait for a response before heading straight for the home office located down the hallway from the kitchen. It took him only a minute or two to find the paper he needed and save the contact information in his phone. When he walked out of the office, though, he almost collided with Veronica as she came down the hallway from the guest bathroom.

"Con permiso," he said as he stepped to the side to let her pass. She nodded and began to walk by, but then she stopped and turned to face him.

"Why didn't you tell me you were Señor Ortega's son?" She asked the question as if it were an accusation.

Tomás shrugged. "I guess I thought you knew. Why?"

"It makes sense, that's all."

"What do you mean?"

"When I threatened to complain to Señor Ortega, you didn't seem too worried. Now I know why."

Irritation burned the back of his neck. He had told himself to play nice so dinner wasn't a disaster. But Veronica had gone too far with her insinuation. "If you're implying that I don't take my responsibilities seriously because I'm an Ortega, then you obviously don't know the first thing about me, my father, or our business. My brothers and I work hard to keep this ranch running. No one gets a free pass around here, especially not from my dad. And I don't appreciate you insulting me or my family just because you don't like how soft the sheets are in your bed. If you have complaints, by all means share them with my dad, Cruz, hell, even my abuelita, for all I care. It's not going to change what I told you the other day."

Veronica opened her mouth as if to say something, but then closed it. And even though he didn't know her very well, he could tell by the narrowing of her eyes and clenched jaw that she was just as irritated as he was. He decided he needed to call a truce—at least just for tonight.

"Look, I understand that this place isn't exactly what you were expecting. But my family is very proud of our ranch and we do want to make sure you're as comfortable as possible so you can do what you came here to do."

"That's all I want," she said after a few seconds.

His frustration began to dissipate. Maybe Veronica could be reasonable after all. "Okay then. Oh, and the dining room is the other way."

She arched her eyebrow and looked down the hallway. Tomás held out his arm to let her walk in front of him.

Then he took a deep breath and followed.

Thirty minutes later, Tomás was feeling less full of irritation and more full of Abuelita's chicken enchiladas. It was one of his favorite dishes and nearly made up for that fact that he'd had to sit through dinner listening to his family ask Veronica a million questions about the sport of equestrian jumping and her home in Mexico. In fact, the only time he'd spoken was to ask if there was more crema for his enchiladas. Even now as he finished off his second plate, Tomás did his best to ignore the conversation happening around him.

Until he heard a familiar name.

"Did you say Victor Rojas?" he asked after swallowing some chicken.

Veronica's head snapped in his direction. The expression on her face told him that she'd probably forgotten he was even there. "Um, yes, I did. We met him last year when we visited a resort in San Miguel Allende for my sister's eighteenth birthday."

"I heard he manages the riding stables for the resort," Cruz added.

She nodded. "Yes, that's right. We went riding every day we were there so we got to talking to him. He's the one who told my father about Rancho Lindo."

Tomás cleared his throat. "And that's why you came here? Because of Victor?"

"Pretty much," she said. "He had lots of good things to say about the...property. I was also really impressed with his knowledge of horses. He says he learned everything while working here. It's obvious that he really misses it."

"Well, we miss him too," Tomás's mom said. "But we understood that he needed to move back home to take care of his parents."

Victor had worked at Rancho Lindo for only two years, but he had been one of the best workers Tomás had ever had. So much so that Tomás had planned to make him his assistant until Victor had received a call that his dad had had a heart attack. Although Victor had originally gone back home to help his mom while his dad recuperated, he eventually decided to stay in Mexico permanently.

Tomás had heard about Victor getting a job at a popular resort, but it was good to also hear that he seemed to be doing well, and that he hadn't forgotten about Rancho Lindo.

The conversation turned again toward equestrian jumping and Veronica's upcoming competition. Thanks to Charles, he knew a little more than everyone else. And as he suspected, everyone was very impressed with the fact that she was hoping to qualify for the Olympics.

"The Olympics? Oh wow," Abuelita said and clapped her hands in excitement.

"You must be very good," Nico added. "I'll have to make sure to stop by the stables sometime and watch you train."

Veronica chuckled. "Sure. But it's really not that exciting to watch, honestly."

"Oh, I highly doubt that," he said with a wink.

Tomás rolled his eyes. His brother was as subtle as a knock on the head.

"So, Veronica, do you have any brothers or sisters?" Nora asked, changing the subject. She knew when to put the brakes on Nico's flirting.

"It's just me and my sister, Valeria," Veronica replied with a quick nod. "We're really close."

"And does she also compete in equestrian jumping?" Daniel asked.

She shook her head. "No, not at all. She's actually in her first year of university in Mexico City. She wants to be a doctor."

"Que bueno," his dad commented, obviously impressed.

"Yeah, she's the smart one in the family," she joked, making everyone laugh.

"Your parents must be so proud of both of you," his mom said.

Tomás noticed that Veronica's smile faltered for a second. "Yes, my dad is our biggest supporter. And in fact, my mom is actually why I started competing in equestrian jumping. She was a very decorated equestrian jumping rider when she was a teenager. She retired when she married my dad, but then she became my trainer once I started to enter competitions. Unfortunately, she passed away when I was sixteen."

"Pobrecita," Abuelita said and reached out to grab Veronica's hand.

Tomás had expected her to pull away, so he was shocked when he saw Veronica hold on.

"I'm so sorry," Nora said. "I'm sure she's watching over you and is still proud of everything you've accomplished."

Veronica's smile came back in full force. "Thank you. I like to think that."

Everyone grew quiet and an uncomfortable heaviness filled the air. He noticed Veronica shift in her seat, and he willed someone to say something and change the subject. So when no one did, he opened his mouth.

"Nico, so did you tell Gabe about who you saw over in Buellton today?"

His younger brother set down his glass and began to share how he had run into a friend from their childhood.

Tomás watched Veronica carefully as she listened to Nico's story. He was surprised to learn that her mom had also been an equestrian jumping rider and that she had passed away when Veronica was just a teenager. Although he wasn't fond of the woman, he still felt sorry for her. Watching his dad suffer through chemo treatments the past few months was bad enough. He couldn't imagine—refused to imagine—what it would be like if his dad wasn't around anymore.

After dinner, his mom brought out two pies for dessert.

"Oh, these look amazing," Veronica gushed. "I didn't think I could eat another bite after those delicious enchiladas, but I might have to make room for a small slice. What kind are they?"

"This one with the crumb topping is apple and the other is chocolate cream," his mom explained. "Our friend Lina owns a diner in town and she makes the best pies in all of the Central Valley. Oh, and the apples are from Rancho Lindo's orchard, so they are especially sweet."

After much debate, Veronica ended up with a piece from both and a cup of freshly brewed coffee.

As Tomás ate his own slice of apple pie, he had to admit that Veronica was almost likable when she turned on her charms. She had seemed to sincerely enjoy dinner and complimented his mother and abuelita on their cooking numerous times. Even now, based on the amount of "yums" she was expressing, this Veronica was down-to-earth and actually fit right in with his family. And maybe because she wasn't looking at him with her usual annoyed expression, he could admit that she was an attractive woman. Beautiful even.

Her black hair cascaded in waves down to the middle of her back, and only when she brushed errant strands away from her face did he catch a glimpse of the small gold hoops dangling from her ears. Tomás also noticed how the dimples on her cheeks deepened when she laughed. He realized that tonight had been the first time he'd ever heard any sound of happiness or amusement from her.

That was when it hit him. It couldn't have been easy for her to come live on a ranch so far away from her family. Guilt washed over him. Yes, she hadn't been exactly friendly with him, but he could've been more welcoming.

By the time Veronica was ready to go back to her cottage, Tomás had decided that he would try to start over with her. And that meant offering to drive her even though Cruz had said he would so he could check the water pressure.

"I can do it," he told his brother, who was happy to let him.

The short ride to Veronica's cottage was quiet. He'd been trying to think of what to say to let her know that he was sorry if he'd made her feel unwelcome. But they arrived before he could get any words out besides, "I'll go check the main water valve around the back."

She nodded, grabbed the containers of food and pie that his mom had packed for her, and headed to the front door.

After adjusting the valve with his wrench, he walked over to the cottage's porch. He almost went inside, then thought better of it and knocked first.

Veronica opened the door a few seconds later but didn't invite him in.

"I was able to open the valve all the way. Sorry about that—we should've checked that before you arrived," he said, hoping she could tell from his tone that he was being genuine.

She nodded. "Thank you."

"Is there anything else I can check for you while I'm here?"

"Well, I did you give a list..."

Tomás cleared his throat. "Right. Well, most of the stuff on your list requires a little more time and supplies.

I was thinking more along the lines of was there any *small* thing I can check for you while I'm here."

"I don't think so," she said.

He nodded. "Okay, then. I guess I'll be going."

"Okay then," she repeated and started to close the door.

"Uh, Veronica," he called out. She opened the door a little wider but didn't say anything.

For some reason, nerves began to prick along the back of his neck and his face warmed. "I, uh, just wanted to say that I'm sorry if I've given you the impression that I don't care about..." He was about to say *you*, then caught himself. "Uh, about Takuache. I promise that I'm going to make sure he's well taken care of and comfortable in his new surroundings. I'm sure it's been hard for him to be away from his home and his usual caregivers. I don't want to make this harder for him. That wasn't my intention at all."

Veronica seemed to study him for a few seconds. Maybe she was trying to decide if he was being sincere. Or maybe she was debating slamming the door in his face. He could never tell with this woman.

Finally, she cocked an eyebrow and nodded. "I appreciate you saying that."

Tomás waited, but Veronica apparently had nothing more to say.

He stuck his hands into the pockets of his jeans. "Good. I guess I'll see you tomorrow."

She nodded again and shut the door, leaving Tomás to wonder if he was ever going to figure this woman out.

When he got back to the house, only Nico and Daniel were still in the kitchen, since they were on cleanup duty. Ever since their dad had started treatments, their mom had taken on most of the load when it came to taking care of him. So to help her out, he and his brothers rotated doing the dishes and cleaning up after each meal since she refused to hire any kind of outside housekeeper. They all had admitted to feeling a little helpless when it came to their dad getting sick. This was the least they could do.

"Did you fix the water pressure?" Nico asked after turning on the dishwasher.

"Yeah. It was only halfway. Cruz probably lowered it after Sal moved out." Sal had been the last ranch hand to live in the cottage. They had to let him go last summer as part of the budget tightening.

Daniel, who had been wiping down the island counter, took a seat. "So, Tomás, everyone has decided that Veronica is pretty great and no one understands why you've got a stick up your ass when it comes to her."

Tomás sat on the stool across the counter from his younger brother. "I don't have a stick up my ass. All I said was that she was high-maintenance."

Nico scoffed. "Why? Because she wanted decent water pressure?"

"No. There were other things." His defenses kicked in as usual when he felt like his brothers were ganging up against him. "Look, I'll admit that maybe I wasn't being completely fair to her. She was actually acting pretty normal at dinner. But also, I've seen her get a little uppity because our stable services aren't what she's used to."

"Well, that's understandable. I mean the woman is training for the Olympics, for God's sake."

Tomás wagged his finger at Nico and corrected him. "An Olympic-qualifying competition."

His brother rolled his eyes. "Same difference. I can see why she might be a little pissed if things get in the way of her training and focus."

"Especially after what happened last time," Daniel added.

"What happened last time?" Tomás asked.

"Show him the video," Nico said, looking over at Daniel.

Daniel opened his phone, then hesitated. "I don't know. Maybe we shouldn't be adding to the views. I feel bad for her."

"I feel bad too. But I think Tomás needs to see it so he can understand where she's coming from. She isn't just training for a chance to get into the Olympics. She's kinda doing this to save her reputation."

That seemed to be enough for Daniel, who typed something into his phone and then set it down on the counter in front of Tomás.

He saw it was a video on YouTube. Daniel clicked the *Play* button.

Tomás watched as a person on a horse came into view in what looked like an arena. He immediately recognized Takuache and then Veronica. Although he had no idea what was going to happen, a knot of apprehension welled in his gut. Because he could see right away that something was off with her. Her position on top of Takuache was stiff, and even the horse seemed uneasy before they took the first jump. His intuition was correct: Soon they began their approach, and he saw Veronica's leg slip as she stood right before Takuache leapt over the rails. To his horror, Veronica seemed to lose her balance. As soon as Takuache touched the ground, she slid sideways off him. Even worse, one of her legs somehow got tangled in the saddle hanging off Takuache and she was dragged a few feet before the horse finally stopped.

"Dios mío," he whispered as the video ended.

"She was in the hospital for a week with a concussion, a fractured ankle, and some other scratches and bruises," Daniel said softly.

Tomás dragged his hand over his face. Although he knew Veronica was physically okay, he couldn't shake the awful feeling in the pit of his stomach. "What happened?" he asked. It was all he could think of to say in the moment.

Nico sighed. "Stirrup bar. It got loose or broke, I guess."

"She hasn't competed since," Daniel said. "That was three years ago."

Guilt snaked through him. Nico was right. This was more than just trying to get to the Olympics. And based on the millions of views this video had already received, no wonder she had wanted to train in private. He couldn't imagine the amount of pressure she must have been under.

He might have gone into dinner with one impression of Veronica, but her behavior and backstory had changed it.

Tomás decided he was going to do whatever it took to help her.

Chapter Six

Veronica didn't need a mirror to know what her face probably looked like in that moment. Annoyance combined with frustration surely had heated her normally bronze complexion into some type of reddened hue.

She had just walked Takuache back into the stable after their training session. It had been another tense and difficult practice. After two weeks of daily training, Veronica knew she hadn't made much progress. And of course, she put much of the blame on her trainer and his stubborn ego. That morning had been filled with argument after argument about whether Veronica was controlling Takuache's reins with too much force. It had gotten so bad that she told Charles she had had enough for the day and ended the practice more than an hour early.

But while she had hoped that would put a stop to his incessant criticisms, all it had done was move the debate from the corral to the stable.

"I'm the one in the saddle, Charles," she said slowly to make sure the man understood her—because based on the past couple of hours, it sure didn't seem like he did. "I think I'd know if I was pulling too hard."

"And I'm the one watching how Takuache is reacting. I'm telling you that you could benefit from handling him a little more gently."

Part of her wanted to remind him how he had once claimed the opposite. But she didn't want to go down that road again. "Look, I'm tired of talking about this," she told him.

Charles shook his head in obvious disappointment. "And that's your other problem right there."

"What is?"

"You're in denial, Veronica. You don't want to even consider the fact that I can help you. Obviously, your dad thinks I can or else he wouldn't have hired me."

And just like that, frustration morphed into fury. She hated when people used her dad as some sort of threat. It was true that she had agreed to train with Charles because her dad had asked her to. But there was another reason and it had everything to do with the promise she'd made to her mom.

It was right after her first equestrian jumping competition—a competition where she had done poorly. She'd been so mad at herself for letting her nerves get the best of her that as soon as they'd gotten home she'd gone to her room, collected all of her practice clothes, her helmet, gloves, and boots, and threw them into a suitcase. A few minutes later she'd dragged the suitcase downstairs to the kitchen and told her parents that she didn't want to compete ever again. They had both looked at each other and then looked back at her and agreed. She'd expected more of an argument, honestly. In fact, there had probably been a part of her that had wanted them to convince her to change her mind. Instead, her dad had picked up the suitcase and said he'd put it in his car and donate everything the following day. But by that night, she'd come into their bedroom way after her bedtime in tears and begged her dad to bring the suitcase back into the house. That's when her mom had told her the story about how her first equestrian jumping competition had been a disaster and that she, too, had wanted to quit the sport.

"So why didn't you?" Veronica had asked at that time.

"Because I realized that the only thing worse than failing was never competing again," her mom had told her. "If that's how you feel about equestrian jumping, then you have to accept the fact that there are going to be times when even though you try your best, it might not be your best day. And if you can't handle that kind of disappointment, then I don't think equestrian jumping is for you."

"It is, Mamá! It is," she had cried back then. "I promise that I will never give it up. Even when I fail, I will always try again."

Her own words were what had made her try to get up twenty years later after she'd taken the worst fall of her life. And they were what made her hold her head up high now and point her finger in Charles's face.

"I can admit that I have things to work on. But don't for a second think that I'll continue to work with you if you're not actually helping me."

If her face was red, then Charles's was now a bright pink. She decided at that moment that he was smarter than she had given him credit for because instead of arguing with her any further, he simply pinched his lips closed and then stalked off.

It was only when he had disappeared around the corner that she finally exhaled. She was so exhausted and upset that she leaned against Takuache for support. Simmering doubts about her ability to do well in the competition threatened to boil over in the form of tears. Part of her wanted to pack her bags and flee back to Mexico. She felt safe there. Protected.

Then she heard her father's voice in her ear telling her not to throw away everything she and her mother had worked for since she was a little girl. Veronica took a long, deep breath and wiped away the wetness that had started to leak from the corners of her eyes.

"He's wrong."

The voice from behind nearly made her jump into the stall. Veronica whipped around to find Tomás standing here.

"Excuse me?" she asked, trying not to show just how much he had startled her.

"Charles is wrong. You're not controlling Takuache too much."

She removed her riding gloves and nodded. "I know. I tried to tell him that, but he doesn't like listening to me."

"Well, you're wrong too."

Veronica put her hand on her hip. "About what?"

"Charles says you're controlling Takuache too much and you say you're controlling him just fine. You're both wrong because it has nothing to do with that."

"Then what is it?"

"He's not comfortable yet. He still needs to get used to the weather and the dirt."

She raised her eyebrows in both irritation and confusion. Tomás might know horses, but that didn't mean he knew Takuache like she did.

Her irritation at Charles and her frustration with her own performance spurred on the sarcasm. "Let me guess, your extensive years as a equestrian jumping trainer have led you to this conclusion?"

He simply shook his head. "I never said I was an equestrian jumping trainer. But my extensive years being around horses and understanding what they need is how I know that's the real issue with Takuache."

The confidence in his wrong assumption was astounding. "Takuache is a champion equestrian jumping horse. He's been all over the world and competed in at least six different arenas. And not once did he ever need time to get used to a new environment." She used air quotes when she said the words *get used to* in order to make him see how ridiculous it sounded. She'd ridden Takuache for eight years already. No one was going to tell her that they knew what he needed more than she did.

"There's always a first time," he said with a shrug. "He's hesitant because he's not comfortable. Maybe it's not the weather or the dirt. But it's something."

She scoffed. "Funny, last time I checked, I'm not paying you for your opinion."

"I'm in a good mood today, so I thought I'd give it to you for free," he said, the sarcasm dripping from every word.

"Well, next time, don't."

"Does that mean you don't want to hear why I

think Takuache performed so poorly the day of your accident?"

Veronica froze. It shouldn't have been a surprise that Tomás had seen the infamous video. After all, millions of people had. What she hadn't expected was him wanting to talk to her about it—something she had refused to do for the past three years. Her dad, sister, and therapist had all surrendered their efforts in trying to get her to open up about what had happened. It was a taboo topic. How dare Tomás attempt to bring it up.

It had been the second-worst day of Veronica's life. What made it worse was the fact that it still haunted her after all this time. It was one thing to fail. It was quite another to have your failure recorded and available to be watched over and over again by strangers. Her dad and sister had protected her from the headlines and news segments while she was in the hospital. But once she was home, they couldn't hide it any longer. She would never forget the day she finally saw the video herself. Someone had linked it in the comments of her Facebook post thanking her fans for their well wishes.

At first, it was like her mind refused to let her accept that she was watching herself. It was as if the rider on the screen were some other woman. But as soon as the fall happened, Veronica felt the impact all over again. That wasn't some stranger being dragged by Takuache on the screen. It was her.

After watching the video, she couldn't get out of bed for days. Her physical pain returned, along with the emotional turmoil of having to accept the fact that her career and Olympic dreams were most likely over.

If possible, that was probably worse than any physical injuries she'd sustained.

It took a long time for her body and her mind to heal. But then once she'd made the decision to return to the sport, the pressure to not throw away a second chance was sometimes too much to bear.

Maybe that was why she was so defensive when anyone questioned whether she and Takuache were up to the challenge.

Veronica took a step closer so she could look Tomás directly in his eyes. That way there would be no misunderstanding over what she was about to say. "How very arrogant of you to think you know anything about me and *my* horse. From now on, worry less about what I'm doing out there and more about what you should be doing in here to get this place up to par with what Takuache needs and what I expect. Got it?"

He didn't look away. In fact, his stare seemed harder than hers. "Oh, I got it."

"Good." With that, Veronica turned on her heel and walked out of the stable.

But she didn't get far.

An overwhelming sense of panic tightened her chest and throat. It was a familiar feeling—but one she hadn't experienced in a very long time. Instead of heading straight for the cottage, Veronica paced in a circle in an attempt to catch her breath. After her accident, the panic attacks had become almost a daily occurrence. Especially in the first few months when she'd get on Takuache. That's when her dad had insisted she start talking to a therapist. Veronica had refused, already inundated with doctor and physical therapy appointments. It was her sister who had finally convinced her to go. It was almost a year before she could ride again.

When she finally had control of her breathing, Veronica leaned against the back wall of the stable and closed her eyes.

Why was she so affected by the fact that Tomás had seen the video? It would've been more of a shock if he hadn't. But the moment he'd mentioned it, it was as if the accident had happened yesterday. All her fears, doubts, and anxiety came roaring back.

Veronica hated how the attack had come out of the blue. At least she'd been able to control the flood of emotions until she was safely out of the vicinity of Tomás. Now, all alone behind the stable, she forced herself to focus on becoming calm and back in control. She also tried to quiet the thoughts telling her that all of this had been a bad idea. Training hadn't progressed as she had hoped, and her environment wasn't exactly helping her feel comfortable or at ease. So far this grand experiment—at least in her eyes—was a failure.

Then go home.

Veronica squeezed her eyes even tighter in an attempt to force the voice out of her head.

She pulled her phone from her sweater and nearly dialed Val's number. But she remembered her sister mentioning she was going to be spending most of the day in the school's lab working on a group project. Veronica put the phone away. She didn't want to bother Val or worry her. This was something she had to get through all on her own.

Veronica made her way back to the cottage and

decided to take a warm shower. Being in water usually helped soothe her nerves and her thoughts. If she'd been at home, she would've gone for a swim. That was when she remembered one of the Ortegas mentioning a nearby creek. It wasn't the indoor lap pool back in Mexico, but maybe it could still do the trick.

The more she thought about the idea, the calmer she began to feel.

A couple of hours later, after a long shower and a bit of rest, Veronica was in a much better frame of mind. The temperature outside had dropped a little, so she would have to save the swim for another day. But she could at least go find the creek in question. Plus, a ride on Takuache where she wasn't having to concentrate on her every movement would be the perfect distraction.

She walked out of the cottage and headed back to the stable.

Chapter Seven

Tomás tried to write the sentence for the third time. And for the third time, he couldn't remember if the word he needed was *except* or *accept*.

He rubbed his eyes and stared at his laptop's screen and the email he was trying to write to a potential new boarder. It had been a long, busy day and his brain wasn't cooperating.

"Maybe I just need to *accept* the fact that I should send this tomorrow," he said to no one.

Tomás nodded as if to agree with himself. He was just about to close his email when his brother Cruz walked into their small home office.

"Hey," he said as a greeting.

"Hey," Cruz answered back. "Mom says dinner is almost ready."

"Okay. I'm done for today anyway."

"Gabe tells me you're going with him to Sacramento on Thursday," Cruz said as he sat in the chair on the other side of their dad's desk. Technically, it was all of their desk now since they each used it more than their dad these days.

Tomás closed his laptop. "Yeah, he said he would need help loading the equipment he ordered. Plus, there's a horse show there on Friday so we were going to check it out. We were talking about coming back Saturday. Why?"

Cruz leaned back into the chair. "I just want to make sure you being gone for two days is not going to be an issue . . . you know . . . with Veronica."

He stiffened in defense. "Why? Did she say something?"

"No," his brother said and shook his head. "But the guys said that you think she's kind of demanding. I guess I just want to be prepared, that's all."

"There shouldn't be any issues. You're working on getting that stuff for the cottage, right? She asked for some new equipment things, but I'm still waiting on them to arrive."

Cruz crossed his arms against his chest. "When it comes to her, everything is a priority, Tomás. You know how much they're paying us, right?"

"I know. But that money should be going to more staff since she keeps expecting me to handle way more than I thought we agreed to."

He didn't share that Veronica didn't appreciate his opinions about her training. But the more he thought about it, the more annoyed he became. Veronica had no right to call him arrogant after he'd been gracious enough to offer some advice, especially since she didn't know him at all. He'd do anything to help the people in his life. In fact, if you proved yourself to be a loyal and trustworthy friend, he'd be that for you and more.

It still grated him when he thought about how

condescending she'd been when all he had done was try to help. So much for trying to be friendly. It was clear that the only thing she wanted from him was to be her personal stable hand.

Cruz shrugged. "If it's too much, then why don't you just ask Gabe or Nico for help?"

"Seriously?"

His brother leaned closer to the desk. "I don't know why you're not seeing the bigger picture here."

"Why is it that before Veronica got here, Gabe and Nico were always way too busy to help me with anything? Now they have all of this free time all of a sudden."

Cruz sighed. "Of course they don't have free time. But we can prioritize around her. Do I need to spell out every reason why it's in your best interest—in Rancho Lindo's best interest—to make whatever Veronica wants a priority?"

"Because of who her father is?"

Cruz nodded.

"Fine. She can be one of my many priorities. But I'm not going to pretend to be her best friend."

"I'm not saying you have to. Just give her what she needs, that's all."

Tomás scoffed. As if it was going to be that easy.

"And what I need is to focus on the stable and bringing in more boarders," he told Cruz.

That's what he got for trying to be industrious. Because if the woman had been anyone other than a world-class athlete with a huge bank account, there was no way he would've let all her sarcastic comments slide. Although, if he was being completely honest with himself, he probably still would have kept his mouth shut. At least, for a little bit more. With their dad going through treatments, he needed to make this boarding side business successful now more than ever. But even he had his limits.

"Exactly, Tomás!" Cruz exclaimed. "Veronica and her dad are part of this equestrian jumping circuit. Hell, they're part of the whole riding competition world. If she has a good experience here and goes on to qualify for the Olympics, don't you think other riders are going to want to know where she's been training? This could open up a whole new level of clients for you, Tomás. And if those clients are willing to pay even a fraction of what del Valle's paying, you could afford to hire more staff and buy equipment—new equipment. This is a huge opportunity for all of us. Don't screw it up just because of your pride."

"What's that supposed to mean?" Tomás couldn't help but be offended.

"I know this stable is everything to you. And I'm sure it's got to be eating at you that Veronica isn't as impressed as you want her to be."

Tomás scoffed. "First of all, you're wrong. I don't care if Veronica is impressed or not. And second of all, aren't you being just a little dramatic about all this?"

That made Cruz shoot up from the chair and begin pacing back and forth. "I don't know, you tell me. We all know that our finances aren't what they used to be. And with Dad being sick, we're basically down another set of hands. You're not the only one around here who could use some help, Tomás. We put our heads together nearly every week trying to come up with other sources of revenue. Well, here is a really big one and you're being a stubborn pendejo pretending not to see it. Which I can't for the life of me..."

Cruz stopped mid-sentence. Tomás watched as his brother turned around and walked back over to the desk. Then he leaned across it to stare Tomás directly in the eyes.

"Are you being like this because she rejected you or something?"

Of all the things he'd expected Cruz to say, that wasn't even in the top hundred.

It was Tomás's turn to stand. "What?" he yelled. "Why the hell would you even think that?"

"Because I don't get why you can't just do what she wants. It's almost as if you want her to leave Rancho Lindo. And that's the only reason I can think of as to why you're acting this way."

Tomás sat back down and put his head in his hands. "You know I would do anything to help the ranch. I want the same thing everyone does. I don't want Veronica to leave, because I know we need her dad's money. I promise you I'm not trying to piss her off on purpose. But I'm not a miracle worker, Cruz. She's used to a level of service that I was not prepared to give."

"Like what?"

"Like setting up and taking down her jumping poles every day. Like not only feeding Takuache, but also making sure he gets all of his vitamins and supplements morning, noon, and night. Like scheduling a fitting for her with some saddlery shop in Santa Barbara."

Cruz chuckled, and he expected another round of pleading or debate. Instead, Cruz plopped back down in the chair and crossed his arms. "You're a smart man, brother. Probably the smartest one of all of us.

If this is going to work, then you need to activate that brain of yours and figure out a way to meet her in the middle."

It was so difficult not to roll his eyes at that comment. But he knew Cruz. At the end of the day, he was a businessman who liked to negotiate. And Tomás knew exactly what to say. "Okay, how about this? I'll talk to Veronica and let her know what I think I can do and what I can't. And I promise I'll keep an open mind about her requests. Then I'll bring those requests to you so we can go through them and prioritize what I can make happen in the next few weeks. In the meantime, you and Gabe rework some things and find me enough money to hire someone part-time who can help her and help me. Agreed?"

"Agreed," Cruz said, offering his hand.

They shook on it and Tomás felt a little bit better about the situation. It wasn't a win. But it wasn't a total blowout either. He'd take it.

After dinner, Tomás set out to complete his part of their bargain. He walked over to the cottage determined to convince Veronica to be reasonable with some of her requests. It was already getting dark and he had wanted to take a shower and relax a little before bedtime. But he knew himself. If he didn't get this over with now, then he'd keep pushing it off. And he wanted Cruz to fulfill his end of the deal sooner rather than later.

Tomás knocked on the front door three times when he finally decided Veronica was not inside. He knew she couldn't have walked to the house, because they would've crossed each other's paths. And since she had no other mode of transportation, she would've had to walk. That left the stables as her only logical destination. But once he arrived, a whole other possibility of where Veronica might be opened up. And it made his stomach drop.

Takuache was gone.

"Shit," he yelled. The other horses snorted back their displeasure at being startled.

Tomás motioned with his hands to the empty stall. "Sorry. But any chance one of you know where they went?"

His question was answered with more snorts. He thought about calling one of his brothers to tell them that Veronica and Takuache were possibly lost. Rancho Lindo was a vast property, and Veronica didn't know it well enough to go off exploring on her own. Especially at this time of day. But the little nag of guilt in his gut told him that this was his problem to fix.

He walked over to his own horse's stall a few feet away. "Sorry, Peanut," he said. "But I guess we're going for a ride."

Just a few minutes later, Tomás and Peanut were headed toward the south side of the property to search for Veronica and her horse. Rancho Lindo was just over twelve thousand acres, and most of it was only accessible by truck, utility vehicle, or horseback. He had no idea if he was headed in the right direction. He only had his gut to guide them. It didn't make sense that Veronica would head toward the ranch's main gate. There was nothing on the road on the other side. Their nearest neighbor was miles away. So he was pretty sure she had to still be on the ranch. Tomás had decided to go south first only because it was in the opposite direction of the main house and her cottage.

But when he didn't spot her or Takuache after about three miles, Tomás began to wonder if he'd made the wrong call.

"I don't know, Peanut. Maybe I better call in the cavalry," he said into the cool evening air.

That's when he realized that wasn't an option anymore. Cell phone service was pretty much nonexistent this far out. He would have to head back toward the stable if he wanted to make a call to anyone. Then he heard hooves off in the distance. Tomás directed Peanut to gallop in the direction of the noise. His relief at seeing Takuache coming toward him was short-lived when he realized the horse was alone.

"Veronica!" Tomás yelled. "Veronica!"

Peanut came to a stop when they reached the other horse.

"Where is she, boy?" he asked Takuache. "Where's Veronica?"

He didn't really expect the horse to turn around and lead him toward his owner. But Tomás had hoped. Accepting that Takuache wasn't going to be much help since he was basically lost himself, Tomás leaned over and grabbed his reins so he wouldn't run off. He clacked his tongue and both horses began to walk again.

The sun had gone to bed by then and Tomás pulled out his flashlight from the bag attached to Peanut's saddle. "Veronica," he yelled again. "It's Tomás!"

Then he thought he heard something.

"Whoa." He commanded the horses to stop so he could hear more clearly.

"I'm over here."

The female voice was coming from his left. He

shined the flashlight in that direction and his chest exploded in relief as he watched Veronica emerge from a row of trees. Tomás dismounted Peanut and led both horses behind him as he walked toward her.

The part of him that had wanted to chastise her for going out on her own was quieted as soon as he got closer. Her usually well-combed and slicked-back hair was unruly. She had dirt smudges on her forehead and chin, and light red scratches on one cheek.

That made him drop the reins and run until he was only inches away. "Oh my God, Veronica," he blurted. "What happened? Did you fall? Are you hurt?"

Her weary eyes blinked back at him. She looked exhausted, and it was taking everything he had not to scoop her up and carry her to Takuache.

"I didn't fall," she finally said. "Once I realized I didn't know how to get back to the stables, I got off Takuache and tried to find a signal on my phone. But then he ran off and I tried chasing after him. But I lost him after I got tangled up in some low branches over there."

Veronica pointed behind her and then started walking toward the horses.

Tomás joined her. "Are you sure you're not hurt anywhere else?"

"I'm sure. Just some scratches. I'm fine."

Her tone was defeated and Tomás decided not to press the issue anymore. He helped her mount Takuache, then got back on Peanut. The two horses walked side by side all the way back to the stables, sometimes exchanging snorts and neighs. Their riders, however, were quiet during the trip.

After getting the horses settled for the night, Tomás

finally spoke. "Come up to the house so we can put some ointment on the scratches," he told Veronica before she began to walk back to the cottage.

"That's okay. I can do it myself."

"I'm sure you could. But I know for a fact that you don't have any bandages or ointment at the cottage."

She shook her head in protest. "You don't have to go to all that trouble. I'm fine."

Tomás let out a long sigh. Why was this woman so damn stubborn? "Veronica, please come to the house. At least let me give you the supplies so you can clean up the scratches on your own. And I'm sure you haven't eaten dinner, so I can also pack you up some of the albondigas soup that Abuelita made for dinner. I know Daniel has been bringing you groceries every week, but I bet this soup is better than anything you can make at the cottage."

She had opened her mouth as if to protest again, then apparently changed her mind and nodded at him.

More silence joined them on their short trek to the house. And it wasn't until she emerged from the guest bathroom several minutes later that she finally spoke again.

"Where's everyone?" she said as she took a seat next to the kitchen island.

Tomás had already set out his abuelita's go-to wound paste and some Band-Aids. "My parents and Abuelita are in bed already. I'm sure Gabe is over at Nora's cottage—he basically lives there now. And the others are probably up in their rooms. Everyone kind of scatters after dinner so they can do their own thing."

She nodded in understanding.

"Okay, here's everything you need to clean up those

scratches. The ointment is a little stinky and it might burn for a few seconds. But trust me, it works."

"Um," Veronica said after surveying the items on the counter. "Actually, if you don't mind, could you do it for me?"

Tomás couldn't stop his eyebrows from lifting in surprise. "Yeah, of course. I already washed my hands, so I can do it now."

She gave him a small smile with her quick nod.

He nodded back and pulled a Q-tip from the old tin cookie container his abuelita used as a DIY emergency kit. Tomás dipped it into a small glass jar filled halfway with an off-white-colored paste and brought out a dollop. Carefully, he moved it close to Veronica's face and gently applied the medicine to the family of scratches on her cheek. She immediately hissed.

He pulled the Q-tip away. "Sorry. The sting will subside soon. Is it okay if I put on a little more?"

"Yes, it's fine. Please continue," she said and closed her eyes.

Tomás applied another tiny smudge across another set of scratches on her chin. This time she didn't react. However, he was suddenly experiencing an acute newfound awareness of how close he was to her. The light, short hairs along the back of his neck came to attention as his eyes fell on the smooth, long arch of her bare neck. He distracted himself by putting down the Q-tip and fiddling with pulling open a package of tiny Band-Aids. But as he carefully placed them on her cheek one at a time, he couldn't help but notice the rise and fall of her chest and how it seemed quicker than before. His own heartbeat sped up as she let out a small breath that passed over his fingers. It was warm, but it heated him in places that had no business being hot. He cleared his throat, as well as the inappropriate thoughts filling his head. He quickly applied the last bandage and told her he was done.

"You can take this back with you so you can apply it in the morning or after you take a shower," he explained as he collected the bottle of ointment and Q-tips and placed them into a Ziploc bag.

"How long do you think I need to use it?" she asked.

He shrugged. "Probably only for forty-eight hours. Once it starts scabbing, you can stop."

"Sounds like you've had your fair share of scratches over the years," she said.

Her tone was light and almost teasing. It surprised him. "I guess I have," he answered with a chuckle. "But definitely not as many as my brother Nico."

She smiled again, but he could tell something was off with her. "Are you sure you're not hurt anywhere else?" he asked.

"I'm not hurt. I'm embarrassed," she admitted quietly.

"Embarrassed? Why?"

Veronica shrugged. "It was dumb of me to go out on my own. I'm sorry for all the trouble I caused."

Tomás could've argued with that, but he knew no good would come of it. "Why did you go out there?" he asked instead.

"I was looking for the creek."

He hadn't expected that answer. "Why?"

"Your brothers had mentioned there was one nearby, so I thought I'd take a ride out to the perimeter and see if I could find it. I thought maybe I could go swim in it one afternoon."

He thought carefully about how to respond to that. "The water is too cold to swim in right now, but I can take you out there one day if you still want to see it. In fact, I can give you the full tour of the property if you're interested."

Tomás hadn't thought she would be, which was why he'd never offered. But it suddenly became clear to him that Veronica might be experiencing some cabin, or rather cottage, fever. She hadn't left the confines of the ranch since she'd arrived.

"I'd like that. Thank you." She nodded her head in appreciation, and Tomás smiled at her.

"Great. Just let me know when and I'll make the time. Now, I can pack up the soup or you're welcome to eat it here—whatever you want to do is okay."

She seemed to think about it for a few seconds before answering. "I'd like to eat it here. I don't feel like eating alone, though." She had rushed out the words, and her eyes darted away from his as if she was embarrassed again by her own admission.

"I could eat some more soup," he said with a shrug.

Several minutes later, they were both seated at the island with bowls and glasses of water. Tomás had also cut up a lemon and fresh cilantro, and warmed some corn tortillas on the stove's comal to go with the hearty meatball-and-vegetable soup. He offered all to her and she accepted.

After only a couple of slurps, Veronica told him what he had known all of his life.

"I think this is the best albondigas soup I've ever had," she said.

He chuckled. "I'm sure it is. Abuelita is known in town for her albondigas. She'll gladly give the recipe to whoever asks for it, but no one can make it like she can. Me and my brothers have a theory that she uses some odd or surprising ingredient and conveniently leaves it off her instructions."

Veronica took a few more sips and then bit into one of the tortillas. "I'll have to get the recipe from her before I leave. Our cook, Soledad, makes a pretty good version too. Maybe she can figure out if there's something your abuelita isn't sharing. If not, I may just have to invite her to come visit me in Mexico and teach me how to make it because I definitely am going to want to eat this again."

Tomás laughed. He was taken by surprise by the warm feeling that spread inside his chest and looked over at Veronica. The welts along her cheeks were a dull pink now, and he noticed that she'd undone her ponytail. Her hair was free and loose—just like she seemed to be in that moment. This was the Veronica that had shown up to dinner with his family the other night. This was the Veronica that made him want to do whatever he could to bring out that laugh and smile of hers as much as possible.

"Is there a dish that Soledad makes that you'd like for Abuelita to make you here? I'm sure she would love to cook you something from home."

Her eyes brightened with joy, and the warm feeling in his chest spread everywhere else.

"I do miss her nopales, especially for breakfast," Veronica said with a wistful smile.

"Well, there you go. I will make sure to ask Abuelita to make some for you one morning very soon. Nora picks the cactus right from her garden, so I know you're going to love it."

That seemed to make Veronica even happier and, in turn, Tomás felt happy too.

They spent the next several minutes chatting about their favorite foods and what they would never eat again. For Tomás, it was raw oysters thanks to an unfortunate incident when he was a teenager.

"If I even get a whiff of one today, I immediately want to hurl," he told her.

"I love oysters," she said. "I could eat a dozen of them all on my own."

He raised an eyebrow at this new fact about her. "Really?"

"Really. Put some lemon and Tabasco or Tapatío on them and I'm in heaven."

"Okay, so what food is your hell then?"

She didn't even hesitate. "Chapulines."

"Grasshoppers?" he asked to confirm. He'd never tasted the insects himself, but knew they were becoming a foodie favorite in the United States and Mexico.

Veronica nodded and then explained. "We met my dad's friends for dinner one night and they'd ordered them as appetizers," she told him. "My dad had had chapulines before and my sister was excited to taste one. She gushed right away about how good it was. Naturally I trusted her and decided to try one too. The flavor was fine, but I just couldn't handle their, um, crunchiness? I wanted so badly to wipe my tongue with my napkin but I didn't want to offend my dad's friends, so I just kept chewing and then swallowed everything down with a big gulp of my margarita."

Tomás nearly choked on his mouthful of soup at the contorted face she made while recalling the experience. He couldn't stop laughing.

80   Sabrina Sol

"I'm sorry," he said after taking a sip of water. "But I was just imagining you trying not to spit it out in front of everyone."

Veronica chuckled. "Believe me, I almost did."

Although he'd found her story funny, he also appreciated that she'd shared it with him since it wasn't exactly flattering. Tomás admitted he liked that. He liked the fact that Veronica felt comfortable enough to tell him about it. And he really liked how it made her seem more genuine and approachable. Maybe his first judgment about Veronica had been rushed. He wanted to get to know her.

That was a good thing, wasn't it?

Tomás finished off his bowl, sat up straight, and cleared his throat. "So, besides the property tour, I was thinking I could also take you into town. I know the stores there aren't exactly what you're probably used to, but you might find some things to help make the cottage more comfortable or more to your liking. And the next time I have to go into Santa Barbara, I'm happy to take you with me. They have a nice mall and other shops that you can check out. We could even get you some oysters."

"I thought you can't even stand the smell of them," she asked with a raised eyebrow.

"I said we could get *you* some. I didn't say anything about being next to you when you eat them."

It was her turn to roar with laughter.

"What's so funny?"

Both of them turned to see Nico walking into the kitchen. Tomás felt his smile fall at the sight of his younger brother. He had been enjoying getting to know Veronica one-on-one. He couldn't help but feel annoyed.

"I thought you were in bed," he said to Nico, who had taken a seat next to Veronica at the island.

"Nah. I was just scrolling through Instagram," he answered. "Is there still some soup left?"

Tomás's annoyance grew at the realization that Nico was going to stick around. "It's in the fridge."

His brother smiled in delight and got up. As he headed toward the refrigerator, he asked again, "So what were you two laughing about anyway?"

Veronica was the one who answered. "Oysters."

"Did Tomás tell you about the time he—"

"I did," Tomás interrupted.

"Yeah, that's a pretty funny story," Nico said as he began to serve himself some soup to heat up.

"It was," Veronica said. "It's too bad, though. I was hoping to convince Tomás to take me to an oyster bar in Santa Barbara."

That surprised Tomás. He glanced over at Veronica, who was smiling at him. "You were?"

Nico walked over and leaned on the counter next to her. "I'll take you. This guy can't even stand the smell of them." He straightened immediately when he focused his gaze on her. "What happened to your face?" he asked her.

She touched her cheek with her fingers. "Oh. Well, I—"

"We were out riding earlier and I didn't see some low branches hanging over the path we took," Tomás rushed. He had decided that no one else needed to know about Veronica's solo exploration.

Nico frowned at her. "Sorry my brother didn't keep an eye out for you. And he should know better than to take you out for a ride at night when you're not familiar with the property yet." With that, his brother walked back to get his soup out of the microwave.

Tomás saw Veronica open her mouth as if to explain further, but he reached out and covered her hand that had been resting on the counter with his. She met his eyes in a question, and he just shook his head. He waited a few seconds more than necessary before removing his hand from hers.

"Well, I think I'm ready to call it a night," Veronica announced.

Nico had just taken his seat again. "What? Are you really going to make me eat all alone?"

"She's tired. Let her go back to the cottage," Tomás said as he stood up to gather their empty bowls.

"Sorry, Nico. It's been a long day... and night."

"Fine. But I'm serious about taking you to Santa Barbara for oysters. Just let me know when."

She gave him a quick smile in response.

"I'll walk you," Tomás said and ushered her toward the back door of the kitchen. When she was in front of him, he turned around and rolled his eyes at his brother.

Nico raised his arms as if to say he had no idea what he had done.

But Tomás knew better. He always knew better when it came to Nico.

He shut the door behind him and joined Veronica on the path back to the cottage.

She hugged herself. "It got chilly," she said.

"Yeah, the temperature drops pretty quickly after the sun is gone. You'll probably need a heavier jacket than the one you have now if you plan on doing any more evening rides."

Veronica folded her arms across her chest. "I'm not planning on it, but it might be a good idea to get one anyway. Do you think that's something I could get in town?"

"Definitely. Like I said, I'm happy to take you one of these days." At least Nico hadn't offered that to her.

"I know you're busy. I don't mind going on my own."

He wondered if that was the real reason why she wasn't agreeing so quickly. Maybe she had wanted Nico to take her instead?

"Well, I guess you could use one of our—wait, do you even have a license?"

She scoffed. "Yes, I have a license. But I don't want to impose by borrowing one of your cars. Do you have Uber or Lyft around here?"

That made him chuckle. Only because he remembered the time when Johnny Lawson tried to start his own ride-share company and only got one client in two weeks. Not only did most adults drive cars in Esperanza, but they also rode their horses into town. There wasn't a real demand for ride-share companies.

"We do not have Uber or Lyft. But Nora usually goes into town at least once a week for supplies. I can ask her to take you with her on her next trip if you'd like?"

"Oh yes, that would be great. Thank you."

"You're welcome," he told her. Then he noticed she had stopped walking.

Tomás turned back to face her. "Did you forget something at the house?"

"No, I, um, I just wanted to thank you."

"You just did. But it's really not necessary. I actually should've offered to take you on your first day here."

"I meant, I wanted to thank you for tonight. I'm

sure you were pretty annoyed that I'd taken off without letting you know. It was dumb of me to think I could find my way around the property without knowing where I was going. So I appreciate you not making me feel more embarrassed or ashamed than I already was. And I want to thank you for cleaning my scratches and giving me soup. You didn't have to do either, and I know it."

Her words did something to him. In that moment, Tomás wasn't sure exactly what it was. But his gut told him that he was starting to see the real Veronica.

And he liked her.

Chapter Eight

After finishing up with Takuache, Veronica grabbed her jacket and began to walk toward her cottage. But then she stopped and headed in the opposite direction when she thought she heard Nora's voice coming from beyond the stable.

As she turned the corner, she saw that her ears were right. Nora was standing outside the corral watching Tomás walk a horse around the perimeter.

"Hey, Nora," she said once she got closer.

Nora turned her head and gave her a huge smile. "Oh, hey, Veronica. How's it going?"

"Don't ask," she said without thinking. Veronica immediately regretted her terse tone once she saw the expression on Nora's face. Another disappointing training session with Charles had left her in a sour mood. But that didn't mean she should take it out on Nora. "Sorry," she offered quickly. "Don't mind me. What's up with you?"

Nora's frown softened. "Um, not much. Tomás asked me to stop by and see his new horse," she replied and pointed to the animal inside the corral.

Veronica looked over and observed the smaller but sturdy horse with a gorgeous cream-colored coat.

"It's a Haflinger," Nora offered. "Tomás bought him from a rancher on the other side of town because the owner was going to put him down."

She balked. "What? Why?"

"The horse bit him, and I guess there have been some other behavioral issues. Olivia, our town's big-animal vet, mentioned it to Tomás yesterday, and he went over there last night to check him out. And then he brought him back here."

"Why would he want a horse with behavioral problems?" Veronica asked. Although she loved horses even more than she loved some humans she knew, Veronica understood there were some that couldn't be helped or saved by even the best trainers.

Nora laughed. "I guess you don't know Tomás that well yet."

She didn't, obviously. Nor had she really tried to get to know him. But she could see that he took a lot of pride in his work and in the stable. And although she had tried not to notice, the man was attractive. His skin was smooth but tanned by a life spent in the outdoors. His hair was dark and cut short, although she'd begun to notice errant wisps creeping from beneath the brown leather cowboy hat he wore every day. He was tall, of course, just like all the other brothers. And even though it looked like he could probably crush something or someone with those rugged, thick forearms, somehow she knew deep inside that he could never do such a thing. There was an air of gentleness he carried with him. She saw it in the way he spoke to Takuache and the other horses in the stable. And the other night after he'd found her in the woods. Of course, there were things about him that irritated her. But his looks and his earnestness would never be one of them.

Not that she was attracted to him, or even really looked at him *that way*. Although she had to admit that her first impression of the soft-spoken man was changing. Especially after that night.

A shiver ran through her thinking about how scared she'd been just minutes before she'd heard Tomás calling for her through the darkness. At first, the ride had been perfectly fine. She hadn't found the creek right away, so against her better judgment she'd convinced herself to keep going. Then Takuache grew more skittish when it became obvious they had no idea where they were or where they were supposed to go in order to get back to the stables. She nearly kicked herself for deciding to dismount and try to find cell service on foot. When Takuache had taken off, Veronica had nearly cried. And when she walked into those branches and scratched up her face, she'd let the tears finally fall.

Then, miraculously, she'd heard Tomás calling for her. And even more miraculously, he didn't scold her or make her feel bad for making such a dumb decision to go off on her own in the dark. Instead, he'd been kind and gentle. He'd cleaned up her wounds, fed her, and then walked her home. It was as if he knew exactly what she'd needed in that moment.

Before then, Veronica couldn't have cared less about Tomás or anything he did outside of taking care of Takuache.

But she was intrigued now.

"What do you mean that I don't know Tomás?" she eventually asked Nora.

"We—meaning everyone in town—believe Tomás is an honest-to-goodness horse whisperer," Nora explained. "He just has this way with them. Horses respect him, if that makes sense. It may not seem like it yet, but eventually Tomás is going to be that horse's new best friend."

Veronica watched Tomás as he continued to lead his new charge around the corral. The animal would take a few steps and then buck his head as if he was about to take off in the opposite direction. Tomás, for his part, would just stay still and wait for the horse to calm down. Then he'd tug gently until the horse took another few steps. She wasn't sure if what Nora said was true, but this horse didn't seem more difficult than any others she'd come across in her life.

But as soon as that thought crossed her mind, the horse bucked again. This time, though, he let out a litany of snorts and squeals. He also kicked up his back legs, and it was obvious that he was trying to take off. So Tomás let him.

The horse made a few laps around the corral and only seemed to grow more agitated that he couldn't find a way out. For a second, Veronica feared that he would actually jump over the fencing. Eventually, he stopped in the middle of the corral and continued to voice his displeasure.

That was when Tomás, who had been quietly waiting on one side, walked over to him and began talking. The horse's grunts and neighs were so loud that she couldn't hear the words Tomás was saying.

"What do you think he's telling him?" Veronica whispered.

"I don't know," Nora whispered back. "But whatever it is, it's what the horse needs to hear."

"How do you know that?"

"Because I know Tomás."

After a few more minutes, the horse did seem a bit calmer. She knew from experience that it would still be a while before anyone could ride him—but Veronica could see a difference already.

"All right, I'm going to get back to work," Nora said, interrupting her thoughts.

"Okay," she replied, still watching Tomás.

"Oh, hey. I'm going into town soon if you want to tag along. Tomás said you need to get a new jacket or something?"

Veronica turned to face Nora. "Yeah, yeah. That would be great. I mean, I don't want to inconvenience you, though."

She waved her hand. "Not at all. Plus I'd love the company."

"Perfect. Let's do it then."

They exchanged phone numbers and then Nora walked away, leaving Veronica at the corral. She was about to head to her cottage but instead decided to follow Tomás, who was leading the new horse into the stable. Like Veronica's, the horse's training seemed to be done for the day.

She waited until Tomás had safely put the stable's new addition into a stall.

"What's his name?" Veronica asked as she approached.

Tomás didn't seem surprised to see her. He just shrugged and answered, "Well, right now it's Ranger. But I don't think he likes it so I'll probably change it."

"How do you know he doesn't like it?"

"Because he doesn't answer to it."

"And how are you going to know what name he'll answer to?" she asked.

"He'll tell me. Eventually."

"The horses talk to you?" she asked, genuinely curious to hear his answer.

But Tomás just looked away while shaking his head.

"What?" Veronica wasn't sure why he hadn't responded.

"Is that a real question or are you mocking me?"

She was surprised at the accusation. "I swear I'm not mocking you. I really want to know why people around here think you're some sort of horse whisperer."

He turned back to look her in the eyes. "I'm not a horse whisperer. I just seem to know what they need."

"Because they tell you?"

"Kind of? Really it's just that I pay attention to them. They give me clues about what they like and what they don't like."

Veronica studied the earnest expression on his face. She wasn't quite sure if she believed that Tomás could communicate with horses unlike anyone else. What she did know in that moment, though, was that he believed it.

"And what clues is Takuache giving you?" Veronica asked.

His eyes widened. "I thought you didn't want my opinion."

She crossed her arms in front of her chest. Based on yet another dismal training session with Charles that morning, Veronica knew she had to do something different. Her progress had been stalled, and tiny seeds of doubt about whether she was ready to compete were steadily growing into weeds of worry.

She was running out of time.

"I didn't. But now I do," Veronica said. When he didn't answer right away, she added, "Please?"

He nodded and motioned for her to follow him into his office. When they were both sitting down, Tomás finally spoke.

"Takuache doesn't know what you want from him."

That made her still. "What do you mean? We've been together for years. He comes from a long line of champions. Of course he has to know what I want, what I expect."

Tomás leaned back into his chair. "I'm not talking about routines or skill. I mean he's getting mixed signals from you, so that's confusing him."

Familiar feelings of defensiveness began swirling in her stomach. It wasn't that she couldn't take criticism. But she didn't like hearing it when she had no idea how to fix the problem.

"What are you saying, Tomás?"

"You and Takuache need to rebuild some trust."

That made her jaw drop. "You're saying he doesn't trust me anymore?" She couldn't help but bristle at the thought. Even after their disastrous competition, Veronica had never once taken it out on Takuache.

"I'm saying you don't trust each other—at least not like you used to."

She was surprised that she didn't just jump up and leave right then and there. But deep inside, Veronica couldn't deny there might be some truth to what Tomás was saying. After all, the worst fall of her career had been the one with Takuache. Not that she blamed him at all. It hadn't been his fault. It had been all hers. But she'd be lying to herself if she didn't admit to the small hesitation she still felt before mounting him. Therapy had helped her overcome the fear. But not the doubt.

It hurt her heart to think that Takuache could sense that.

"So what do we do about it?" she asked.

It didn't escape her that Tomás visibly relaxed. His shoulders sagged and his jaw untightened. Had he expected her to scream or protest? That was when she knew that both of them hadn't trusted the other either.

"I think you should take Takuache out after your training sessions—just the two of you."

Veronica pointed to the cheek with the scratches. "Did you forget where these came from?"

He chuckled. "I'm not saying to go for another late-night adventure. Obviously, go out when the sun is still up. I think it will be good for both of you to become familiar with the ranch and with each other again. You're not the only one who's far from home."

She really wanted to believe that Tomás's advice would help. But she couldn't ignore her own experience.

"I get that horses can feed off your energy," she said, trying very hard not to sound annoyed or disbelieving. "But it's not like I just started riding him. How much more comfortable do we need to get with each other?"

"You both went through a big trauma together. The past three years, you've had to relearn each other's rhythms and signals. But things have changed again. Both of you are under a lot of stress to perform. You may know how to handle him after all this time, but right now you are not in sync with him, and unless you fix that, you're not going to get what you need from Takuache."

Later that night, Veronica told her sister over Face-Time what Tomás had said.

Val had listened intently without interruption. It had been nice to get out everything that had happened—had been happening—with her training and Charles. She may not have known yet what to do about it all. But she definitely felt like a load had been lifted off her shoulders and her heart.

Talking to her sister was always its own form of therapy.

"Do you trust him?" Val asked.

"Takuache? I thought I did but maybe I don't, according to Tomás."

"I meant Tomás, silly. Do you trust Tomás?"

Veronica had to think about the question for a few seconds. Her answer might have been different a few days ago. That night after he'd found her, she sensed a growing connection between them. And it was more than the fact he'd tended to her cuts. He seemed to genuinely care about her and if she was okay. "I think I do," she admitted.

"Wow," Val said, her eyes wide and eyebrows arched. "That's new, right? Isn't this the same guy you were complaining about a few weeks ago?"

Her cheeks burned with a touch of shame. "It is. But he's not who I thought he was."

That made her sister raise her eyebrows even higher. "Oh, really now?" she asked in a teasing tone.

Veronica rolled her eyes. "All right, all right. Rein in that wild imagination of yours. Why are you always try-ing to steer our conversations to my dating life lately?"

"Because it's been nonexistent ever since Sebastian."

Veronica was about to reply to that *nonexistent*

comment, but she snapped her mouth shut at the mention of her ex. She could have lied and told Valeria that she was wrong and that she hadn't been dating because of her training schedule. But she knew Valeria would see right through it. So rather than make a big deal out of nothing, she shrugged and responded with only honesty. "I haven't met anyone that I would want to date."

The expression on her sister's face softened. "But you haven't really been looking, Vero. Not all men are pricks like Sebastian. Did I mention that I heard from some friends that he's totally single right now—has been for several months, actually."

Veronica uncurled her legs from underneath her and sat up straight. "And? Why would I even care?"

"Oh, that's right. I forgot that you are the only woman in the world who wouldn't take joy in knowing that the ex who cheated on her was also cheated on himself." Her sarcasm dripped with more sarcasm. She also made sure to roll her eyes as much as physically possible.

"She cheated on him?" She blurted the question without thinking, going against her own rule that she would never ever ask anyone about how Sebastian was doing. Not only had he broken her heart, but he was the reason she'd been so distracted the day of the competition. So distracted that she hadn't checked Takuache's bridle that afternoon. Maybe if she hadn't found out that morning he had been sleeping with another rider, she would've noticed the broken buckle and she wouldn't have fallen off Takuache for all the world to see.

That was the last day she'd seen or talked to her ex.

And up until that moment, she'd been successful in avoiding any conversations about him.

But while she really couldn't care less about the man, she admitted to her sister that it gave her a little kernel of satisfaction to hear that karma had finally caught up with him.

"I knew it would," Val said with a chuckle. "Now let's get back to the more important conversation. I think you need to get off that ranch one night and go find yourself a cowboy to ride. You need to find a guy who's looking for a no-strings, no-commitment hookup. You need someone to screw all that stress right out of you."

She nearly spit out her drink. "Valeria del Valle!"

"Sorry, but I can't help it. I'm dating a really great guy and I want you to date a really great guy too. If that's not possible right now, then what's the harm in having a little fun?"

Sex without a relationship? Veronica had never done that in her life. She believed in soulmates and happily ever after. How could she ever hope to find either if she was busy sleeping around with men she knew didn't want the same? Sure, last year, there were a few first dates and second dates with others in between. But if she couldn't see a possibility of forever when she looked in their eyes, then that was it. Her time was valuable—especially when she was training—so she wasn't about to waste it on relationships she knew would never go anywhere. The kind of fun Val was talking about would only be a distraction. And Veronica couldn't afford to lose focus on getting ready for the competition.

"There will be no riding unless it's part of my

training," she told her sister. "Besides, the only cowboys around here are the Ortega brothers and that's not happening. Ever."

Not that they weren't all handsome, of course. Even she could admit to herself that sometimes she'd lose a breath or two when she'd happen to spot Tomás from across the corral working during a training session. Like his brothers, he was tall with sturdy shoulders. But his serious and determined features gave him a more understated attractiveness. The kind that could catch a woman off guard and make her forget for a second where she was and what she was supposed to be doing.

Her sister blew out a big breath in disappointment. "Why do you insist on always rejecting my ideas?"

"Because that's what big sisters do. Seriously, though, what do you think I should do about the Tomás thing—and you know what I'm talking about so don't even go there."

"I don't know, Vero. What is your gut telling you?"

Veronica considered her sister's question. "That he's proven to me that he might know what he's talking about." She waited for Val to continue with her interrogation. Instead her sister shrugged at her through her phone screen.

"Then why don't you try out his advice?" she asked. "It can't hurt, right?"

"I guess not."

"Why do I sense an unspoken *but*?"

Despite her age, Val could sometimes be as intuitive as a wise, all-seeing abuelita.

She hesitated for a few seconds, afraid that speaking her fear would manifest it.

Veronica let out a long sigh. "What if it doesn't work? What if I never get back to where I was before the accident? What if all of this—therapy, new trainers, coming to Esperanza—is going to be for nothing?"

"Vero, you can't think like that. You have to be positive. You have to believe that you can and you will."

And that was the problem right there, Veronica thought.

Could she believe in herself again?

Chapter Nine

Tomás heard the laughter before he even came down the stairs.

But he was still surprised when he entered the kitchen. Because he had expected to see Nora and his mom as the source of the giggles. Instead he found Veronica sitting with his mom at the island counter with a plate of pan dulce and two mugs in front of them.

"Mijo!" his mom called out. "I was just about to text you. I brought back some conchas and orejas from the church bake sale. Come sit and I'll make you a cafecito."

It was just after eleven o'clock on a crisp Sunday morning. Although he and his brothers had come back to the ranch right after Mass, their mom and abuelita had stayed behind to chat with friends. His dad had stayed home.

He nodded and did as his mom directed. "Buenos días," he said to Veronica and tipped his cowboy hat in her direction.

"Buenos días," she replied before lifting a mug to her lips.

Tomás watched as his mom poured the already brewed

coffee into another mug. "I told Daniel that Abuelita would make you stop at the bake sale," he said. "She can't ever pass up the opportunity to get something sweet."

His mom laughed and handed the coffee to him. "That's true. But actually it was my idea. I wanted to get some in case your father wanted a concha."

"Did he eat one?"

A deep frown transformed his mom's face. "No. Well, not yet. Maybe he'll want one later."

Tomás's stomach churned at this information. His dad hadn't been eating very well. And the fact that he hadn't even wanted some Mexican sweet bread—perhaps his favorite Sunday treat—was a bad sign.

"I'm sure he will," he said to his mom, trying to lighten up the worry he saw in her eyes. "I'll eat an oreja then so he can have a few conchas to choose from." Tomás picked up one of the crisp, flaky pastries covered in sugar and twisted into a shape resembling an ear.

"Those are my favorite," Veronica said, holding up the last half of her pastry before taking another bite.

"Tomás really loves los besos," his mom said.

He nearly spit out the coffee he had just sipped. Although he knew his mom was referring to the variety of pan dulce where two half-dome-shaped sweet breads appeared to "kiss" through a layer of jam, it still sounded embarrassing.

Especially when he glanced over and noticed the sly smile now expanding across Veronica's face.

His mom, oblivious to her own son's mortification, announced she was going to go check on his dad upstairs.

"I'm sorry to hear your dad isn't feeling well today," Veronica said after his mom left the kitchen.

Tomás wasn't sure how to respond to her words so he

just nodded. After all, Veronica didn't know the entire story, and he wasn't going to offer any details. He and his brothers had agreed months ago not to share their dad's cancer diagnosis or treatments with anyone outside the family. The last thing they needed was their employees or business clients worrying about the head of the Ortega family, and by default the stability of Rancho Lindo.

She stood up after a few seconds of silence. "Well, I guess I'll head back to the cottage. I had just stopped by to see if my clothes were done drying."

He swallowed the last piece of his oreja. "You did your own laundry?"

Veronica raised an eyebrow. "Yes. I do know how to use a washing machine."

"Oh. I guess I didn't realize since you..."

"Since I asked about laundry service on the first day," she finished for him. Veronica picked up her mug and took it to the sink. "In my defense I only asked because most of the places I've stayed at offer it," she explained as she rinsed the mug before placing it in the dishwasher. "However, I'm perfectly capable of washing my own clothes. If needed."

Now that she had explained it, Tomás felt bad about judging her request. He decided it was time to make good on a promise.

"So, if you have some time after your laundry is finished, I'm free the rest of the afternoon. I could take you on that tour. You know. If you still want to go for a ride."

He watched as her eyes brightened with excitement. In fact, her entire face seemed to be glowing.

"Yes, I would love to do that. Could we meet at the stable in about thirty minutes? I need to take my clothes back and change."

"Sure. I need to change as well. I'll see you there."

She gave him one last quick smile before heading toward the laundry room off the kitchen.

Tomás smiled, too, even though Veronica couldn't see it.

"That's very nice of you to take her around the property."

His mom's voice from behind him startled him.

"I thought you were upstairs," he said, picking up his mug to rinse off.

"Your dad is taking a nap, so I came downstairs to ask if your abuelita wants to go to Lina's for lunch. I was going to ask you, too, but now I hear you have other plans."

The light amusement in her tone didn't escape him. He knew teasing when he heard it.

"It's just one ride," he said. Technically, it would be their second together. But he wasn't about to give his mom any more fodder for her curiosity.

She walked over and sat back on one of the island stools. "I know. I'm just saying it's a nice thing to do. I think the poor woman is bored. Pobrecita."

"Bored?"

"Okay, maybe not bored. But I do think she's lonely. She's all by herself in the cottage when she's not training. Even though she does come for dinner more regularly, the only other time she's here is when she needs to do laundry. She even stayed a few hours after her clothes were done last time to play cards with us. And although I know she would never say it, I somehow doubt she really wants to be hanging out with me or Abuelita—we're too old. Veronica needs friends her own age. Like you and Nora and the rest of the boys. All of you should be inviting her out to places."

The guilt from before rammed back into his chest like a charging bull. "I know, I know. I promise we'll make the time to do that."

"Good. I'm glad that you like Veronica."

Tomás stilled. Had Cruz said something to his mom? Did she think Tomás had some sort of crush on Veronica too? "I don't like her," he blurted.

"Que?" his mom gasped.

He shook his hand as if to wave away the words he'd just spit out. "No, I mean, yes. I just meant that I don't *like* her."

When it was clear that his mom was still confused, he tried to explain. "I want Veronica to have a good experience at Rancho Lindo, so I'm going to do everything I can to make sure that she feels welcome. It's true we may have gotten off on the wrong foot, but I think we understand each other better now. And I don't mind spending time with her."

He could've sworn one of his mom's eyes twinkled with that amusement again.

"That makes me happy, Mijo."

Tomás almost questioned what she meant by that. But if he did that, there was a chance he could ruin the moment they were having. Because ever since his dad's diagnosis, there wasn't a lot that made his mom happy—or at least made her say that she was happy.

So he wasn't about to take that away from her. Whatever she was thinking or assuming, it didn't matter. All that mattered was that she was feeling something other than sadness or worry.

♘

One of Tomás's favorite things to do was to show off Rancho Lindo.

Not that he had many opportunities—or the free time—to give guided tours. But when there was a request, Tomás would take it in a second.

So the nerves rolling around in his stomach confused him as he and Veronica made their way around the property. In fact, he was so wrapped up in his own thoughts, he hadn't realized that Veronica was talking to him until she waved a hand at him from her saddle on top of Takuache.

"You still with me?" she asked.

Tomás quickly nodded. "I am. Sorry, just thinking of something I need to do later," he said. It wasn't exactly a lie. The ride had reminded him that he needed to talk to Cruz about clearing some overgrown brush along the property's fence. "Did you ask me something?"

Veronica rolled her eyes at him. "I asked you a few somethings." Then she chuckled. "I was just wondering about how long your family has owned Rancho Lindo."

"Since 1837. We're one of the last remaining family-owned ranches established by a Mexican land grant. Me and my brothers are the fifth generation of Ortegas to own and work Rancho Lindo."

Tomás knew the pride had come through in his words. He wasn't embarrassed or ashamed, though. He *was* proud. And he always considered it a privilege to be able to carry on the legacy of the Ortegas who had come before him. His dad and his tío Jesus had taken care of Rancho Lindo together until his tío had died in a car accident when Tomás was only four. It had always been expected that Tomás and his brothers would follow tradition and run the ranch together.

But his brother Gabe had had other ideas and went on to have very successful career in the army. Then last year he'd been injured in an accident and had to come back home. It wasn't until late last year that Gabe had decided to stay for good.

Now the five of them were working Rancho Lindo together—just like his dad had always wanted.

"What's that over there?" Veronica asked, pointing a finger to the left of them.

Tomás followed Veronica's gaze. "Those are the ranch's old bunkers," he explained as their horses meandered toward them. "That's where Rancho Lindo's temporary or seasonal workers used to stay back when my abuelo ran the place. It's basically three buildings set up in a triangle. And each one used to have a set of bunk beds and a kitchen—you know, just the basics. If you want, I could talk Cruz into fixing it up for you if you're still not happy with your current living accommodations."

He couldn't help but laugh out loud at his own joke. Veronica even chuckled.

"I didn't realize you were such a comedian, Tomás Ortega," she said.

They rode past the bunker buildings and headed south on the path that would take them to the southernmost perimeter of the ranch.

"Gosh, I knew the property was big. I guess I just didn't realize it was vast," Veronica said, the awe obvious in her voice. "How is it you don't get lost yourself?"

"Oh, I've gotten lost before. Mainly when I was younger. But even a few times as an adult. After a while, some of the land starts to look the same—almost like a house of mirrors. But with cow manure."

"Then how do you find your way home?" she said after a loud, bellowing laugh.

"I look for the familiar. Like that valley over there. That's how I know we're headed south," he explained. The valley was his own beacon of sorts. It centered him and let him know what direction to take whenever he questioned his own judgment.

He noticed after a few minutes that Veronica hadn't said anything.

"Everything okay?" Tomás asked.

She finally looked over at him. "Yeah. I guess I'm just thinking of my family's home back in Mexico. It's nowhere as big as Rancho Lindo, but I used to look for little landmarks on the property when I was a little girl to give me a sense of where I was when I went riding. It's silly, but I kind of miss them."

Even though he knew it didn't make sense, he felt bad for asking the question. Only because he hadn't meant to make her sad. He thought about how he could turn the conversation.

"How old were you when you first started riding?" he asked.

"If you ask my dad, he'll say I wasn't even born yet. My mom rode when she was pregnant with me for as long as her doctor would let her. But the first time I actually remember getting on a horse? I was probably four or five. What about you?"

Tomás considered the question for a few seconds. "Well, I'm sure I was on a horse before I could even walk—not riding, of course. But Abuelita says my dad would hold us on his horse for a few minutes when we were babies just so we could get used to it and the horses could get used to us."

"And how old were you when you realized you could talk to them?"

"I don't talk to them. I just listen, remember?"

"Okay, then how old were you when you realized you could listen to them?"

"I was nine."

As they continued along the south perimeter fence, Tomás told the story about how it was actually his brother Cruz who had announced to their parents that Tomás seemed to have a special knack for dealing with the ranch's horses.

"Why did he think that?" she asked.

Tomás shrugged. "I guess because I seemed to be the only one who could get them groomed and exercised without that much of a fuss. They liked me better than my brothers. People usually do too."

That made her laugh even louder this time. "Again with the jokes. Why did I think that Nico was the funny brother?"

The mention of his younger brother—the one who had flirted with Veronica on more than one occasion—bristled his nerves. But he brushed away the irritation he had no business feeling.

"Nico *thinks* he's funny. I *am* funny," he said. "All right, my turn for a question. When did you decide you wanted to try out for the Olympics?"

She let out a long sigh. "Probably as soon as I knew what the Olympics were. My mom used to display all her trophies and ribbons in a glass cabinet in my dad's office. Before she discovered equestrian jumping she was a very successful escaramuza."

Veronica must have seen confusion on his face because she continued with an explanation. "Escaramuzas are what the female riders are called in Charreria. They perform very difficult choreography riding sidesaddle."

Recognition finally dawned on him. "Oh, okay, now I know what you're talking about. A few years ago Cruz and I saw a performance at a horse show up north. I was so impressed with that level of skill."

"Yeah, it's a pretty difficult sport. My mom competed for a few years before switching to equestrian jumping. So one day—I think I was six or seven years old—I asked her why there was an empty clear box also in the cabinet. She told me she had always wanted to fill it with an Olympic medal. But she never got the chance. That's when I decided I would win a medal one day and give it to her."

A wave of sadness overwhelmed him. His heart hurt—actually hurt—for Veronica. He knew the feeling of wanting to give something to a loved one, but not being able to. Tomás would do anything to be able to tell his dad that he and his brothers had come up with a plan to bring more money to the ranch. He would do anything to remove that burden from his parents. It wasn't an Olympic medal, but Tomás knew how happy it would make them.

Part of him wanted to tell Veronica that he knew how she was feeling. But he couldn't—not yet. It wasn't easy for him to open up to people. He was careful expressing his feelings even with his own family.

"I'm sorry," Tomás said instead.

Veronica looked over at him with a raised eyebrow. "For what?"

"I'm sorry your mom isn't around to see everything you've accomplished—and will accomplish."

"I appreciate you saying that," she said softly. "I

like to think that she's still around me, training me...
guiding me."

The crack in her voice stung him. He had the sudden urge to take her into his arms and comfort her. But she cleared her throat and stiffened her back. Tomás could practically see the emotion bounce off her. He tried to change the subject—and the mood.

"Guess what? I got a very exciting email just before I met you at the stable."

"Really?" she asked with an attempt to smile. "And what did this exciting email say?"

"That your new wardrobe-slash-dresser has been shipped and will be delivered to the town's general store in a few days."

She showed her genuine excitement by clapping. "Wonderful news. Now that I have somewhere to put my clothes, I can finally unpack."

Tomás scoffed. "What happened to the dresser that was in the bedroom?"

"Oh, it's still there. I use it to store my makeup and hair things."

Although he wanted to say something else to tease her, he decided to keep his mouth shut. Veronica had actually offered to pay for the new piece of furniture, which she had picked out from the catalog Cruz had shown her earlier that week. Of course, he refused to take her money since the wardrobe would stay in the cottage after Veronica left for the competition. A strange feeling overcame him in that moment thinking about her filling up the wardrobe only to have to empty it in a couple of months.

Chapter Ten

Veronica had just served herself a glass of orange juice when her phone vibrated on the kitchen counter.

"Hola, Apa," she singsonged after answering.

"Hola, Mija. How are you doing?"

"Good. How about you? How's London?"

"London is wet and cold. I'm ready to go home already."

She rolled her eyes. "You just got there last night. You're just grumpy because you're tired. Have you eaten today?"

It was their usual banter. Her dad would complain about something and Veronica would try to do what she could to fix it. And most things could be fixed with a long nap or a hearty meal.

"Yes, I had a sandwich a few hours ago. But I'm about to head to dinner with the team. And you?"

"I was just about to make myself some breakfast."

"Que? Don't they feed you on that ranch?"

Veronica laughed. "Yes, I usually have dinner with the family most nights. But I try to do breakfast and lunch on my own here in the cottage."

"And what about everything else? The equipment? Takuache? Is that stable manager taking good care of him?

"His name is Tomás."

"Who?"

"The stable manager is named Tomás. And, yes, Takuache is doing well. He has everything he needs."

"I'm relieved to hear that. I was getting a little concerned after talking to Valeria before I left on my trip. She had said you weren't too happy with things there."

It shouldn't have surprised Veronica that her sister had said something to their dad. After all, Veronica had never told her not to. And Valeria would have shared it only with the hope that maybe their father could do something to fix it.

Still, she couldn't help but feel a small twinge of worry. She didn't want Tomás or his family to have to deal with her father. Her father wasn't known for having an easygoing nature. He also was a problem fixer. So if he ever believed that the Ortegas were a problem—a problem that could hurt his daughter's chances of making the Olympic team—then he wouldn't waste any time severing ties to Rancho Lindo. She wouldn't be able to forgive herself if she was responsible for hurting the family financially. Tomás—well, all of them—didn't deserve that.

They continued chatting for a few more minutes before she heard a knock at her door.

"Apa, I'm going to let you get ready for dinner. I have a few errands to run, okay?"

She expected him to argue, but to her surprise he told her to call him the next day so they could talk more. After she hung up, Veronica opened the door to find Nora standing on the porch stairs. Today was the day they were going into town so Veronica could pick up some things. It would be nice to do a little retail therapy. More important, she was excited just to get off the ranch for a few hours.

Nora waved at Veronica. "Sorry, I'm a little early. But I finished my morning tasks sooner than I expected. Do you want me to come back later?"

Veronica shook her head. "No, it's fine. I just need a few minutes to finish getting ready. Come on inside."

About fifteen minutes later, they were on their way in Nora's truck. Although she had already explained it wasn't technically hers—it belonged to the ranch. She just happened to be the one who used it the most.

"If you ever want to take it out on your own, I'm sure the Ortegas wouldn't mind."

Veronica shook her head. "I don't know about that. Tomás didn't seem very excited about that idea."

Nora scoffed. "That's only because Tomás barely goes anywhere. He doesn't understand that not everything we need is here on the ranch."

She couldn't help but laugh at that. It was clear that Tomás was more of a homebody than his brothers— whenever she needed to find him for whatever reason, he was either in the stable or at the main house.

"He really loves Rancho Lindo, doesn't he?" Veronica asked, looking out the closed passenger-side window as they drove down the ranch's main driveway onto the main road.

"We all do," Nora answered.

She looked over at the other woman and was surprised by the emotion written all over face. "How long have you worked on the ranch?"

"Only about two years now. But I basically grew up on Rancho Lindo. My tío and tía worked here and I used to stay with them during the summer. I've known the Ortega boys since we were all kids."

"Really? And were you and Gabe a couple back then too?"

That made her sputter with laughter. "God, no. We were friendly, of course. But he was too busy being a moody teenager to even notice me. I was closer to Nico and Daniel. And Tomás, too."

"I can't even imagine Tomás as a teenager. Did he spend every waking minute in the stable like he does now?"

"Oh, well, he was pretty much already running the stable back then even though the Ortegas had a full-time stable manager. But if he wasn't there then he was with Mia."

"Mia?" Veronica couldn't hold back the surprise in her voice. She wondered who this Mia could be. Tomás had never mentioned her. Although it wasn't like they were best friends—he didn't have to share anything with her that didn't have to do with the stable.

"His ex-girlfriend," Nora explained. Veronica felt a tiny sense of relief and quickly told herself it meant nothing.

"They started dating when they were both high school freshmen and all through college. Everyone was sure they were going to get married one day."

Out of nowhere, a little ember of annoyance sparked in her chest. She shouldn't care that Tomás almost got married to someone she'd never heard about until that moment.

"So what happened?"

Nora pulled into a small parking lot and turned off the ignition before answering. She twisted in her seat to face Veronica, who could see the regret written all over Nora's face. Nora was obviously very protective of Tomás. She recognized it because she was just as protective of Valeria. That's when she realized that Nora was an older sister just like her.

"I'm sorry," Veronica told Nora. "It's none of my business. You don't have to tell me anything."

Nora shrugged. "No need to apologize. I'm the one who's just been blabbing away. I'm normally not a gossiper. But honestly, I've never heard the full story—I don't think anyone has actually. All we know is that they broke up right after Mia graduated from NYU. She still lives in New York and Tomás says they don't keep in touch at all."

Veronica was still thinking about what Nora had shared as they walked into Esperanza's general store. She thought it was odd that Tomás hadn't told his family about what had happened with his ex. She wondered if it was because he had been embarrassed or because she had broken his heart pretty bad. Something Veronica knew a lot about unfortunately.

"Tomás said you wanted to look at the jackets?" Nora's question cut through her thoughts.

"Yeah, I need something a little thicker," Veronica replied, not sure how she felt about Tomás instructing Nora on her behalf. "I also want to get some warmer pajamas."

"Clothing is upstairs. Then I can meet you down here to get the rest of the things you need. I'm going to go across the street to pick up my supply order. Unless you want me to stick around?"

"No, I'll be fine," Veronica said. "Go do what you need to do."

Nora gave her a smile and a quick wave before heading out the store's front door.

Veronica walked upstairs and was met right away with a round wooden table covered in folded sweaters. She picked up a hunter-green turtleneck and a pretty white one with black stripes. She wandered over to the other side of the table and a heather-gray men's waterfowl sweater caught her eye. Veronica thumbed through the stack and held up one she thought might fit Tomás. It was a good-quality sweater and she knew the color would look nice on him.

What on earth am I doing?

The thought hit her so hard that she dropped the sweater back onto the table. She had no business buying Tomás a sweater or any other type of gift.

After folding the sweater and placing it gently back on the stack, Veronica moved on to the racks of winter coats located in the center of the room. She picked through the hangers until she came across a black insulated one that looked nice.

"All our jackets are twenty-five percent off."

She looked up and noticed a small older woman with salt-and-pepper hair standing across the rack from her. "Oh. Great. Do you know if this one is water-repellent?"

"Yes, ma'am. All of those on that side are. How long are you in town for? Are you sure you don't need something heavier?"

Veronica smiled. "Is it that obvious that I don't belong here?"

The woman shrugged. "Sweetie, I know every person

in Esperanza. And since I don't know you, then I figured you're just visiting. Question is, though, who are you visiting?"

"Me. She's visiting me. Veronica is a friend from high school."

Before Veronica could say anything, Nora was at her side.

"Miss Nora!" the woman exclaimed. Her whole face lit up and she put her hands on her hips. "Well, you should've said so, sweetheart. Any friend of Nora is a friend of mine. I'll give you thirty percent off that coat if you want it."

Luckily, another customer walked over to ask the woman a question and she eventually went back downstairs, leaving Veronica and Nora on their own.

"Sorry about Frances," Nora told her. "I love her but she's the town's biggest gossip. I hope you don't mind pretending that we're friends."

Veronica couldn't help but smile. "Well, we *are* friends. But I do appreciate you saying I was visiting you instead of telling her the real reason why I'm staying at Rancho Lindo."

Nora shook her head vigorously "Gabe and Tomás are adamant about making sure we protect your privacy. And if Frances knew the truth, then the whole town would, too, by dinnertime."

Knowing that Tomás and his family were continuing to keep her stay a secret made her trust in them grow even more. Veronica felt safe and at ease.

"I really appreciate that, Nora. Thank you."

She reached out and squeezed Nora's hand to show that she meant what she had said. Nora squeezed back.

"You're welcome," she told Veronica. "Now, let's do some shopping!"

Veronica ended up buying four bags' worth of merchandise from the general store. They hadn't found everything on her list though, so Nora promised to take her into Santa Barbara on the weekend. For the first time in weeks, Veronica felt light and even giddy. It had felt wonderful to go shopping, but also just to hang out doing something other than training. It was almost as if she was drunk on happiness. That was the only reason why, after loading her bags into Nora's truck, she went back into the store for one more thing.

When they arrived back at Veronica's cottage about fifteen minutes later, they weren't alone. Tomás and Gabe were waiting for them on the porch.

"Did you clean out the store or what?" Tomás teased as he helped carry her shopping bags into the house.

"Of course not. I left the tools section perfectly intact," Veronica replied. They put the bags on the couch while Nora stayed outside with Gabe.

"Well, I have a feeling you made Frances's day," Tomás said.

"Speaking of Frances, she asked where I was staying and Nora told her that I was her friend from high school."

"Are you saying Nora actually lied to someone? And they believed her? Because she has the worst poker face in the world."

Veronica playfully slapped his arm. "Don't say it like that. Now I feel bad that I put her in that position."

"I'm teasing, Veronica," Tomás said and took a step closer. "You don't have to feel bad. I guess we never really discussed what we should say about why you were here. Although I don't see why anyone would question it—well, besides nosy Frances."

"I told Nora that I appreciated all of you making the effort to protect my privacy. I really am grateful to you—to all of you."

He nodded but didn't say anything right away. So they stood there just staring at each other for a few seconds. Tomás seemed to be studying her in those moments. It was as if he was trying to figure something out. Or rather, it looked like he was trying to figure her out.

Then whatever it was that was hanging in the air moved on.

"All righty then," he said, finally. "Did you get my text? Gabe is going to haul away all of that dead brush on the side of the cottage. And I'm going to fix the screen on the bedroom window. It's getting colder so I don't imagine you'll need to leave the window open much, but just in case. Although I don't recommend it. We can't have you catching a cold now, can we?"

Why did him not wanting her to be cold make her warm?

"No, we can't." Veronica looked over at the bags sitting on the couch. "Listen, Tomás. I really meant it when I said I hope you know how much I appreciate you—and your family."

She walked over and reached in to pull out the sweater she'd bought for him.

"I'm glad to hear you say that, but it's really just part of the job. We want to make sure all our customers are happy."

Customers.

Of course. That's all she was to him after all. He'd only been nice to her these past few weeks because she was his customer. Veronica shoved the sweater back in the bag.

"Well, that's what I am. Happy."

He tipped his hat at her and told her he was going to go get the new screen out of the golf cart parked outside.

Suddenly, the euphoria from before was gone. The bags on the couch didn't elicit any feelings from her at all. She left them where they were.

Chapter Eleven

Tomás hated money.

He hated how necessary it was. He hated how it could corrupt people. And he especially hated that Rancho Lindo never seemed to have enough of it these days.

"I thought we expected to make a profit this quarter because of the expansion of the microgreens contract," his brother Daniel said.

They were all sitting in the home office for their monthly finance meeting. Cruz had just let them know that if they weren't careful, they were bound to show a loss at the end of the quarter. He'd had the same thought as Daniel. Rancho Lindo's contract with the Green Grocery Store—a growing organic and locally sourced grocery chain—had expanded thanks to the popularity of the microgreens cultivated in Nora's garden. Their production was about to double in size during the spring. Tomás didn't understand why that wouldn't make the ranch even more money.

"The microgreens contract is going to make us a profit," Gabe explained. "But it's going to be offset by our losses everywhere else."

Cruz stood up from behind their dad's desk. "We need some new income revenue, guys. Because if we don't have at least one quarter where we're in the black this year, then we're going to have to start looking at getting a business loan."

"Dad isn't going to like that," Nico warned.

"Well, Dad doesn't need to worry about this," Cruz said, pointing at Nico. "We're going to figure things out on our own. So let's come up with a few more ideas."

They spent the next hour going around the room and brainstorming ways to bring in more money to the ranch. The last resort would be selling off some equipment and letting go of another ranch hand. The very last resort would be a loan.

When they were done with the meeting, Nico jumped up and announced, "I think we all need a shot after talking about this crap."

Tomás wasn't in the mood, but he also knew there was no arguing with his brother. So he joined Daniel and Gabe as they walked out to the backyard and took their usual seats around the firepit. Oreo and Shadow followed—always ready to go where the boys went. After it became obvious no one was going any farther than the patio, they lay down next to the circle of chairs.

A few minutes later, Nico and Cruz joined them—one carrying five shot glasses and the other a brand-new bottle of tequila.

"Boys, we're trying something new tonight," Nico announced and raised the skull-shaped glass bottle.

"Where'd you get that?" Gabe asked.

"Picked it up a few weeks ago when we were up in Nevada for that auction."

"Let me guess," Tomás said. "You also taste-tested it."

Nico shrugged. "Pues, of course. I always try before I buy."

"Tequila is just tequila," Cruz explained as he passed out the shot glasses.

Nico literally gasped. "How on earth are we related, man?" he asked Cruz.

"As long as it goes down smooth, I couldn't care less about what the bottle looks like or what kind of container it comes in."

Cruz took the bottle from Nico and walked around the firepit to serve each brother. The rest of them stood up and raised their shot glasses in the air.

"All right, who's going to start us off?" Cruz asked as he took his place next to Gabe.

"I will," Daniel said. He cleared his throat and continued. "To Rancho Lindo, may it always be our home."

Nico went next. "To friends and familia, may we never be alone."

"To the loves we've lost and those we have yet to find," Nico added.

"To lessons learned and leaving mistakes behind," Gabe said.

The brothers all turned to Tomás. He nodded, raised his glass, and said, "And to forgetting the bad, so we can always remember the good."

"Salud," they all said.

After two more rounds they sat in silence, leaving only the sounds of the crackling wood and usual animal noises to fill the uneasy night air. Tomás knew they were all thinking of the same thing. They had to do whatever it took to make sure Rancho Lindo was around for the next generation. So whatever sacrifices had to be made or whatever last resorts had to be taken, then so be it.

And no matter what, their dad couldn't know that the finances were so unstable.

"So, Tomás, how's it going with Veronica?"

Nico's question pulled him out of his dark thoughts. He shrugged and set his glass on the table next to his chair. "It's going fine."

"Fine? That's it?" Gabe asked.

"What else do you want me to say?"

"Well, what do you think she's telling her father about Rancho Lindo?" It was Cruz who had the question this time.

Tomás crossed his arms over his chest and leaned farther back into his chair. "I have no idea. Why?"

"Why? Tomás, we talked about this. If Enrique del Valle is happy with the services here at Rancho Lindo, it could open up a whole new source of income."

"I get that, Cruz. But what do you want me to do? Ask Veronica if she's saying nice things about us to her dad?"

Cruz nodded. "Uh. Yeah. That's exactly what I want you to do."

"Well, Nora mentioned that Veronica did say she was very grateful for everything we were doing for her," Gabe added.

"See?" Cruz told Tomás. "That's what I wanted to know. Now maybe you can ask if she could share her positive thoughts with her dad."

Tomás rolled his eyes. "I am not going to do that."

"Didn't you just promise less than an hour ago to do whatever it takes to make sure the ranch shows a profit next quarter?"

That wasn't fair. Tomás was already doing everything he could to help. Plus, he didn't want Veronica to think that was the only reason he was trying to make sure she had everything she needed. Tomás was making the effort because he wanted to.

"I'm going to keep my promise, Cruz. I just think that asking Veronica to convince her dad to give us more business isn't very professional. In fact, it reeks of desperation."

Cruz shrugged. "Desperate times and all that, brother."

"All right, this conversation is both boring me and depressing me. I'm heading to bed," Daniel announced.

"Me too," Tomás said, looking directly at Cruz. "I'll see what I can find out and let you know."

Cruz nodded and stood up. They each picked up their own shot glass, while Nico grabbed the nearly empty bottle. "Damn. This is the last time I'm sharing my tequila with you greedy bastards."

"That's why I keep the good stuff up in my room," Cruz said as they began walking toward the house.

"Tomás, hold up." He felt someone tug on the sleeve of his sweatshirt to stop him from walking through the door.

He turned around to find Nico right behind him. "What's going on?" he asked.

Nico waited until they were the only two left on the backyard patio. He cleared his throat. "I wanted to ask you a question. But I need you to be honest with me, like one hundred percent honest."

Tomás nodded. "Okay. What is it?"

"Do you think Veronica would say yes if I asked her out?"

"Are you joking?" Tomás already knew the answer because he knew his brother like the back of his hand. It was obvious that he'd been interested in Veronica since the day she'd arrived. Still, for some reason he didn't want to make this easy for him.

"Not joking. Come on. I don't joke about stuff like this."

Tomás rolled his eyes. Nico had never been serious about dating because he was never serious about relationships. The only reason he was interested in Veronica was because she hadn't shown any real interest in him. She was a challenge. She was something he wanted just so he could prove to himself and others that he could get her.

Irritation heated the back of his neck even in the chilly night air. "I don't think it's a good idea."

"Well, I didn't ask permission, Tomás. I just wanted to know if you think she would go."

Tomás threw up his hands in frustration. "How the hell would I know that?"

"Because you see her every day. You talk to her, don't you? Pretend she's one of your horses and you're trying to figure out what she needs."

Anger exploded from within. "You're an asshole, Nico."

His brother raised his arms. "Whoa. Calm down, big brother. I just meant that you're the one who probably knows her the best by now. That's all."

"That doesn't mean I know what kind of guy she likes or if she's dumb enough to go out with you."

"Hey now. No need to be mean. Why are you so worked up about this?"

"Because I'm not the Veronica expert, okay? You

and Cruz seem to think we have the kind of relationship where she spills her secrets to me. She barely likes me. Why on earth would she confide what her dad thinks or about her love life?"

As soon as he said the words, Tomás realized what he was really irritated about. After their ride the other day, he'd thought they had gotten closer. He thought maybe they were even becoming friends. But then she kept telling him how grateful she was for what he and his family were doing for her. It was almost like she'd been surprised he could actually be nice.

At least, that's how it had made him feel. And he wasn't exactly sure why he'd been so disappointed by it.

Chapter Twelve

DOES DEL VALLE HAVE WHAT IT TAKES TO BE A CHAMPION?

The online article's headline was nearly identical to the handful of other articles that had been popping up in the last couple of days.

Veronica had expected it. As the weeks leading up to the competition ramped up, so would the speculation about the competitors.

And, of course, she was the media's favorite topic when it came to speculation.

"You'd think they'd at least try to go with something a little more creative," she told her dad, who was on the other end of the line. Veronica scoffed one more time and shut her laptop.

"It's good when the stories are the same. That means we're controlling the message—we're not giving them anything new to report."

Veronica shook her head. That was his go-to sound bite when it came to publicity. "So articles questioning my mental health mean we're controlling the message?"

"Right now? Yes. This is all superficial analyzing. We have no reason to answer rehashed questions at this point. But the closer we get to the competition, the tougher those questions will get. And the more hard-hitting the headlines will be. That's what we need to prepare for. In fact, our team is already narrowing down which reporter we want to give your exclusive interview to."

Her stomach twisted at the thought of having to go through another media circus. She wanted to tell her dad that she wasn't going to do any interviews. But she knew that was a losing battle. Enrique del Valle knew how to use the media to his advantage. He did it for his business and he would do it for her. Veronica trusted his judgment. So if he said she had to sit down in front of Oprah, then she was going to sit down in front of Oprah. And if he wasn't upset about the silly articles, then Veronica knew she didn't need to be either.

"All right," she said. "That's enough news for this morning. What else did you want to talk about?"

Although she couldn't see him, Veronica imagined her dad leaning back into his Escalade's soft leather seat. He was on his way to the airport for yet another business trip. "Well, there's still the matter of you coming home for a week before you need to fly to Kentucky to prep for the competition. I need to know which specific days you'll be here so I can have my assistant book your ticket. I could even have the team set up some nice publicity shots of you here on the estate."

Veronica scrunched up her face. "I don't know, Apa. I think I should just worry about training that last week. We already have enough publicity photos."

"What about a location shoot at the town's stables? We could set up some sort of donation PR thing where you personally deliver equipment and other items."

"You know I prefer to keep donations anonymous."

Veronica hated using her charity work as some sort of publicity stunt. Before she'd started training again, she'd become a volunteer at the local stables. She helped take care of the horses and even offered training to children who otherwise couldn't afford lessons. It had been a sort of therapy for her. And she'd enjoyed it so much that she hoped to go back once she retired from equestrian jumping for good.

As usual, her father didn't understand. "But why? This is the type of press you need right now. The team thinks—"

"I don't care what the team thinks. I'm telling you what I think."

She hadn't meant to raise her voice and she hadn't meant to pick a fight. Especially since she wanted to bring something up that her dad was not going to be happy about.

"I'm sorry, Apa. I know you're just trying to do what's best."

"Then why not let me do what I know needs to be done?"

Veronica sighed. "I will. For everything else. But I don't want to taint what I've done at the stables. It doesn't feel right."

"Okay, Mija," he said after a pause. "Look, I don't mean to argue. I just want to make sure everything goes smoothly for your comeback. We won't do anything at the stables. Will you at least come home so we can do everything else?"

She knew this was the opening she needed to broach an uncomfortable subject.

"Fine, I'll come home first before going to Kentucky. But I need to ask you for something in return."

"Anything. Tell me."

Veronica exhaled before saying the words. "I want you to let Charles go."

There was silence on the other end of the phone. But Veronica knew better than to think her father was going to keep quiet. She braced herself.

"You know that's not possible. Not when the competition is less than two months away. There's no way we'll be able to find another trainer at this point."

"But I've made no progress with Charles," she explained. "We need to hire someone else. Call Jorge or even Richard."

"They're not available."

Veronica refused to accept what he was saying. "Call them anyway. They'll be able to give you some names."

"Vero..."

"I know," she rushed. "You can call Stephen over in Connecticut. He might come out of retirement if the money—"

"Veronica! There's no one else. I already asked them all. Jorge, Richard, even Stephen. I asked them all and Charles was the only one who said yes."

"What?" She honestly didn't understand what her dad was telling her.

"Vero. Mija. I'm sorry to have to tell you like this. There are no other trainers that are interested in working with you." He paused for a second before continuing. "Now do you see why I can't fire him?"

"No, I don't see," she said. "I know that I'm a perfectionist. But I'm sure I'm not the only rider out there who is. Why is it so hard for people to get that?" She'd worked with three other trainers before Charles. None of them had given her what she'd needed in terms of instruction or motivation. How could she be expected to win any competition with trainers who couldn't inspire her?

She hated that she was still under a microscope after all these years. Every move, every decision was going to be analyzed and dissected. Although it wasn't fair, Veronica always knew that the road back to the Olympics was going to be scrutinized. And instead of articles and interviews about her abilities and experience, the media would focus on the fact that she'd fired four trainers in less than a year.

Scandals made for great headlines. Veronica had to do whatever it took to make sure she controlled the narrative.

"Don't worry, okay?" her dad said. "You need to focus on your training. I'll talk to Charles and let him know that he needs to step it up."

Her chest heaved with anxiety. "No. Don't."

"Why not?"

Because Veronica had just begrudgingly realized that she couldn't risk Charles quitting like the others. Not because he was a good trainer; she just didn't want to add fuel to whatever media frenzy would be awaiting her once the competition was under way.

She sighed into the phone. "It's been a long day and I'm tired. I was just feeling frustrated, that's all. I can make this work with Charles."

"That makes me happy to hear. But you tell me if I need to step in, okay?"

Veronica agreed even though she knew full well she wouldn't be saying anything to her dad about Charles again. The viral video of her fall, and now this personal goal to stay away from controversy, threatened to overshadow everything she had worked for her entire life. She needed to take control.

After the phone call with her father, Veronica couldn't focus or stay still. She was a bundle of emotions and needed to clear her head. She needed to go for a ride.

It was just after four in the afternoon when she finally made it to the entrance of the stable. As she walked in, she saw Tomás at the last stall, talking. At first, she thought one of his brothers was on the other side. Then she saw the horse from the other day peek out over the gate.

She watched quietly as Tomás pulled an apple from his pocket and brought it up to the horse's mouth. Veronica involuntarily winced in anticipation of the horse bucking or doing something worse. But it was for nothing. Instead, Tomás was left unscathed as the horse seemed to happily chew the apple right from his hand.

It was hard to believe this was the horse from that day in the corral. He seemed so calm, and it was obvious that he trusted Tomás. She had to admit she was impressed by the transformation.

Veronica walked over to where Tomás was standing. "Wow, I can't believe how docile he is now. You've done a great job with him," she told Tomás.

He looked over at her and seemed confused. "Are you actually giving me a compliment?"

"Maybe. Or maybe I'm talking to the horse."

They both laughed at that and for a few seconds she'd forgotten about the phone call with her dad.

"His name is Ranger," Tomás said after a few seconds. "I decided to keep the name after all."

"Why?" she asked.

"While he's definitely calmer, he still doesn't like being around the other horses."

"Oh, I get it. He's the Lone Ranger, right?" she said with a chuckle.

"Exactly."

"So how did you get him to change?"

"I didn't."

Veronica turned her eyes back to the horse. "Well, you definitely did something. Because he's not the same horse I saw that other day."

"All I did was show him that I understood him. And because I took the time to get to know him, he then slowly began to trust me. The way he acted before was just a defense mechanism because he didn't like anyone to get close to him."

When Veronica didn't say anything right away, he blurted, "I know it sounds weird. I'm sure you don't understand."

But that was the thing. She did understand.

After her fall, the last thing Veronica wanted was to be around people. Those first few weeks were a very dark time in her life. She pushed away her dad and even Valeria. She spent most of the days in bed and no one really questioned it because she was also recuperating from her injuries. So she used that as an excuse for not wanting to go downstairs and eat dinner with her family or declining invitations to go to the movies or even just for a walk on their property. When Valeria had had enough of her self-pitying party, Veronica had lashed out.

Just like Ranger.

"I know all about pushing people away," she

admitted to him. "I thought I'd gotten better about trusting people. The accident kind of stirred up all of these defenses. I don't always realize that I'm being... not nice."

To his credit, Tomás didn't agree with her right away. "I'm the same way, I guess. I can also be not nice when I think someone is judging me. And I apologize because I know I acted like that with you when you first got here."

"I accept your apology if you can accept mine. I know I didn't make it easy to be nice to me."

He gave her a quizzical look. "Are we being adults now?"

"I think we are. But I'd like to think that we're friends too."

"I'd like that," he said.

Veronica smiled at the rush of warm emotion swelling inside her chest. When she'd arrived in Esperanza, making new friends wasn't on the list of things she wanted to accomplish during her stay there. But she was glad it was happening.

Chapter Thirteen

The smell hit Tomás as soon as he opened the back door to the kitchen.

And as he took a few steps inside, his eyes began to burn and water.

Whatever it was, it was minty, spicy, and funky.

A stranger might have run for the hills rather than find out the source. But he had a lifetime's worth of bad smells and eye irritation to know where it was coming from and who was responsible.

Abuelita.

"Please tell me that whatever you're cooking is not for lunch," he said after a couple of coughs to clear his throat.

He walked over to the kitchen island, where his abuelita and Nora were sitting. Baskets of different-colored plants, fruits, vegetables, and chiles covered the island's marbled counter. He figured that most, if not all, of those items were inside the large pot on the stove and that, based on the steam escaping from the lid, they were being boiled into some sort of healing concoction created by Abuelita.

"Not for lunch, but you can taste it when it's ready if you want," Abuelita said.

"I don't want," Tomás said and grabbed a nearby napkin to blow his nose. "What is it, anyway?"

Nora, who had been reading something on her laptop, looked over at him. "It's a tea."

"Another one?" he asked, scrunching his nose. "I thought you both were done experimenting?"

Nora and Abuelita had cooked up at least three different medicinal teas in the past month for his dad. Abuelita's lifelong experience with homemade remedies—or remedios as she called them—combined with Nora's vast knowledge of herbs and other plants had conjured up some pretty powerful concoctions. Unfortunately, they had had little to no impact on his dad's energy levels and appetite.

"We never said we were done," Nora replied. "Plus I found this website that lists all of the herbs and their medicinal benefits. I was telling your abuelita that she needs to be taking some of these too."

Abuelita stood up and walked over to check the pot on the stove. "And I say that I don't need them. I'm very healthy. Healthy like a . . . ? Come se dice?"

"Healthy like a horse," Nora answered.

"Yes. I'm a caballo."

Tomás laughed. "If you say so, Abuelita."

Judging by her emphatic nod, Abuelita did.

"Mijo, we are going to make as many tés as we can until we find one that will help Santiago," she said as she stirred.

"I know, Abuelita. But why do they have to stink so much?"

"It no stink," she scoffed.

He looked over at Nora and mouthed, *It does*. She rolled her eyes in response.

"And why is it making my eyes water?" Tomás complained, wiping his eyes again.

"It's because of the garlic... or maybe the chiles," Nora explained. "And it's only because they just started boiling. The smell will ease up after it cooks for a while."

Tomás shook his head in disgust. "It better. Because I can already tell you that my dad will refuse to drink anything that smells like that."

"He's going to drink it—I will make sure," Abuelita said. She came back to the kitchen island to sit down. "I told your mamá that she needs to talk to the doctor because he doesn't want to eat."

"Abuelita, it's the treatments. Once he finishes this round, his appetite will come back," Tomás said.

"Chale. He needs to be eating now so his body can stay strong to fight the cancer." Her voice broke at the end and she quickly grabbed a napkin to cover her mouth. And although his heart was breaking to see Abuelita so emotional, Tomás knew he had to keep it together. For all of their sakes.

"Just put some tequila in the tea and he'll drink it right up," he said, attempting some lighthearted humor to dissipate the sadness that now permeated the air as strongly as the smelly tea.

Nora let out a small chuckle even as she wiped away a tear from her cheek.

"Speaking of teas, I picked some lavender from the garden this morning and was going to bring it over to Veronica. She mentioned the other day that she likes to drink a cup of lavender tea before going to sleep.

I'm going to take her one of my steepers so she can make it herself."

"That's very nice of you, Nora," he said genuinely.

She smiled at him, and he was glad to see there were no more tears on her cheeks.

"How is her training going?" Nora asked.

He shrugged. "I don't know. She's out there every morning with Charles, but..." He almost said that he didn't think she liked the man very much. But it wasn't his place to talk about it.

"But what?" Nora pressed.

Tomás cleared throat. "But, uh, I think she and Takuache are still getting used to their surroundings. I'm sure it's been hard for her, and for him, to be away from their home and family. Especially since she's kind of stuck on the ranch."

Nora nodded in understanding. "She really enjoyed our shopping adventure in town. And we made plans to go into Santa Barbara on Saturday. We're going to do some more shopping, get some manis and pedis, and grab some lunch."

"You are?" He wasn't sure why he was surprised. After all, it had been his idea for Nora to take Veronica into town. He also didn't understand why a small part of him was glad that Veronica was going with Nora and not Nico.

"She's not at all like you described her, Tomás," Nora said.

"Quien?" Abuelita asked.

"Veronica, Doña Alma," Nora explained. "Tomás doesn't like her."

Tomás cringed at Nora's explanation. "I never said I didn't like her."

Abuelita waved a wrinkly finger in his direction. "Ella es una buena mujer. No seas tonto, Mijo."

"Yes, I know she's a good woman," he admitted, a little hurt that his abuelita would scold him for being silly about his first impression.

Nora looked up again from the laptop and eyed him suspiciously. "You do?"

He threw up his hands. "Why is everyone making a big deal out of this? All I ever said was that I thought she was demanding. I understand now where that was coming from and I'm trying to be more accommodating and patient. I'm trying to be her friend, too."

"That's good to hear. I mean, I'm sure all of us were a little intimidated at first because of her dad and the fact that she's training for this Olympic event. But as soon as I spent a few minutes talking to her, I could tell she was just a regular person."

Tomás wouldn't go as far as to call Veronica a regular person. Her world was so much different than the world on Rancho Lindo. Although he did like her, he had no misunderstandings: They were two very different people.

"Okay, Mijo. I think this batch is ready," Abuelita said as she poured some of the liquid she'd been brewing into a glass mug. "You can taste-test now."

He was just about to make up an excuse to leave when his phone rang. The caller ID let him know who was calling and for a second he debated answering. Then he decided the conversation he was about to have was still going to be less painful than whatever Abuelita had in that mug.

"Sorry, Abuelita. I need to take this call," he said and then walked out to the back porch.

"Hey, Mia," he said into the phone.

There was a pause. Then, "Hey, Tomás."

Old emotions stirred within him as soon as he heard her voice. It had been almost a year since the last time he'd seen and spoken to her during her last visit to Esperanza. It had been short because he really didn't have anything to say to Mia other than the polite niceties because their parents were friends. He had no idea why she'd be calling him now.

"What's going on? Everything okay?" he rushed to ask, immediately thinking that only some emergency would be the reason for her to want to talk to him like this out of the blue.

"Yeah, everything is good. Real good, in fact."

The slight concern eased and was replaced with increasing curiosity. "Glad to hear that."

She cleared her throat. "I'm coming home next week for my parents' anniversary party."

He leaned his left shoulder against a porch pillar in an attempt to relax the sudden nerves he was feeling. "I figured. I'm sure they're happy you're going to be here. Your mom is planning a real shindig."

Mia laughed. He'd almost forgotten how it had sounded. "You have no idea. I've been trying to help with what I can from here in New York, but I have a feeling she's got a To Do list for me that's at least a mile long for when I'm in town."

"I'm sure. Again, that's really good that you can be here to help."

"I'm glad I will be," she said. Then after a few seconds, she added, "And I'm actually bringing someone with me."

"Yeah? Well, I'm sure Lina will appreciate an extra set of hands."

"Well, that's the reason I'm calling, actually. I wanted to be the one to tell you myself. I'm bringing my fiancé. I got engaged a few weeks ago."

He heard the words perfectly clearly. That didn't mean they made sense. Part of him had always preferred to believe that she'd turned down his proposal all those years ago because she didn't want to get married. Ever. Old feelings of regret and embarrassment came rushing back.

"You're getting married?" he asked.

"I am. Next year. Probably. We haven't set a date, but yeah, probably next year."

Unfamiliar emotions made him unsteady and Tomás reached out to hold on to the porch pillar. Of all the things he could've guessed Mia needed to tell him over the phone, this one wasn't even in the galaxy.

He had to compose himself and make sure Mia didn't tell her mom, who would then tell his mom, that their conversation was awkward.

He took a long breath and willed his voice to be smooth and even. "Congratulations, Mia. I'm happy for you. I really am."

She let out a soft sigh. "Thank you, Tomás. I know it's been years since the two of us, well, you know. And I'm sure you've moved on and barely think of me at all. But my parents insisted that I personally tell you my news before their party. They love you like their own son and they just want to make sure we stay friends."

Were they still friends? It surprised him to hear her classify their nonexisting relationship like that. There was a time when he would've done anything to be with her again. But that was one lifetime and one fiancé ago. Not that he had any right to feel stunned by her announcement anyway. Mia had moved on from him a long time ago. And he had done the same.

Except for the very few times they happened to run into each other over the past eight years, he and Mia had had no contact. He never really knew what to say to her on the handful of occasions she'd come to town to visit her parents. He mostly tried to go for casual and nonchalant. He was polite and respectful for the sake of their families. The only reason he knew anything about her life in New York was because of her mom. The fact was, Mia stopped being his friend the minute she told him she wasn't in love with him anymore.

It had been his biggest fear when he'd learned she wanted to go to NYU instead of the University of California at Santa Barbara like she had originally planned.

And the more she had talked about moving and what it meant for her, the more he realized she'd never once mentioned how good it would be for *them*. For their relationship.

Rather than giving her an ultimatum—mainly because he was afraid of making her choose—he told her that he supported her decision and wanted them to stay together. He told her he would still go to Santa Rosa Junior College to get his certificate in equine management as planned so he could manage the stable at Rancho Lindo. That had always been his dream and he told her to go follow hers.

Then four years later he flew to New York for her graduation with an engagement ring in his suitcase only for her to announce she wasn't flying back with him to Esperanza.

So he'd asked her if she wanted to end the relationship too. The question hadn't even thrown her. In fact, she looked relieved. She told him that even though she would always love him, she wasn't in love with him anymore. Mia said that she couldn't see a future with him. Correction. She didn't want a future with him on Rancho Lindo.

Tomás wasn't the kind of man to hang on to someone who didn't want to be with him.

He said they should end things. And the ring he'd saved up for a year to buy never left his suitcase.

His only saving grace that day was that neither Mia nor her family knew that he had planned to propose. Of course, his entire family knew. Part of him thought his mom was just as devastated as he was when he broke the news to everyone after his trip. She had wanted to say something to Lina or, even worse, call Mia herself. Luckily, his brothers and dad had convinced her to stay out of it. And they respected his request not to talk about all the details.

He had been too embarrassed about the entire situation. Tomás didn't know what Mia had hurt worse— his heart or his pride.

"There's nothing left to talk about," Tomás had told everyone. "She doesn't love me anymore and that's it."

He'd done a good job of keeping his feelings of hurt and anger to himself. Over time, they'd disappeared and he got over the fact that Mia and he were over. But because of who their parents were, he had to accept the fact that she would always be a part of his life in some way.

Even he could admit that running into her now and then and treating her as if they hadn't been intimate or in love all those years ago was always an awkward dance. That was the only reason he always made their interactions quick and superficial. Because even though he held no romantic feelings toward her, Mia had still hurt him. He would be a fool to forget that.

So when it came to her, he made sure to keep his distance as much as possible. Physically and emotionally.

And now she was marrying someone else.

He knew she was waiting for him to say more. But words failed him. And the uneasiness from before grew with every second of silence between them. What was left to say anyway? They'd hashed it out eight years ago. She'd wanted to stay in touch and try to be friends. He didn't. He had expected Mia to come back after a week and beg him to take her back. She didn't.

Even now, he wasn't sure he wanted to be friends like she'd said. Not because he was still in love with her, but because it would be weird. Wouldn't it?

"How are things on Rancho Lindo?" Mia finally said. "And how is your family?"

"Everything is good. We're good," he answered.

"I heard Gabe and Nora are dating. I couldn't believe it when my mom told me."

"Yeah. It was kind of a surprise to everyone. I still don't get what she sees in him."

Mia chuckled. "Well, she did have a crush on him when they were teenagers. Guess they just needed time to realize there was something there."

He wasn't quite sure how to respond to that comment. Especially since out of all of his brothers, Gabe was the last one he'd ever imagined would be in a serious relationship at this point.

"And what about you?"

"What about me?" he asked.

"Anyone special that you're seeing?"

He was about to tell her there wasn't, but then he remembered a conversation he'd had with Nora. She had point-blank asked him if he was still in love with Mia. And the only reason she thought that was the case was because he hadn't really dated anyone significant since her. But it had nothing to do with leftover feelings for Mia and everything to do with the fact that he was wary of getting blindsided again. After all, he was the idiot who was going to propose to his longtime girlfriend and hadn't seen that her feelings had changed for him somewhere along the way. Sure, he had felt the emotional distance at times, but he had chalked it up to their physical distance. He'd known Mia all his life, but it turned out he didn't know her at all. How could he trust himself again and risk losing his heart to someone who would just throw it away eventually?

He dated here and there—mainly because he did get lonely. His brothers loved to set him up, especially Nico—though only when Daniel wasn't available and he needed another guy for his date's friend. But he tried to be realistic and not go into anything looking for a relationship. And because he hadn't had a serious girlfriend for years, everyone just assumed he was still hung up on his ex.

Tomás did not want Mia to think the same thing.

"Uh, yeah. I'm dating someone. It's still new, though, so we'll see where it goes."

"Oh, that's good. I'm happy for you."

"Thank you."

There was some more silence until she finally said

she needed to get back to work. They ended the call with Tomás saying he was looking forward to meeting her fiancé.

"Why did I say that?" he questioned himself after disconnecting the call.

Because now there would be no getting out of doing exactly that. He opened up the calendar app on his phone to double-check the date of the party.

Tomás thought about the concoction cooking inside the house. Maybe he should ask Abuelita for some after all. He could save it in case he decided he needed to have an upset stomach in about two weeks.

Chapter Fourteen

Why on earth was she so nervous?

Veronica rearranged the throw pillows on the couch for the third time in an attempt to distract herself. It wasn't like she hadn't had this conversation with someone before.

But Tomás was an entirely different story. Deep down she knew he was going to be the key to a successful showing at the competition. There was something in his eyes that allowed her to trust him completely. That was what she wanted—what she needed. Tomás wouldn't bullshit her, and he wouldn't try to control her either. He would be the partner she had been looking for. The problem was, he couldn't know what she knew with certainty.

In other words, she had to make him believe what she did.

And there was a good chance he would refuse her anyway.

A loud knock startled her.

Tranquila, Vero. Tranquila.

She took a deep breath and opened her front door.

"Hi, Tomás. Thanks for coming over."

He took off his cowboy hat and walked inside. "Of course. You said it was important."

She motioned for him to take a seat on the couch. He looked at it, paused, and then sat down in the armchair instead.

Veronica smiled to herself as she picked up the brown paper gift bag that had been sitting on the small coffee table.

"This is for you," she said, holding it out to him.

"For me?" he asked instead of taking it. Tomás raised his eyebrow at her questioningly.

She nodded quickly and moved it closer until he finally accepted it. Veronica watched with eagerness as he pulled out the sweater.

"I wanted to get you a little thank-you gift. Your advice about Takuache is really helping. I definitely feel like he's settling in and getting more comfortable."

Tomás held the sweater up in front of him. Then he put it back in the bag.

"Thank you. It's very nice, but you didn't have to buy me a gift."

"I know I didn't have to. I wanted to."

He looked down at the bag and for a second she was worried he was going to say he couldn't accept it. God, that would be so embarrassing.

Instead, he stood up. "Thank you, Veronica. I appreciate it. Uh, I guess I better get back to work." He headed for the door with the bag in his left hand.

"Are you really busy today?" she asked, walking after him.

"Yeah. I have a few things to finish up before lunch. Why? Was there something else you needed?"

Veronica clasped her hands in front of her. "Well,

I didn't mean to interrupt your work. I just wanted to talk for a few minutes, but it sounds like this isn't a good time. I'll catch you later."

He stepped away from the door and closer to her. "I didn't realize. You're not interrupting me. What did you want to talk about?"

She'd almost changed her mind about asking him her big question. She could barely handle the possibility of him rejecting the sweater. How on earth could she handle him rejecting her?

Still, this was important. Veronica needed to suck it up and just ask.

"It's about Charles," she began.

"What about him?" he asked.

"He's not giving me what I need, you know, as a trainer. I want to hire you to be my, um, secret trainer."

"Secret?" he said with raised eyebrows.

Veronica cleared her throat. She was too embarrassed to go into all of the reasons their arrangement had to be off the books. "I just meant that I'd still keep Charles as my official trainer, but I'd like to work with you...um, after hours. And we'd keep it just between the two of us."

Tomás looked at her as if she'd just grown a second head. And then he roared with laughter. "Good one. You're very believable, you know that? For a second I thought you were serious."

Veronica squared her shoulders. This was not the reaction she'd expected from him.

"Tomás. I am serious."

The amused expression that had covered his face morphed into pure confusion. "You realize I have absolutely zero experience as an Olympic trainer, right?"

She took a step closer so he could see exactly how much thought she'd given the idea. "But you do have experience working with horses. I want you to do with me what you did with Ranger."

"Do what, exactly?"

"Bring out my best. Bring out Takuache's best."

"That's what Charles is for."

"You're not understanding. Charles is not who I need. He doesn't get me or Takuache. He's more worried about doing things the way he's always done them rather than adapting to me and my style. It's frustrating."

"So, fire him and hire someone else—a real trainer."

"I don't need a real trainer. I need you."

Heat warmed her cheeks after realizing how that sounded.

Fortunately for her, Tomás didn't seem fazed. "Why on earth would you think that I could do something like train you for an Olympic qualifying equestrian jumping competition?"

"Because I believe that you can."

It was the truth. Even though she had doubted Tomás's expertise when she'd first arrived at Rancho Lindo, he had more than proven to her that he could help her.

Tomás dragged his hand over his face before meeting her eyes. "Veronica, I really am flattered. And I promise I will do what I can to help you...from the sidelines. But I can't be your trainer. I'm sorry."

Veronica's heart dropped. Tomás was rejecting her.

As soon as he'd left, she plopped down onto the sea of throw pillows. She considered calling her sister to wallow in her defeat.

Then she remembered that she was Veronica del Valle and she never gave up without a fight.

Chapter Fifteen

Cruz announced his arrival by slamming the office door.

Tomás jerked his head up. "What the hell, Cruz?" he yelled. "I just fixed the doorknob."

His oldest brother crossed the small room in one long stride. "Did you really tell Veronica that you wouldn't be her trainer?"

Irritation burned the back of his neck. Damn Nico. He knew it had been a mistake telling him about what happened with Veronica. But his younger brother had been in the kitchen when he'd come back from the cottage. Nico could tell something was up and Tomás just blurted it out.

He'd been thrown by Veronica's proposition. How had she come to the conclusion that he could be her trainer? It was ridiculous. That was exactly the word he'd used when he'd told Nico about it. And then almost immediately ordered him not breathe a word of it to Cruz.

"I don't know the first thing about being an equestrian jumping trainer," Tomás said.

Cruz threw up his hands. "So you watch some YouTube videos and learn. I honestly cannot believe you are throwing away this opportunity. It could really change our luck, Tomás. Why would you turn it down?"

Tomás shot up from his chair. "Because I don't have the time. I already told you I need help. Who's going to pick up the slack if I'm training Veronica?"

"We'll figure it out. Why can't you at least consider it? Obviously, Veronica thinks you can do the job."

But he didn't. And that was the real point. Because what if he did agree to it and Veronica didn't make it to the Olympics? No other equestrian trainer would want to come to Rancho Lindo knowing that its first and only rider failed. Tomás didn't want to be responsible for disappointing Veronica or hurting the ranch's reputation.

"It was a dumb idea, Cruz. We need to focus on the more realistic opportunities to bring in more money. I need to focus on getting more boarders."

"Tomás, why are you so stubborn? Just because this wasn't your idea doesn't mean it's a bad one. Do you really think Veronica would risk her career if she didn't think you could really help her win? I'm telling you, you need to think—"

Cruz was interrupted by Nico and Daniel bursting through the door.

"I just fixed the doorknob," he said again.

Daniel slammed his palms onto Tomás's desk. "Why didn't you tell us?"

He sighed. "Because I turned her down, so there's no need to have a whole big discussion about it."

"Who?" Daniel asked.

"Veronica."

"What exactly did you turn down?"

"She asked him to be her trainer and he said no." An obviously annoyed Nico filled in the blanks.

"Really?" Daniel still looked confused. "Hold up. I wasn't talking about Veronica. I was talking about Mia!"

The realization of what his brother was really referring to unsettled Tomás. He had no interest in having this conversation either.

"What about Mia?" Cruz said.

Daniel turned his attention to their oldest brother. "She's engaged."

"And she's bringing her fiancé to the party next weekend," Nico added.

Cruz nodded in understanding. "Oh," he said.

Tomás dropped back onto his chair. "No, there's no *Oh* needed. It's not a big deal. Why are you all acting like it is?"

"Because it's Mia," Daniel explained. "Also, because you've known for days and you didn't say a word to any of us. We know you, Tomás. You don't like to talk about Mia."

His usual frustration pricked the back of his neck. "It's not that I don't like to talk about her. It's that I have no reason to talk about her. She's not a part of my life anymore. So why would I care if she's engaged?"

"I think you protest too much, actually," Nico said.

"And I think all of you are trying to make something out of nothing. Trust me. I'm not secretly falling apart because my ex-girlfriend is getting married. That's what ex-girlfriends do, right?"

Nico sat on the edge of the desk. "By the way, Mom

is beside herself. Lina told us and we said something to Mom because we thought she already knew."

Now Tomás's gut wrenched with regret. He kicked himself for not saying anything to their mom. "Oh my God," he said and covered his face with his hands. This was so not how he had planned for his Monday to go.

He felt a hand on shoulder. It was Nico. "You okay?"

Tomás shook his head. "She's probably so mad at me."

"She is," his brother said matter-of-factly. "But she'll get over it. Are you really okay about this Mia news, though?"

"I'm fine," he said, trying to make them believe he was telling the truth. "Yes, it was a surprise, but only because we haven't really kept in touch. That's all. I told Mia that I was happy for her and I am. Really I am."

"We don't believe you," Cruz said and the others nodded in agreement.

"Well, it's the truth," he insisted. "I'll go talk to Mom right now and apologize for not telling her."

Tomás stood up again, but Nico pushed him back into the seat. "Hold up. That's not the only thing you're going to have to apologize for."

He jerked his head up. "What are you talking about?"

"Aren't you forgetting to tell us something else?" Daniel added.

Dread filled Tomás's gut. What was his brother talking about?

"What else isn't he sharing?" Cruz asked for him.

"Apparently our brother is secretly dating someone," Nico said with a sly grin.

"Spill it, Tomás," Daniel ordered. "Who's the lucky woman?"

Shit. This was much worse than not telling his mom about Mia. Panic made his heart start to race. Why had he lied to Mia? Now he was going to have to apologize to his mom for that too.

He needed some air.

Tomás leapt from his chair and walked past the unwelcome trio into the main stable. Unfortunately, they followed him.

"Where are you going?" Cruz said from behind him.

"To the house." He stopped walking and turned to face his brothers. "I have to talk to Mom about this."

"No, you don't," Nico said.

"Yes, I do. She's probably furious."

Daniel sighed. "You don't have to tell her because we didn't tell her. We wanted to talk to you about it first."

"Yeah. So now you can't leave until you tell us who she is," Nico said.

He threw up his hands. "I lied. I told Mia I was dating someone so she wouldn't think I was some pathetic loser. I'm not dating anyone."

A huge grin crossed Nico's face and he slapped Daniel on the arm. "I told you. You owe me twenty bucks."

Cruz shook his head. "Really, Tomás? So what are you going to do when you see Mia at the party? Introduce her to your invisible girlfriend?"

He hung his head. "I didn't really think that far ahead. I guess I'll tell her the truth."

"No you won't."

They all looked at Nico. "What? Did you not hear me? There is no girlfriend." Tomás let out a long, deep sigh.

"Not now. But there can be. I'll just make some calls and get you a date for the party. I'm sure I could find at least one woman in all of the Central Valley who wouldn't mind being your plus-one."

Tomás shook his head. "Absolutely not. I am not going to fake-date one of your exes."

He didn't need to complicate the situation any more than it already was. Yes, it might be awkward at first, but he would figure it out.

"Like I told you before, I'm perfectly capable of being in the same room with her. And I'm not about to do something stupid that could ruin the party. It will all be fine."

He looked at his brothers for confirmation that everything would in fact be fine.

But instead he only saw the scheming going on inside all of their heads.

"We could hire someone to pretend to be your girlfriend," Cruz said.

"Yes, great idea!" Nico shouted and then gave Cruz a high-five.

"But where are we going to find a woman willing to play along?" Daniel asked.

"I'll do it. And you don't even have to pay me."

All of them turned around to see Veronica walking out of Takuache's stall.

Chapter Sixteen

All of them started talking at once.

Veronica just stood there amused by the chaos she'd just unleashed.

She had taken Takuache for a short ride after their usual training session and had just come back when she'd overheard the brothers talking inside Tomás's office. She couldn't quite make out every word, and part of her was tempted to put her ear against the door. Instead, she'd gone inside Takuache's stall to remove his saddle. Several minutes later, the conversation from inside the office had carried out into the main area of the stable. This time she could hear every single thing.

Veronica had been shocked by Tomás's admission. And she'd also felt bad for him. Then a lightbulb turned on inside her head and she knew she had to share her brilliant idea.

Of course she should pretend to be Tomás's girlfriend. And she was serious about them not having to pay her. After all, there was something else she'd accept in return.

The guys were still talking—or maybe it was arguing?

So Veronica put her fingers to her mouth and blew. The high-pitched whistle did its job, and finally silence came to the stable.

Tomás stepped closer to her and simply said, "No. Thank you. But no." He then walked away from everyone and went back inside his office.

Daniel waved at her to go follow him. "He's stubborn. Go talk to him."

"I don't think it's a good idea," Nico announced.

"You're the one who offered up your exes," Daniel said. "Veronica is a much better option."

"Thanks. I think?" she said before turning around to follow Tomás.

By the time she got to his office, he was sitting behind his little desk. Papers were stacked in towers of various heights, and a row of cups and mugs lined one side. For someone who was so meticulous about his horses and stable, Tomás was the opposite when it came to this area.

He didn't acknowledge her presence at first. Maybe he thought if he ignored her then she'd leave. He should have known by now that she didn't scare that easily.

Veronica sat down in one of the chairs across the desk from him. "Why do you like telling me no?"

Tomás looked up, opened his mouth, shut it, and went back to scribbling on the notepad in front of him.

"I was serious, Tomás. I'll be your fake girlfriend at the party."

"No," he said without looking up.

"Why? Am I not pretty enough to be your girlfriend?"

That made him finally meet her eyes. "Don't be ridiculous. You're gorgeous and you know it."

Veronica hadn't been fishing for a compliment, so she didn't know how to respond to that. But it emboldened her to keep going.

"Then let me do this for you. Your brothers think it's a good idea."

"Well, I don't," he said and went back to studying the papers in front of him. "I shouldn't have lied to Mia in the first place. I don't want to keep lying once she's here."

Veronica sighed. Normally she would've stopped pushing by now. She wasn't the kind of woman who begged for someone to date her—fake or not. But she was determined to convince Tomás to train her. Helping him out with his ex situation would be a bonus.

She decided to tell Tomás something she hadn't told anyone in a very long time.

"I want to help you because I know where you're coming from."

He looked up at her again. "What do you mean?"

"I understand having to face an ex who has already moved on," she confessed after a long sigh. "And if you pretend it's not going to affect you, then you run the risk of getting hurt again. Well, in my case, it actually landed me in the hospital and in the starring role of a certain embarrassing viral video."

His eyes widened in shock. "Are you telling me that what happened to you three years ago was because of a guy?"

"Yep," she scoffed, heated embarrassment starting to creep up her neck. "How basic is that?"

"What happened?" he asked softly.

Veronica allowed herself to go back to that moment in time when her entire world shattered.

"I was with Sebastian for two years. We broke up a few days before the competition. I was sad, but I decided to just focus all my energy into my training. And I thought I was fine. Then the morning of my event, I had just finished a TV interview at the hotel and as I was walking back to my room, I ran into him. He was coming out of the elevator with Lorena Silva—one of my biggest competitors. It was obvious they were together, probably had been for a while."

"Dammit," Tomás said.

"He basically admitted my assumption was right, but just blamed me for being too focused on the competition and ignoring our relationship. Which was bullshit since I'm sure Lorena was just as focused. Anyway, I somehow kept my cool, but once I arrived at the arena, I was a mess. I didn't do my usual safety check and missed that Takuache's bridle had been damaged during my practice ride the day before. It broke during my first jump."

"I'm so sorry you had to go through all that. That Sebastian guy was obviously a selfish jerk."

Her chest warmed at the tense expression on Tomás's face. He looked angry for her.

"He was," she admitted, trying to dismiss the uneasy feelings that were being stirred up by bringing up that horrible day. "I realize that now. But my point is that I understand how hard it can be to see that your ex has moved on. So if I can do something to help make it easier for you, then I want to do it."

Tomás sighed. "I really appreciate the gesture. But Mia and I broke up years ago. And I've seen her a couple of times since then. It's no big deal."

"But she didn't have a fiancé at that time," she said.

Veronica didn't mean to be so blunt, but she knew Tomás was being a little naïve. Based on what Nora had told her, she had a sneaking suspicion that his heart hadn't completely healed from Mia. She had been his first girlfriend, his first love, probably his first everything. How could she not still have a tiny hold on his heart? He was in store for a rude awakening if he didn't think he'd be affected by seeing Mia with the man she was planning to marry. She tried to soften her explanation.

"You may think it's not going to be a big deal, but it *is* going to be different. Why not just be prepared, that's all."

He regarded her with an impressed nod. "You make it sound like pretending to be my girlfriend would be so easy. That's kind of a huge favor. And it could become complicated because my family would have so many questions—especially my mom. How can you be so nonchalant about it?"

She was also impressed that she wasn't arguing with him to let her do it. "I am, aren't I? That's because I want you to see that this can be just another business arrangement between us. Except no payment necessary."

He leaned back into chair. "But you do want something in return, don't you?" he said.

"Not really," she said with a shrug. "Let's just say that I'll do this favor for you and maybe you can do a favor for me one day."

He looked at her. Really looked at her. An uncomfortableness slowly began to rise inside her. But she wasn't going to back down. Not when something as important as her career was on the line.

She folded her arms against her chest. "Fine," she admitted. "I'm still hoping you'll agree to be my trainer."

"*Secret* trainer," he emphasized.

Why did he say the word as if it was something horrible? "Yes, *secret*. I can't fire Charles, so yes, you'd have to train me after hours."

"Why can't you fire him?"

"It's complicated. It just has to be this way, that's all. So let's help each other out."

"I already said I don't need your help. I got over Mia a long time ago."

She met his eyes in a challenge. "Then why don't you date?"

"Excuse me?" he asked. His entire posture stiffened in apparent defense.

Veronica pressed forward. "People say you haven't had a real girlfriend since Mia, and they think it's because you're not over her."

"People need to mind their own business. And so do you," he said sternly and pointed at her.

"Tomás," she answered, trying to ignore the pang of hurt that pinched her heart. This conversation was taking a turn that she didn't like. "I swear I'm not judging you. I promise. I haven't had a real relationship since Sebastian either."

Her admission seemed to surprise him. "Really? Why?"

"Well, for the first few months after the accident, I was still recovering from my injuries. And then even after my body healed, my mind didn't. I kind of just shut down. I didn't want to talk to or be around anybody. I even pushed away my sister and my dad. And it was another several months before I even stepped into a stable again. I was in a dark place and all I kept thinking about was Sebastian's accusation that all I cared about was being in the Olympics. I had sacrificed so much for so long and it had all been for nothing."

"It wasn't for nothing," he said matter-of-factly. "Not many people get as far as you did."

"Yeah, but I didn't see it like that. Therapy finally helped me pull myself out of that funk. And when I did, I promised to only do things that made me happy. I spent as much time as I could with my family and I even started volunteering at our town's equestrian center. By that time, dating just wasn't a priority. And I'm sure part of that was a fear of getting my heart broken again. Then I decided to go for a comeback. Romantic relationships aren't my priority right now. Instead, I try very hard to let the people in my life know that they are what truly matter to me—Olympics or no Olympics."

"I guess we are the same—that way," he said and leaned toward her. "Still doesn't mean I'm afraid of seeing Mia with her fiancé."

She shook her head furiously. "I don't think you're afraid, Tomás. I just think you're trying to convince yourself that it's not going to be hard."

He threw up his hands. "Fine, it's going to be hard. I can still handle it . . . on my own."

"Maybe. Maybe not. Your brothers think this plan could help you, you know, if Mia saw you with someone else. Hell, maybe it might even attract you a real girlfriend. You know women always want what they can't have."

He laughed at her bluntness. "I'm sure my brothers—and maybe Nora—have spun quite a tragic tale about why I don't have a girlfriend. But I have this handled, okay? Besides, you once told me I annoyed you. What makes you think that's going to change if we pretend to be dating?"

Veronica didn't have a response to his words. She could've told him the truth. She could've told him that he didn't annoy her anymore. In fact, she had grown to enjoy spending time with him. But for some reason she felt like he wouldn't believe her and would think she was only saying that to get what she wanted.

Instead she told him that she'd drop it and walked out of his office.

She would have to come up with a Plan B to get him to be her trainer.

Chapter Seventeen

The morning of the anniversary party seemed to arrive out of the blue.

Although it had been on Tomás's mind for the past several weeks, he still couldn't quite believe it was already here.

He told himself the day didn't have to be a big deal. He would go to the Mass with his family and then come back home and get ready for the party. Of course, he knew he'd have to talk to Mia at some point. He just kept reminding himself to make sure whatever conversation they had was light and friendly. It didn't have to be more than that.

No big deal at all.

The Ortegas arrived at the church about fifteen minutes before the Mass was scheduled to start. They were all dressed in their Sunday best despite it being a Saturday. Even Tomás's dad. He was happy that his dad seemed to be feeling good enough to join them. The night before, he and his brothers had discussed who would stay at the house with him in case he didn't feel up to going. Nico had volunteered, but his dad had insisted he would be fine. And so the entire family, including Nora, were now walking toward the church from the parking lot.

Tomás, who had been focused on the small group of people congregated at the entrance doors, was surprised when he felt a hand slip into his. It was his mom.

"You look so nice today, Mijo," she said, then gave him a gentle tug as if to slow down his pace. "I'm glad all of you decided to get haircuts. Well, except for Nico, of course. He says he's going to grow his hair down to his butt!"

Tomás laughed. "He only tells you that because he knows how much you hate it."

"I do hate it. One night I'm going to sneak into his room and cut it myself."

"If you do, let me know and I'll hold the flashlight."

She laughed, but then her expression turned serious. He arched his eyebrow in an unspoken question. As the rest of the family continued to walk ahead of them, she said softly so only he could hear, "You okay?"

Tomás gave her a quick nod. "Yeah. Are you?"

She smiled. "I am. I have a feeling it's going to be a wonderful day. I'm so happy for my friends."

He nodded again in agreement. He also knew her positive attitude had a lot to do with how his dad was feeling that day. "I'm glad you're happy, Mom." It was the absolute truth. The last several months had obviously taken a toll on her. It was good to see her like this.

"And you? Are you happy?" she asked.

"Of course. I'm happy for them too."

"That's not what I meant."

Tomás stopped walking so he could look his mom in her concerned eyes. "I already told you. I'm fine. I don't want you worrying about me or anyone else today. I want you to enjoy yourself, okay?"

"I can't help it," she admitted. "I hate seeing my boys hurting."

"Mamá. I'm not hurting. Please stop worrying about me and Mia. It's going to be a good day for everyone."

She opened her mouth as if to say something else, but his dad called out to her. Instead of continuing the conversation, she pulled him in for a quick hug and whispered, "You're a good son, Tomás."

Then she left him standing on the sidewalk.

A few minutes later he joined the rest of the family inside the church. They were all seated in the same pew, just a few feet away from the altar. Most of Esperanza's residents filled the rest of the seats. Then everyone stood up as an organist began to play.

Omar and his wife with their baby walked down the aisle first. He gave his old friend a customary nod and got one back in return. Tomás still couldn't believe Omar was a dad now. Omar was the same age as Nico and he still thought of him as his brother's partner in crime when Daniel was either not around or too smart to agree to whatever chaos Nico was planning. Abuelita had referred to Nico and Omar as Travieso Uno and Travieso Dos for as long as he could remember. They were troublemakers through and through. And now one of them was responsible for a tiny human.

Unbelievable.

He smiled at the thought and was about to lean over to say something to Nico, but then he spotted her.

Mia.

She was walking arm in arm with her dad down the aisle. His heartbeat quickened with each step she took. It didn't matter that he'd seen her a handful of times over the past several years. It was as if he was seeing her for the first time after she'd basically broken his heart. In a way, she had done it again.

Emotions slammed into him like a wave, knocking down every defense he'd been trying to fortify ever since Mia had told him that she was engaged. Everyone had been right. This time was different. He had lied to himself just like he'd lied to everyone that he was fine. Not because he still loved her, but because it was a painful reminder that he hadn't been good enough for her. The past eight years was more than enough time to get over her betrayal. But he realized it had helped that she'd also never really had a serious boyfriend after him. She was committed to her career, her mom liked to tell him. And that gave him the excuse he needed to accept that it wasn't him—it was her. She didn't want to marry him because she didn't want to get married. Period.

But now she'd met someone who had changed her mind. Mia hadn't said no to him because she didn't want to get married. She just didn't want to marry *him*. And he couldn't help but feel rejected all over again.

Luckily for Tomás, she was too busy waving to people across the aisle to notice him. And then just like that, he was staring at the back of her head.

Determined to shake off his unexpected feelings at seeing Mia, he turned his attention to Lina, who had just entered through the church's doors. The organist began playing the traditional wedding march as she began her procession. It seemed that Lina had been very serious indeed about getting the wedding she had always wanted—right down to the white dress and veil.

The rest of the Mass passed in a blur. Because the more Tomás tried not to think of Mia and when he was finally going to have to talk to her, the more he thought about it.

Luckily for him that wouldn't happen right after Mass. He and his brothers were tasked with rushing back to Rancho Lindo to finish setting up for the party. Since the Riveras lived in a small house behind the diner, the Ortegas had offered to host the event in their backyard.

About thirty minutes after they came home, guests began arriving.

Including Veronica. She had walked into the backyard with Nora, and his breath caught at the sight of her. She wore her long dark hair down in soft waves again, but he had never seen her so dressed up. Or looking so beautiful.

He waved at them and met them by the door leading into the house.

"Hey there. You look . . . you both look nice."

Nora beamed and gave him a big smile. "You already told me that. But thank you again."

"Thank you. You look nice too," Veronica said. "Are you sure it's okay that I'm here? They don't even know me."

Tomás nodded. "Of course it's okay. You're a guest of Rancho Lindo, so you automatically get an invite."

"See, I told you," Nora said to her. "All right, I'm

going to go find that boyfriend of mine. I have a feeling he's already scoping out the food. I swear that man is always hungry."

They all laughed and then Nora left in search of Gabe, leaving Tomás and Veronica alone.

After a few seconds of silence, she asked, "So how was the ceremony?"

"It was nice. And the church was packed, so I'm sure there are going to be a ton of people here in a few minutes."

"And how was it seeing Mia?"

Tomás probably should've lied and told her it was fine. But he wasn't sure he could sell it, and that would just bring up more questions. So he told the truth. "You were right. It was weird."

Veronica reached out and touched his arm. "I'm sorry."

"I was more nervous than I thought. Why is that? It's been eight years, for Pete's sake. How pathetic am I?"

"You're not pathetic, Tomás. You're human," she said and then grabbed his hand to squeeze it. The kind gesture told him it was safe to let out all the things he'd been feeling during the Mass.

"I know I don't have romantic feelings for her anymore," he began. "But why does it bother me that she's engaged?"

He lowered his head to look at the cement under his feet. Veronica took a step closer and looked up to meet his eyes. "You loved her once. She was part of your life for a long time. It's normal for these old feelings to come rushing back."

"That's the thing, though. This has nothing to do

with old feelings. I think...I think I'm embarrassed that she's found someone to spend her life with and I haven't. It's almost as if I'm still the same guy she broke up with."

Veronica shook her head. "You're not the same man you were eight years ago."

"I kind of am."

"What do you mean?"

"I'm exactly where I was when she broke up with me—working in Rancho Lindo's stable. Mia told me she couldn't see a future with me because she didn't want to live the rest of her life in the same small town. She wanted adventure and to experience new things and she knew if we stayed together then she wouldn't be able to fulfill her dreams. And she was right. Because while she's traveled all over the world and achieved success in her career choices, I haven't done any of those things. I'm exactly where I was when she left me."

Tomás shook his head in shame. Everyone had been right. He hadn't moved on at all. And that pissed him off. Not because he still loved Mia. It was because he was embarrassed to have confirmed that she'd made the right decision all those years ago.

"You're being too hard on yourself," Veronica told him. "You're doing what you love, Tomás. How many people can say that?"

He met her eyes and saw the genuineness reflected in them. Her words touched him, and a warmth spread through his chest. He wanted to tell her how much it meant to him to hear her say that.

"Veronica, I—"

"Hello, Tomás."

A woman's voice behind him interrupted his words.

He knew it was Mia without even having to turn around. He glanced at Veronica for a second in a panic. She winked at him and squeezed his hand again before letting go. Then she was gone.

"Hello, Mia," Tomás said after he came face-to-face with his ex and a man he didn't recognize. He assumed it was the fiancé. She confirmed it a few seconds later.

"This is Brian, my fiancé," Mia said.

Brian was taller than Tomás by at least a good inch. He had red hair and blue eyes. He reminded Tomás of one of the sons of England's Princess Diana—the spare, as his abuelita called him.

Tomás held out his hand and the man took it and gave it a firm shake. "Good to meet you, Tomás."

"Same. It's nice to see you...both."

Brian nodded as a ringing sound erupted from his pocket. He took out a phone, glanced at it, and told Mia he would be back in few minutes. She smiled and then turned back to Tomás.

"It's nice to see you, Mia," he said.

"You said that already," she reminded him.

He laughed. "I did, didn't I?"

"Is this weird?" she blurted. "Because it feels a little weird and I don't want it to be."

"It's only weird when we talk. Guess it's going to be a very quiet week."

"Guess so," she said with a laugh.

"Your hair is shorter." He had no idea why he said that.

She touched the ends of her straightened bob, almost defensively. He hadn't meant for the comment to sound like an accusation. He was never good at small talk.

She told him she'd cut her medium-length locks on a whim.

"It looks good on you," he added. The simple compliment came easy.

"Thanks," she said. "Your hair is...the same."

So is everything else about me, he thought. He attempted a smile and hoped he didn't seem as nervous as he was feeling.

Then she surprised him when she told him, "Thank you."

Tomás looked at her and raised an eyebrow. "For what?"

"For being so polite. I'm sure I'm not exactly your favorite person these days."

He shrugged. "I don't hate you, Mia."

"I'm glad," she said with a nod. "I also want you to know that I'm not here to stir up the past. I probably shouldn't tell you this, but I kind of dread having to come back to Esperanza because I never know how things are going to be between us. But I wouldn't have missed this for the world, and that's the only reason I'm here. For my parents."

In other words, he was just another person who lived in town. Not that he expected to mean anything more to her than that.

Brian came back and immediately wrapped his arm around Mia's waist.

"So how was the reunion?" he asked Mia.

"Good," she said.

He winked at her and then turned to Tomás. "I have to tell you that I've been very curious to meet you."

"Really?" he replied, purposely not adding that he was curious to meet Brian.

"Yeah, of course. I wanted to meet my competition." Brian laughed at his own joke, but he could tell Mia was embarrassed.

Tomás held up his hands. "Not competition."

"Oh, I know. I'm just messing with you. Besides, Mia says you've got a girlfriend. Is she here?"

Mia looked around. "Oh yeah. Where did she go? I would love to meet her."

Tomás's anxiety shot up. He had planned to tell Mia the truth in private—not in front of her fiancé and the rest of the party guests.

"Uh, funny story, um," he stammered.

"I'm back, honey. Sorry, I had to go help your mom with something."

Tomás felt an arm link through his and he turned to make sure it really was Veronica by his side. He still couldn't find any words to say.

As usual, Veronica took control of the reins. "So nice to meet you, Mia. I'm Veronica. Tomás's girlfriend."

And then she promptly kissed him on the cheek.

Chapter Eighteen

Tomás nearly choked on his own saliva.

After a few coughs, Veronica unhooked her arm and looked at him with concern. "I'm going to get you some water."

"I'll...go...with...you," he spit out and followed her into the house.

He was still coughing when she handed him a glass of water. He took it, grabbed her hand, and pulled her in the home office. After taking a few gulps, he was able to speak again.

"Why did you say that?"

To her credit, she did look surprised. "I thought you had changed your mind about the whole fake-girlfriend thing. I thought that's what you were trying to tell me before she showed up."

He shook his head. "What I was trying to tell you was what I was telling you. That's all. I hadn't changed my mind."

"Oh," Veronica replied.

"What am I going to say now? I'm going to look like an idiot. Actually I'm going to look like an idiot that lies."

Tomás couldn't believe what was happening. How was he going to fix this?

Veronica took a seat on the small leather love seat inside the office. "Look, I'm sorry. I jumped the gun and read into things. But this isn't a disaster. It's only for one night, remember?"

It didn't matter if it was one night or ten. Tomás didn't like being caught off guard or being forced into something he didn't want to do.

"Let me guess," he said bitterly. "This means I'm also roped into being your trainer. Oh, excuse me, *secret* trainer."

The secrecy thing still irritated him. If she needed him to help her so badly, then why not tell her dad or anyone else? He didn't want to be something she had to hide. If she was ashamed of having a trainer who wasn't experienced, then why ask him at all?

She studied him for a few seconds. "I'm not roping you into anything, Tomás. I'm offering to do this for you tonight. No strings attached, okay? But if you happen to change your mind, then I wouldn't mind it."

He walked away from her to look out the office's window. It was all too much.

"Can I ask you something?" she asked him.

Tomás turned around but stayed where he was. "I guess."

"Is there something else that's bothering you... about me?"

"You? No. Why would you ask that?"

"Because I don't understand why you're so against this training proposition. Why are you so opposed to it?"

"Because if you're going to be too ashamed to tell people I'm training you, then why even ask me?"

Tomás wasn't quite sure why he'd decided to tell her the truth. The last thing he wanted Veronica to think was that he cared about things like that. Even though a part of him did.

She stood up and walked over to him. "I would never be ashamed of that, Tomás. The reason I can't say anything is because I don't want any sort of controversy hanging over me in Kentucky."

Tomás didn't understand. Veronica was a highly respected equestrian jumping champion. "What are you talking about?"

Veronica exhaled. "I can't fire Charles because it will only add fuel to the rumors that I'm…difficult. Charles is the only trainer left in the world who is willing to work with me. And if I let him go, then that's the only thing that the media will focus on—that's the only thing I'll get asked about at the competition. And I don't need another scandal overshadowing me. Not again."

He was moved by the vulnerability in her tone. He believed her pain, and he didn't want to be the reason she experienced any more. He could see now how important this was to her.

Tomás took a step closer. "Okay, I'll train you. In secret." She was about to hug him when the door to the office flew open and Nico walked inside the room.

"What the hell, guys. You realize you basically just set off a bomb and left."

"What?" Tomás took a step away from Veronica to face his brother.

But Nico turned his attention to Veronica. "That was quite the show. Everyone is talking about it."

"Oops," she said, glancing at Tomás.

Cruz and his mom walked in next.

He nearly cursed out loud. Nico muttered something about finding Daniel and then he was gone. Classic Nico.

Tomás looked at his mom and other brother. He took a deep breath to begin to explain.

Before he could say anything, though, Veronica spoke. "We were just heading back to the party."

His mom arched an eyebrow. "Is there something you two forgot to tell me?"

Tomás cleared his throat and Veronica attempted a small smile. "There is, Mom," he began, "but now's not the time. I promise you can ask us all the questions you want in the morning. Let's just enjoy the party, okay?"

His mom wasn't a dumb woman. She obviously knew he was trying to deflect, but she also knew better than to push the issue. Especially tonight of all nights.

"Fine," she said with a roll of her eyes. "We'll talk tomorrow."

When the door closed behind her, Tomás focused his attention back onto Veronica. He walked over to her and said, "I can't lie to my mom, Veronica. She's…"

He stopped himself. This wasn't the time or place to tell her about his dad. "She's Lina's best friend. She won't be happy about this."

Veronica looked up at him, and he tried to ignore her slightly smeared lipstick and the fact it was his cheek that had smeared it. "Look, I understand this just got more complicated. But we can figure things out later. I think the best thing right now is for us to get back to the party."

Tomás wanted to figure things out now. But if he knew his family, the rest of them would come barging through those doors any second now. He needed to get her out of there as soon as possible.

"All right," he said. "But it might be best if you stay close to me. I'll bet good money my abuelita and Nora are going to try to corner you and pepper you with questions. We need to get our stories straight before that happens."

Veronica grinned. "Wait. Does this mean we're really fake-dating?"

"I told you from the beginning that I wasn't comfortable with this. But you can't unring a bell. So for tonight and tonight only, yes, we are fake-dating."

She reached out to tug on his tie. "You're welcome."

He took her hand off him. "I didn't thank you."

"You will. Eventually."

He walked to the door and opened it. "Let's get back to the party and deal with the repercussions of your little stunt."

Chapter Nineteen

Veronica always loved a good party, and the Ortegas really knew how to throw a great one.

She guessed that there must have been at least a hundred people under a large white tent set up in the large home's sprawling backyard. The patio held stations for all sorts of food, desserts, and drinks. And laughter and animated conversations competed with instrumental music played by a live band.

It reminded her of the parties her parents used to host at both their estate in Mexico and their home in Colorado. She pushed away the lilts of sadness that seemed to drift through her whenever she thought of what used to be. It hit her then that the Ortegas reminded her of her own parents, especially Señora Ortega. She'd only had a handful of conversations with the woman, but she could tell that she was kind and generous and loved her children unconditionally.

"Are you okay?" Tomás whispered as they walked from the patio toward the tent to find a seat for dinner.

She swallowed down her unexpected emotion. "Yeah. I'm good. How about you?"

"I've been better. Is it just me or is everyone watching us?"

"Oh, definitely. I think we are the pre-dinner entertainment."

Veronica smiled and then took Tomás's hand. He flinched and instinctively tried to pull it out of her grip, but she held on tight. "We're onstage, remember? We need to put on a good show."

She felt his hand relax and then instead of her holding him, he was now holding her hand.

His hand was rough. Which was understandable given his work. But it wasn't so brusque that it irritated her. In fact, it felt nice. Comfortable even.

Then his brother Cruz walked up to them and Tomás let go.

"We need to put out another table and six chairs," Cruz said.

Tomás looked at Veronica. "I'll be back in about five minutes."

She smiled. "Okay. I'll go get us some drinks. Beer?"

He nodded and then walked off with Cruz. Veronica headed over to the bar cart set up in the corner of the tent. She asked for two Modelos and watched as the bartender pulled them from a tub of ice.

A large, bald man came up beside her. "Good choice," he said as the bartender handed her the two bottles. "But don't tell me those are both for you."

She laughed. "No. Although it's still early, right?"

That made him bellow and he turned to face her head-on. "I don't think I've had the pleasure of meeting you, miss," the man said, reaching out his hand. "Although you do seem familiar to me. I'm Eduardo."

Veronica shook his hand. "Hello, I'm Veronica."

"Are you sure we don't know each other?"

"No, I don't think so. I'm just in town to visit my friend from high school, Nora."

As far as Veronica concerned, she was going to stick to the story they'd already created as to what she was doing at Rancho Lindo. Plus, it would come in handy to explain when she eventually left.

The man frowned. "Hmm, I don't think I know her. I don't get to Esperanza often. But I'm an old friend of the happy couple," he said, pointing to Mia's parents, who were dancing.

"Oh. Where are you from?" she asked, then took a sip of her beer.

"Canada. But I travel all over, so I feel like I have many homes. In fact, I'm headed to Guadalajara in a few weeks."

Veronica nearly choked on her beer. No wonder she had seemed familiar to the man. She was pretty sure that he was a business associate of her father's. They had never met in person, but her dad always spoke fondly of his friend Eduardo from Canada. And knowing her dad, he probably had shown off photos of her and her sister to him at some point.

She had no idea if this man would eventually make the connection like she had. Nor could she trust that he wouldn't tell people that he'd run into Veronica del Valle at some party on some ranch in Esperanza.

"Oh, there's my boyfriend," she said, pointing to Tomás, who had just entered the tent carrying some folding chairs. "I better get him his beer before it gets too warm."

And before the man could say anything else or put a name to her face, Veronica walked away.

Several minutes later, the panic she'd felt had calmed down. It helped that she was back at Tomás's side at one of the round tables inside the tent.

"So, I got cornered by Abuelita when I was grabbing the chairs," Tomás said in a low voice so only she could hear.

Veronica gasped. "Oh no. What did she say?"

He chuckled. "That she knew something was going on a few weeks ago."

"What? Are you serious?" she asked.

"I am. She insists that we can never hide anything from her. She said, and I quote, that we make eyes for each other whenever we're in the same room."

Veronica let out a laugh. She knew his abuelita was a character. But this was too much.

"Glad you find this all so amusing," he said. "I'm never going to be able to look her in the eye again."

"It's not that horrible, Tomás. She'll forget all about us once she gets distracted by the next juicy piece of town gossip to come along."

"Are we gossip?" he said, looking horrified. "Gosh, that sounds so bad."

She touched his arm to reassure him. "It'll be fine. We just need to make it through tonight and then all of this attention will go away and you can go back to focusing on growing your stable's business and I can just focus on making the Olympic team."

Veronica knew she was right. This fake-dating scheme was temporary. And it had gotten her exactly what she'd wanted. Tomás had agreed to train her. As far as she was concerned, that was what mattered. They both could put up with a few more hours of questioning eyes and whatever else Tomás's abuelita thought she saw or didn't see.

Chapter Twenty

It was late when Tomás woke up that Sunday morning.

The stress of everything that had happened the day before had left him feeling exhausted and anxious. So he'd stayed home while the rest of the family had gone to Sunday Mass.

Voices and other noises coming from downstairs let him know that they were home, though, and he figured it was time to face the music. In other words, it was time to come clean to his mom.

He finally made his way to the kitchen just after ten. His mom, his abuelita, Gabe, and Nora were sitting around the island drinking coffee and eating their breakfast.

"Good morning, Mijo," his mom said. "There's some machaca con huevos on the stove and tortillas in the warmer on the counter."

"Thank you," he said and walked over to serve himself a plateful of the eggs scrambled with shredded dried beef, onions, chiles, and tomatoes.

Everyone was very quiet by the time he joined them at the kitchen island. And he felt eight eyes on him as he took his first bite of food. He knew he wouldn't be able to enjoy his breakfast until he cleared things up. He just hoped his mom wouldn't be too angry.

Tomás set down his fork, wiped his mouth, and began. "About last night—"

"I'm so happy for you, Mijo," his mom interrupted.

He raised an eyebrow in surprise. "You are? But I haven't told you—"

"Mom was just telling us how much she likes Veronica and is glad that you two are dating." This time it was Gabe who cut him off.

Abuelita clapped her hands in obvious excitement. "Sí, I am happy too. She's a good woman. I think she is good for you."

"But we're not . . ."

"Listen, Mijo. I know why you probably thought you had to keep this from us. But you don't have to do that anymore, okay." His mom's smile could've reached the heavens. Tomás felt mixed emotions watching her positively giddy with the idea of him and Veronica as a couple. He felt shame for deceiving her, yet it made him happy to see her like this. It had been a long time.

Maybe he could let her be this happy for one more day. He would tell her the truth tomorrow.

As his mom and abuelita chatted away about the party, he noticed that Nora hadn't said a word to him. In fact, she wouldn't even meet his eyes. And he knew her almost as well as he knew his brothers. Nora was upset with him.

"Hey, can you come with me to town in a few minutes?" Gabe asked. "I talked to Carl last night and he said he just got the delivery of those pavers we've been waiting on. I could use an extra hand."

"Yeah, sure. Just let me know when you want to go," Tomás said.

"Okay, give me a few minutes. I'm just going to go change."

Gabe kissed Nora on the side of her forehead and told her he would call her later. She nodded and then told his mom that she'd clean up and do the dishes. His mom thanked her and she and Abuelita said they'd finish their coffee out on the patio. But before she left, his mom came over and hugged him.

"What was that for?" he asked after she pulled away.

"Just because." Then she gave him a big smile and walked outside to join his abuelita.

After the door closed, Tomás stood up and told Nora, "I'll help you do the dishes."

"That's okay. I got it."

Her cool tone confirmed to him that she was pissed.

He followed her to the sink. "All right, Honora. What's wrong?" Tomás used her full name to let her know he was serious.

"I don't like this," she said without looking at him. "I don't like being a part of a plan that makes me have to lie to your mom and abuelita."

"Gabe told you," he said after a long sigh.

Nora turned to face him. "Of course. He told me last night at the party. Then he begged me to go along with it because it was only for last night. But now this morning? I don't like lying to them. You know that."

"But you're not the one lying, Nora. I am."

"I know the truth and the fact that I'm pretending not to is the same as lying. Gabe said you were going to confess everything to her today."

Tomás threw up his hands in frustration. "I was. But then she started going on about how happy she was, and I didn't want to take that away from her. Not yet. You know how sad she's been the last few months because of my dad. When was the last time you saw her so excited, so giddy about something like she was just a few minutes ago?"

Gabe walked back into the kitchen. "You ready?" he asked Tomás.

When he didn't answer, Gabe must have noticed the glare coming from his girlfriend's eyes. "What happened?"

Tomás gestured toward Nora. "She's mad at me about the Veronica situation."

"Actually, I'm mad at all of you Ortega brothers," she said. "It was a stupid idea, and you all are fools for coming up with it."

Gabe raised his palms. "Whoa. I already told you I had nothing to do with this. I only found out from Nico yesterday and I told you immediately."

"And I was against it from the very beginning," Tomás quickly added. "But then Veronica kind of improvised and I couldn't stop the train, I guess."

"Maybe," Nora replied. "But aren't you the one who told Mia you had a girlfriend in the first place?"

Damn Nico. He really had a big mouth.

"Yes, that was dumb and I take full responsibility for that. I swear, Nora, this isn't what I wanted. I'll tell my mom the truth tomorrow."

Nora crossed her arms against her chest. "Fine. I'll just make sure to keep to myself today. I don't want to run into her again and have to keep lying when she tries to ask me questions about you two."

"Thank you," Tomás said.

She wagged a finger in his direction. "Don't thank me. I'm not doing it for you. I'm doing it for your mom. You're right. It is nice to see her so happy and

I definitely don't want to upset her. But what I don't understand is why Veronica would agree to this."

"Because she wants me to help her train for the competition."

"Really?" Gabe asked. "I thought Charles was her trainer."

"He is and he still will be. I'm just going to be helping her after hours. But no one else can know about this, okay? Especially Cruz. I don't need him announcing it at the next city hall meeting."

"All right," Nora yelled and held up her hand in a stopping motion. "That's it. You two get out of here. I don't want to know anything else about anything I'm not allowed to talk about. I've had my secrets quota filled for the day." Then she turned her back to them and began washing dishes.

Tomás and Gabe arrived in town about fifteen minutes later and headed over to Carl's Landscaping to pick up their order. Gabe was planning to install the new pavers along the path leading from the main house down to Nora's garden.

As they waited for Carl to bring the pallet over to the truck, Gabe told Tomás not to worry about Nora.

"She's not going to stay mad at you forever," he said. "You know how protective she can get. She's just worried this little charade is going to blow up in your face."

"I thought it had. But the hard part is over. I'll tell Mom tomorrow that Veronica and I decided it would be best to just stay friends. I don't want her to know that I tried to trick her or Mia."

"I think that's best. She was pretty excited about you finally dating someone. And since I'm with Nora now, she only has three sons left to worry about ending up alone."

"Except it's all fake. Veronica and I are not you and Nora. And Veronica is leaving next month anyway."

"Then you go and find yourself a real girlfriend. I may not have been in on this plan from the beginning, but I see why you ended up agreeing to it. Nora will see it too."

Tomás wanted to believe Gabe. He wanted to believe that everything was going to work out and no one was going to be hurt by his deception in the long run.

After they loaded up the truck, the brothers walked over to the general store to pick up a few items, including a few pieces of Almond Roca for their abuelita. Nora snuck it to her secretly about once a week.

"I don't understand why it's still a secret if most of us know about it," Tomás said.

"Because Abuelita doesn't know that we know. Nora told Mom because she wanted to make sure she wasn't doing something that could hurt Abuelita. And Mom told Nora it was okay since it was only a few pieces and she knew Abuelita liked the fact that she shared this secret with Nora."

"So we all have to pretend it's still a secret because it makes Abuelita happy?" Tomás asked.

"Exactly."

It wasn't lost on Tomás that he was basically doing the same thing when it came to him and Veronica.

After the party, they'd talked for a while back at her cottage. She had apologized again for jumping the gun on their fake-dating plan. And she had also apologized for kissing him on the cheek. He said she didn't need to apologize. Truth be told, he hadn't minded it . . . that much.

"Hey, Mia," Gabe announced.

Tomás and Gabe had just walked out of the pharmacy and apparently right into Mia and Brian.

Tomás froze at the sight of them. Last night, Mia had mentioned that she was taking Brian into Santa Barbara for the day. It was the only reason he hadn't even considered seeing them in town.

"Hey, guys," she said with a big smile. "What are you doing in town?"

"Just picking up some things," Tomás answered. "What about you? I thought you were spending the day in Santa Barbara?"

"I asked her to show me around Esperanza," Brian said. "We'll go to Santa Barbara tomorrow."

"Yeah, my parents wanted to go with us, but I guess they partied a little too hard last night."

Gabe laughed the loudest. "I tried to cut your dad off once he kept asking me to dance the Macarena with him."

"He asked me too," Tomás said with a chuckle.

Mia covered her face with her hand. "Oh dear. Sorry about that."

"No need to apologize. I'm just glad he had a good time," Tomás said earnestly.

"Well, he did," Mia said. "They both did. And now they're paying for it."

Brian nodded. "We were all supposed to go to dinner tonight over in, what was it called again? Buellton? I have a feeling they're going to cancel on us for that too."

"I was thinking that too," Mia added. Then her eyes widened and she pointed at Tomás and Gabe. "Why don't you guys come with us and bring your girlfriends? Our reservation was for six because my brother and his wife were also going to come, but the baby has been teething and is running a fever, so my sister-in-law doesn't want to take her out."

Tomás was so thrown off by Mia's invitation that he nearly blurted, *What girlfriend?* Then he remembered she was talking about Veronica.

"Oh no, that's okay," he stammered. "We don't want to intrude on your plans. Besides, your parents might still want to go."

Mia shook her head. "Trust me. They're going to need at least another day to recuperate. You wouldn't be intruding at all."

"Then we'd love to go," Gabe said. Tomás whipped his head to look at his brother and called him all sorts of names telepathically. But Gabe just stood there with a goofy grin on his face. What on earth was he doing agreeing to go out with Mia and Brian?

Tomás asked him exactly that once they were back in the truck and Mia and Brian had disappeared into a nearby store.

Well, he didn't really ask him. Instead, he socked his brother in the arm.

"Oww!" Gabe yelled, "What the hell was that for?"

"For agreeing to dinner with them. Veronica was my fake girlfriend for one night only."

His brother shrugged. "I'm sure she won't mind. Nora, on the other hand, might have something to say about it. Might as well hit me again for her."

For a second Tomás couldn't decide what was worse—Veronica saying no to the dinner date or saying yes.

Chapter Twenty-One

It wasn't easy for Veronica to let someone else take control. Especially when it came to her training.

She put up with Charles in the beginning, thinking he knew better than her. But it was harder than she thought it would be to not challenge Tomás. His training style was all about feeling and senses. She had always been more tactical. Veronica did better with specific instruction and outcomes. She needed to know actual steps.

Telling her she should "sense" what Takuache was feeling wasn't exactly helpful.

So even though she wanted to question Tomás's methods—she kept her mouth shut. After all, she was the one who had come to him for help. Veronica couldn't give up after just one training session.

As much as a part of her wanted to.

"Sometimes you have to know when to quit," he told her.

Wait. Was Tomás reading her mind?

"Excuse me?" she asked. They had been out riding for about an hour. It was their first official training session. Veronica hadn't expected to get started so soon. But Tomás had texted her to meet him at the stables once he returned from town with Gabe. And although she'd been excited to start, the last sixty minutes had been more than frustrating.

"I'm just saying I think that's enough for today," Tomás said as he guided his horse, Peanut, to turn around.

"But why? When I train with Charles during the week, we usually do two or three hours." Veronica hated that she sounded like she was whining.

"Exactly. I don't want to push Takuache today when he's going to have a full workout tomorrow."

"Then why even suggest we start today?" Her frustration was building. And she didn't like feeling like she wasn't in control.

Tomás cleared his throat. "I guess I figured, after last night, that you'd want to get the training going."

He was right. But something still nagged at her. "All right. But since when do you do things because I want to?"

She watched him as they rode a few more feet. It was apparent to her that he wanted to tell her something but was struggling with getting it out.

"What is it, Tomás?" Veronica said. "Just tell me."

He waited a few more seconds and then said, "When Gabe and I were in town, we ran into Mia and Brian."

"Okay?"

"And dumb Gabe accepted Mia's invitation for him and Nora and me and you to have dinner with them tonight in Buellton."

"Oh," she said. Then she realized what he was

asking. "Ohhhh. So you want to do this pretend-dating thing one more time?"

"I don't want to. But I guess I have to."

Veronica blamed her already-building frustration for the spark of annoyance that shot through her at Tomás's tone. He made it sound like going on a fake date with her was going to be as enjoyable as a root canal.

"Gee. You really know how to charm a woman."

"You know that's not what I mean," he scoffed. "I'm not looking forward to spending a couple of hours with Mia and Brian, that's all. I should just tell Gabe that we're going to cancel."

"Do you think that's the best call?"

"Are you saying you want to go out to dinner with them?"

"Honestly, I couldn't care less," she said with a shrug. "I'll do whatever you want to do. But going out of your way to purposely avoid spending time with them might raise some eyebrows. You said your mom and her mom are best friends, right? What are you going tell your mom about why you didn't want to go to dinner with them?"

He was quiet for a few seconds before letting out a long sigh. "I hate when you're right."

"Likewise."

"Is that why you're mad at me?" he said after a pause.

She furrowed her eyebrows in confusion. "What? I'm not mad at you."

Tomás laughed. "Yeah, right. You've basically had steam coming out of your ears for the past hour."

The irritation was back in full force. "I have not. I've been listening to your advice, haven't I?"

"Judging by the tight expression you've had on your face all morning, you didn't like what you were hearing. Am I right?"

Disappointment roiled her stomach until it cramped. It was the same thing all her other trainers had complained about to her dad. She thought she'd been doing a good job of being more open to criticism, but he might as well have called her difficult. She didn't like the categorization—especially when she was making the effort not to be that way.

Veronica sat up straighter in her saddle. "All right, all right. Maybe this has been enough training for today."

"Veronica..." Tomás said.

Without looking at him, she gripped Takuache's reins. "Text me what time I need to be ready." Then she ordered her horse to move and rode away.

But as fast as Takuache ran, she still couldn't escape the feeling that maybe the fake-dating and the training arrangement were bad ideas after all.

Chapter Twenty-Two

Outside, the spring night air was cold. But it was nothing compared with the chill inside the SUV.

Tomás glanced over at Veronica, who was sitting next to him in the back seat. Gabe and Nora were in the front, and they were all on their way to the restaurant in Buellton.

She had engaged in some small talk with Nora, but basically ignored Tomás. His stress level was through the roof. How on earth were they going to be a convincing couple if Veronica insisted on giving him the silent treatment?

It was obvious that he'd pushed a button with that attitude comment. And the more he thought about it, the more he wanted to kick himself. Veronica had confided how much it had hurt her that others saw her as difficult. And he had assumed the same in the very beginning. But as he got to know her, Tomás began to understand the pressure she was under to salvage her career with the upcoming competition.

He had expected her to tell him she'd changed her mind and didn't want to go to dinner. But she'd replied to his texts and was ready when they arrived at the cottage to pick her up. Underneath her heavy jacket, she wore a white shirt, tight-fitting blue jeans, and knee-high black boots. She smelled like lilies—his favorite flower. The simmering attraction to Veronica that had been building over the past several weeks was now threatening to boil over into something he wanted to act on. Even now, as she sat stoic and closed off, he couldn't deny how beautiful she looked.

Her passion for her sport and determination were sexy as hell. Veronica was a woman who would move mountains to get what she wanted. A thrill ran up his spine just thinking about the remote possibility of him being something she wanted. It had been a long time since such lustful thoughts kept him awake at night. Veronica had become a regular visitor to his feverish dreams, and sometimes he had to force himself to stop staring at her while she trained. In fact, the other afternoon he'd basically had to run back to the house and take a cold shower.

Now he was going to have to spend an entire night beside her pretending they were a real couple. He couldn't help but be excited.

And terrified.

Tomás shook his head in attempt to brush off the inconvenient emotions he was feeling. He had no business thinking of Veronica in that way. And definitely not when it was apparent she thought the exact opposite of him.

Gabe pulled into the parking lot of Sawyer's Steakhouse and everyone got down from the SUV. But before Veronica could start walking, Tomás reached out to hold her elbow. She turned around with a raised eyebrow. "I'm sorry about what I said today," Tomás said. "I know you probably didn't want to come tonight, so thank you for showing up anyway."

She looked down at where he still held her elbow and he immediately let go. "You're welcome."

And then she walked away. Tomás let out a long sigh and braced himself for a long night. But as soon as he entered the restaurant, Veronica grabbed his hand. For a second, he thought that maybe it was her way of saying that she forgave him. Then he realized Mia and Brian were seated on a bench right in front of them. He dismissed the small pang of disappointment and again reminded himself he had no right to feel anything toward Veronica except friendship.

The small group was seated within five minutes. Tomás pulled out a chair for Veronica and she gave him a bright smile. "Thank you, honey," she said before sitting down.

"Anything for you, sweetheart," he replied. His suspicion that maybe he was overdoing it was confirmed when he looked over at a Gabe and he discreetly made a gagging motion.

Tomás distracted himself from having to look at Mia or Veronica by reading the menu. It was full of the usual steak-house dishes and he quickly decided on the rib eye, along with a baked potato and steamed vegetables.

"Honey, did you want to split the spinach and artichoke dip?" Veronica's question prompted him to put down the menu. Before he could answer, though, Mia said, "Since when do you like artichokes?"

He saw Veronica's eyes widen with regret. She wouldn't have known that he despised the vegetable. Tomás knew he had to answer carefully. "It's still not my favorite," he explained. "But Veronica is encouraging me to try new things."

"Yes, that's right," Veronica blurted. "I'm trying to show him that there are more interesting things to eat than steak and potatoes."

They all laughed, and Tomás was relieved. Although now he definitely needed to change his order and picked up the menu again.

"So, Veronica. What do you do for a living?" Brian asked.

Tomás stilled. Why on earth hadn't they prepped for tonight?

"I, um, I also work with horses," she said.

Mia raised her eyebrows. "Really? What a coincidence."

"It was. I guess that's why we connected so quickly. Horse people are drawn to horse people." Veronica glanced over at him and smiled. This time, though, he felt the warmth behind it.

"Well, Tomás is definitely horse people," Mia said. He bristled a little, though, at the way she said it. "Oh my gosh. Did he ever tell you about the night of our senior prom?"

Embarrassment heated his cheeks at the memory. "I'm sure Veronica doesn't want to hear this."

Veronica looked at him with a wide grin. "Oh, but Veronica does want to hear this."

He let out a sigh and sank down in his chair as Mia began recounting that night.

"Well, we were at Rancho Lindo and had just finished taking photos with our friends. We were about to get into the limo that would take us to the hotel in Santa Barbara for the prom, but one of the ranch hands ran up to him and said that one of the mares was struggling. So, Tomás being Tomás, he told me to go ahead with our friends and that he'd meet me there after he checked on the mare. But I decided to wait for him."

"It was her first foaling," he explained to Veronica. "I was worried that she was having complications."

"And what happened?" she asked. He was surprised at her genuine interest and concern.

"What happened was we missed the prom," Mia blurted. "Tomás had to physically pull the foal out so his rented tux was ruined."

"All I had to do was change into a regular suit," he said, trying very hard not to show the old irritation bubbling up. "We still could've gone."

Mia had been so upset about missing their senior prom. It wasn't the first time she had accused him of caring more about horses than people. Although Mia used to tell him how much she supported his duties at the ranch, she still got mad when those responsibilities caused him to postpone or cancel plans with her.

"I thought you would understand. You work for your family's diner," he'd told her after one fight.

"My waitressing job at the diner isn't twenty-four seven," she'd yelled at him. "I can walk away when I need to. Why can't you?"

"Because Rancho Lindo isn't a job, Mia. It's my life," he'd said.

"Well, you better decide soon if that's a life—a future—you really want."

Soon after that argument, Mia had announced she'd applied to NYU and had been accepted. She had told him he could use the next four years to figure out what he really wanted. And because, at the time, he'd only wanted her, Tomás had agreed he'd think about it.

So they stayed together. He saw her during her

holiday and summer breaks when she came home to Esperanza. And although she invited him to visit her in New York, there was always a reason he couldn't make a trip. If he was being honest with himself, maybe that's why he thought it would be a good idea to propose when she graduated. He wanted to prove to her that he was still committed to the relationship. He thought if he gave her a ring then she would have to move back to Esperanza and build a life with him.

Instead, she chose the life she had built on her own in New York.

Even now, he could feel Mia's annoyance about prom night.

"Was the foal okay?" Veronica asked, pulling him from his thoughts.

"He was and so was the mamá," he said with a huge smile. He had been so proud of himself that day. That is, until it became clear that Mia was furious with him. They'd nearly broken up that night.

Veronica reached over and covered his hand with hers. Then she looked over at Mia. "I missed my homecoming because my horse came down with acute laminitis. It's when the hoof gets so swollen—"

"It becomes painful for the horse to stand," Tomás finished for her.

Mia opened her mouth as if to say something, but instead she gave Nora a small smile. Then she changed the subject. "So, what's everyone going to order?"

A surge of gratefulness warmed Tomás all over again. He glanced sideways at Veronica and wondered if she could sense just how much her story had meant to him. He was sure she made it up in order to show that Tomás wasn't the only one at the table who would drop everything to take care of a sick animal. It had definitely quieted Mia before she went on to list all the other times he'd disappointed her as her boyfriend.

That alone was worth it.

After everyone placed their orders with their waiter, Tomás excused himself to go to the restroom. And when he came out, Veronica was waiting for him in the small corridor leading back into the main dining room.

"Everything okay?" he asked.

"I want us to call a truce," she said quickly.

"A truce?"

"Yes. Let's forget about what happened earlier today. I promised to make sure Mia believes we're a couple and I still plan on doing that. I just wanted to make sure you still knew that."

"I really didn't mean to hurt your feelings," he said.

She nodded. "I know. And I'm sorry. I'm not used to your methods, but I know that I have a really good chance of doing well in the competition. I think I need to shake things up when it comes to training. I need to be open to doing things outside of the box."

Tomás let out a sigh of relief. "I appreciate that. How about we start tomorrow with a clean slate?"

"Deal. I'll follow your lead during training and you're going to follow mine tonight. Okay?"

His heart rate immediately sped up. "Why does that make me nervous?"

"Because it should," she said in a teasing tone. "I'm going to make sure there is no shred of doubt in Mia's mind that we're a couple. In fact, I'll consider this a successful night if Gabe and Nora start believing it too."

A zing of thrill went through his body at her

determination. Whatever she had planned, he somehow knew he wasn't going to be mad about it. In fact, he was looking forward to it.

"Thank you also for making up that story about your homecoming. You were very convincing and it shut Mia up. I almost wanted to high-five you right at the table."

Veronica tilted her head in confusion. "I didn't make it up."

Her admission almost surprised him. Almost. Because he could definitely believe Veronica caring so much about her horse that she'd skip some dance.

"Oh. Okay. Well, I guess we have a deal then," he said and stuck out his hand.

Hesitation crossed her face for just a split second before she accepted it. She barely grasped his hand before letting go. Their contact was brief, but the warmth and softness of her small hand inside his was enough to stir up all kinds of longing. He needed a minute.

"I'll meet you at the table. I'm going to get a beer at the bar. Did you want one?"

"Sure." He watched as she walked back to join the others and then headed to the other side of the restaurant where the bar area was.

"I'll take two Modelos," he told the bartender.

"I'll also take two."

Tomás turned and saw Mia standing next to him. "Since when do you drink beer?" he asked her. "I thought you preferred those fruity cocktails?"

She shrugged and smiled. "I guess I'm trying new things, too, these days."

He laughed and tried to make small talk as they

waited for their drinks. "I like Brian. He seems like a very laid-back kind of guy."

She nodded. "He is. When I first met him, he kind of reminded me of you."

"Really," Tomás said in surprise.

"Yeah. He doesn't let things bother him too much. Whereas, you know, I let everything bother me."

He had to laugh at that because it was true. "Well, then I guess you guys are a good match."

"Thanks for saying that. And for what it's worth, I'm sorry I hurt you. I really tried to make it work for a long time."

"But we wanted different things," he said softly.

"We did. We probably still do."

He shrugged. "I can't change who I am. Rancho Lindo is my home. And I love what I do."

Tomás thought he could see pity reflected in Mia's eyes. "I know," she told him. Then she looked over at where Veronica was sitting. "You and Veronica seem to get along pretty good."

"We do? Uh, yeah, I mean, we do."

She raised her eyebrow and narrowed her eyes. "Is there something you're not telling me, Tomás?"

He willed the panic in his gut to calm down. "No. Why would you ask that?"

Mia shrugged. "I don't know. Just call it women's intuition. Something just seems off, that's all. Anyway, let's get back."

Tomás smiled and motioned for her to go ahead of him. He definitely wanted to make sure she couldn't see the worry that was probably etched all over his face now.

Chapter Twenty-Three

Dinner had turned into dessert and then that had turned into hitting a local bar.

Veronica wouldn't have minded it so much if Tomás hadn't told her, Nora, and Gabe on the drive there that Mia seemed to be doubting their fake relationship.

What the hell had she meant about *women's intuition* anyway?

She wished Tomás would've found a way to tell her that before she'd happily agreed to Brian's suggestion that they go somewhere else for drinks. Veronica thought she'd handled dinner pretty smoothly. But that was before she realized Mia was analyzing her and Tomás under a microscope.

"Let's just text them and say one of us isn't feeling well and we had to go home," Tomás said.

"See, this is what happens when you lie," Nora accused. "You can't stop."

Gabe looked at him through the rearview mirror. "It's your call, brother. If you don't want to go, we don't have to go."

Veronica turned in her seat to face Tomás. "I agree with Gabe. This is your decision."

Although part of her couldn't ever turn down a challenge, she knew this wasn't something she could control.

Tomás seemed to think about it for a few minutes. "Let's go. She can't prove anything tonight. Might as well have a good time while we can."

"Hell, yeah!" Gabe yelled.

Tomás met Veronica's eyes. "Are you still in this?"

She smiled and yelled, "Hell, yeah!"

By the time Veronica had finished her third beer, she was ready to hit the dance floor. The band at The Flamin' Oak was pretty good, and she'd been tapping her foot to the beat of every song so far. It had been a few years since she'd been out dancing. And she quickly decided she didn't want to wait one second longer, especially since Mia had been peppering her with questions since they'd gotten there. It was as if she was interviewing for the job of Tomás's girlfriend.

And with every beer, she'd moved her chair closer and closer to Tomás. He smelled so good. She didn't know if it was his cologne, his shampoo, or just him. Whatever it was, she couldn't get enough of his scent. Desire was burning her skin, and a familiar ache electrified every nerve. If she didn't stand up soon, she was going to end up on his lap.

"Let's dance," she yelled into Tomás's right ear.

He whipped his head in her direction and looked at her as if she'd just asked him to take her to the North Pole. "You want to dance? With me?"

"Um, yeah. That's why I said that." Veronica shook her head at his silly question.

Tomás's eyes flicked over at Mia, who was now chatting with Brian. "I'm not really a dancer," he said.

Before she could question him, his brother leaned over him and said, "Don't believe this guy. He's probably the best dancer in the family—well, after Mom anyway."

That surprised Veronica. "Well, now you have to dance with me. I need to judge you myself. Come on!"

She grabbed Tomás's hand and tried to pull him out of his chair. It took a few tugs and a big strong push from Gabe to finally get him on his feet. The band had just started a new song, and many other couples flocked to the dance floor.

At first, Tomás just stood there still as statue. So Veronica took his hands and placed them on her shoulders. Then she wrapped her arms around his waist and stepped closer. "All right. Let's see what you got, Mr. Horse Whisperer."

For a second, she thought he was going to drop his grip and walk back to the table. But she saw something flash behind his eyes and felt his fingers dig into her flesh a little more. He pulled her against him, but tensed up a little at the initial contact of their bodies. Slowly, he slid his hands from her shoulders down to her hips. He gripped them softly and began to move.

The feel of him against her revved up her desire even more. He was strong and steady, but her knees felt weak and she moved her hands to his shoulders and hung on to him as if he were her lifeline.

The sound of a single trumpet filled the bar as a familiar banda song began to play. Veronica and Tomás stepped in perfect unison to match the beat. At first, Veronica watched as their feet moved backward and forward. Then she focused on Tomás's long legs, his hard chest; finally she met his eyes. He was watching her too.

Veronica's pulse quickened as if it were trying to keep time with the music. All of a sudden, she was breathing too fast, but also not fast enough. The room around them blurred out of focus until it seemed as if they were the only two people on the dance floor. He held her eyes with his searing gaze. Veronica couldn't help but feel like she was the only person or thing that mattered to him at that moment.

She was taken aback by her body's response to his. She decided to make some light conversation to get her mind off all the ways it was imagining how Tomás might hold her in other positions.

"I wasn't sure if you were just going to leave me here and go back to the table," she admitted.

Tomás pulled back to meet her eyes. "Really?"

"Well, I basically had to drag you."

"I don't dance a lot. That doesn't mean that I don't like to. Especially if I have a good partner."

He pulled her a little closer. To her relief, he didn't stiffen again, and she couldn't help but notice how nicely her body melded against his.

"I'm a little nervous now," she blurted out.

"About dancing with me? I swear I won't step on your feet."

She shook her head. "Not about dancing. About, you know, keeping up this charade. I just want to make sure Mia is buying all of this. Do you think she's changing her mind?"

"I don't know."

"She's been interrogating me. I tried to be as vague

as possible so I'm lying but not really lying. I think she's suspicious. Maybe we need to be more handsy."

It was a risk given her current state of desire for the man pressed up against her. Veronica blamed the music and the alcohol in her system for suggesting such a thing. But she convinced herself she could handle some extracurricular touching. It didn't have to mean anything. She sure as heck didn't even have to enjoy it.

Okay, that was a lie. Given the heat coming off her own body, she was definitely going to enjoy whatever Tomás was willing to do.

He chuckled. "Handsy?"

"More PDA, you know. We have to sell it."

"You'd be okay with...that?"

Veronica wasn't sure if she was. But another part of her body was making the decisions thanks to the drinks she'd had earlier.

Tomás didn't wait for her to answer. "How about this? Let's dance first, okay? No pressure. We'll figure out what comes next later."

It turned out that later came about half an hour later.

All three couples ended up on the dance floor at the same time. Veronica decided this was the perfect opportunity to convince Mia.

As soon as Tomás pulled her into his arms again at the beginning of the song, she made sure to lean her head against his shoulder. He smelled like cologne and a hint of alcohol. Feeling emboldened, Veronica reached out and touched the vee of his T-shirt, then slid a finger down his chest, stopping just above his belly button. Tomás jerked, so she pulled her hand away. He surprised her then by putting her hand back where it was.

"You look very beautiful tonight," he said after a few minutes.

Veronica's head spun. Was he flirting with her? Perhaps he'd had more to drink than she'd first thought.

"Thank you. You look very handsome."

She felt him take a breath. "Is this okay?" he asked. "Being this close to me?"

"Yes. It's fine. It's nice," she admitted.

Veronica looked over and noticed Mia looking in their direction. "Maybe we should do more," she whispered.

Tomás whispered back. "Like what?"

"You could kiss me." She'd said it without thinking. But deep down she knew it was because she wanted him to. It had nothing to do with putting on a show for Mia.

He raised his eyebrows. "Now? Here?"

She tilted her head up just a fraction, her lips inches from his. "Mia is just a few feet away. I think this is the perfect time for some handsy-ness. Unless you want to wait until—"

"Sometimes you talk too much."

Tomás whispered the last few words against her mouth. When she didn't protest, he pushed in for a kiss. It was warm, soft, and tentative.

It was nice, but nothing she couldn't walk away from. That is until his tongue swiped her bottom lip and jolted alive every sense and every nerve, making the rest of her resolve shatter in his arms. Sighing, she grabbed his shirt with both hands and kissed him back with fervor. His arms wrapped around her body, hugging her as if she might be pulled away at any moment.

And then it was over. Just like the song.

Veronica needed a few minutes to cool down in more ways than one. Instead of taking her seat immediately, she announced that she was going to go to the ladies' room. Nora said she would go with her.

There was a line, of course, so they took their spots behind five other women.

"You guys looked amazing out there," Nora said. "Almost like professionals."

Veronica felt her cheeks begin to warm all over again. "It was all Tomás. He's very good."

Her friend nodded enthusiastically. "He's always been a good dancer. I've seen him dance with his mom and abuelita at family parties, but not like how he danced with you. You're a good partner for him. Also, I'm pretty sure he enjoyed that kiss too."

She looked over at Nora and saw that her friend had a huge silly grin across her face. Veronica's face burned even hotter. "Well, um, we had to make it convincing. You know, for Mia's sake."

Nora raised her palms. "I believe you."

She wasn't sure how to respond to that, so she just smiled at Nora as they both took a few steps closer to the restroom door. She'd been a fool to think she could handle this. They'd only kissed once and her response to it was far from fake.

It was as if he'd flipped a switch in her. She'd gone from thinking Tomás was attractive to wanting Tomás.

They might be on a pretend date tonight, but Veronica was starting to have real feelings.

Chapter Twenty-Four

There you are," Tomás said.

"Did you need something?" Veronica asked.

He closed in on her and cupped her face with both of his hands. "Yes. I needed this."

His lips crashed into hers. Relentless. Searing. Their sighs of pleasure filled the empty stable. Tomás eased her against a wooden pillar, determined to finally explore her body.

"I want you, Tomás," Veronica sighed as he moved his lips to her neck and then collarbone.

Her words catapulted his desire and he moved one of his hands down to her hip. "I want you too," he groaned as he continued to suck and nip.

"Tomás."

He didn't answer because he didn't want to stop. He was going to have Veronica tonight.

"Tomás."

"Tomás!"

Tomás jerked his head off the desk. He was confused to see Nico standing in front of him and not Veronica.

"No time for beauty sleep, brother," Nico said. "We have been summoned."

Tomás stretched out his arms above his head and yawned. Although he'd actually made it to bed before one in the morning, he hadn't slept a wink. Because every time he closed his eyes, images of that kiss with Veronica woke him—and other parts of his body—all the way up.

When she'd first suggested they have more physical contact, he'd had his doubts. But the moment she mentioned the idea of them kissing, any hesitation had flown out the window.

Even now he could almost still feel the way her lips had pressed hard against his. She'd tasted so sweet and perfect. And it was way too short.

He couldn't help but wonder if the kiss had affected Veronica the same way. She had seemed more affectionate after, like sitting very close to him at the table and holding his hand as they walked out of the bar. But then when they dropped her off, she had simply waved to the three of them, said good night, and then disappeared into her cottage.

Wondering what she was thinking about their kiss had kept him up as well.

It was only eight in the morning and he had hoped to talk to her before her training session with Charles. But now, apparently, he was being summoned.

It turned out that Cruz had needed him and Nico to go with him into town to pick up their lumber order. At first he didn't mind, since some of the pieces were to fix one of the stalls. But he regretted the trip as soon as the interrogation began.

"So how was your big date last night?" Nico teased from the front passenger seat of the truck.

"It was fine," he replied tersely.

"According to Gabe, it was more than fine. In fact, I heard there was a very passionate kiss on this big date."

Cruz looked at him in the rearview mirror. "You kissed Veronica? Like for real?"

"No, not for real. Well, I mean, yes I kissed her, but only because Mia was getting suspicious."

"And?" Nico said.

Tomás looked out the window, not wanting for either brother to see the heat that was burning his cheeks. "And nothing."

"Look," Cruz began. "I admit I was all about this plan, especially once I found out that Veronica was playing along in return for some training. But maybe it's time to stop. You know, before things get too complicated between you two."

Tomás sighed. He didn't want to admit that Cruz had a point. Although he knew his brother's concerns had everything to do with how those complications might affect Rancho Lindo rather than how it would affect him or Veronica. It was the main reason he hadn't wanted Cruz to know about the arrangement. Of course, Nico had blabbed as usual.

But he had decided not to say anything anymore to his mom. His dad had an important oncology appointment coming up in a few days. And Tomás didn't want to add to her stress. Eventually, he would find the right time and the right words.

Just not now.

"Don't worry. I've got it handled," he told them both.

Whether or not they believed him was to be determined.

Luckily, they didn't press the issue any further once they'd arrived at the lumberyard. It took them three trips to load everything into the back of the truck.

"Need some help there?"

Tomás turned around on his last run and nearly knocked out Esperanza's mayor.

"Whoa," Mayor Walker said as he ducked to miss getting hit by the bundle of two-by-fours Tomás had been carrying on his shoulder.

"Mayor! Oh wow. Sorry about that." Tomás set the pieces of lumber on the ground next to him. "Are you okay?"

Mayor Walker waved his hand at him. "I'm fine. I'm fine."

James Walker was rail-thin and about seventy years old. Tomás figured that even a slight bump could have sent him flying into the nearby bushes. He doubted the mayor would be able to lift the pieces of wood even with Tomás carrying most of their weight. Mayor Walker was also the town's bank manager and Tomás had heard he'd had some sort of heart procedure done last year. The man had no business doing any sort of lifting or carrying at all.

"Good," a relieved Tomás told him. "And thanks for the offer to help, Mayor, but these are my last two pieces and my truck is right over there." He pointed across the street to where Cruz and Nico had just unloaded their share.

"Ah, I see." The mayor nodded. "How about I walk with you—I need to talk to Cruz about something."

Tomás nodded and then hoisted the wood back onto his shoulder. Mayor Walker followed a few feet safely behind him.

"Hey, Mayor," Nico said as they approached. "Don't tell me my brother nearly knocked you out over there."

Mayor Walker chuckled. "He tried to, but I'm quick with my reflexes."

As Tomás arranged the lumber onto the stack on the truck's bed, he heard the mayor ask Cruz if he could have a few words with him. They walked a few feet away and started talking. The hustle and the bustle of the road and nearby park prevented Tomás from hearing their conversation.

After securing the load with ratchet straps, he walked over to Nico, who was leaning against the hood of the truck. "What do you think that's about?"

His younger brother shrugged. "I don't know. I guess money stuff."

"Well, obviously. But what's so urgent that Mayor Walker needs to pull Cruz to the side and talk to him this minute?"

"I don't know, Tomás. Why don't you ask your brother when he comes back?"

"Aren't you curious?"

Nico shrugged. "Honestly, I'm not. Money stuff is not my thing. I'm going to trust that Cruz will let us know when we need to know."

Mayor Walker and Cruz walked back to the truck after another five minutes or so.

"All right then, you boys have a good afternoon. I'm glad to hear you're working hard to fix things."

"Always," Nico replied.

The mayor seemed to like his answer based on the proud smile that stretched from one of his ears to the other.

Tomás was about to ask the mayor what he and his brothers were supposed to fix. Because he got the sense that the mayor wasn't referring to the lumber. But someone yelled his name from the corner and Mayor Walker said he needed to go talk to the person too.

After they were back inside the truck, Tomás asked Cruz, "What did Mayor Walker need to talk to you about?"

"Just some stuff about our accounts," Cruz replied.

"Should we be worried?" Tomás didn't like the vagueness.

"Not any more than you should be already. I already told you guys we have some loans coming due. Mayor Walker just wanted to check in to make sure we were going to be able to make the payments."

"And what did you tell him?"

"I told him that we would be fine."

"Cruz…"

His brother sighed in exasperation. "I said I'll handle it. But if you really want to help out then you're going to make sure this little arrangement with Veronica doesn't turn south—for all of us. Okay?"

"Okay," Tomás agreed.

What else could he say at that moment?

Now he had to make sure he did exactly that.

Chapter Twenty-Five

Veronica's first-ever kiss had happened when she'd least expected it.

Mathew Anderson, her sixth-grade crush, had passed her a note during science class asking her to meet him by the water fountain outside the gym during lunch. She hadn't been able to concentrate after that and the last thirty minutes before the bell rang seemed to tick on forever.

Finally, lunch recess arrived and Veronica quickly walked to the meeting place.

Mathew didn't show up for another ten minutes.

"So, here's the thing," he'd said off the bat. "Julie Lawrence wants to be my girlfriend, but Davey Cagle says you want to be my girlfriend too. Is that true?"

Instant embarrassment had made Veronica want to dissolve into a puddle right there on the asphalt. "I... um... I." She couldn't even make an intelligible sentence. That's how mortified she was.

Mathew didn't seem to notice. "Well, in order for me to choose, I need to kiss both of you. Julie let me kiss her before school already. So now I want to kiss you."

His words shocked her into being able to speak again. "Oh. Um, okay."

She'd barely uttered the second syllable of that last word when Mathew's chapped lips pecked her vanilla-Chapstick-covered ones. It was quick. It was basic. It was fine.

Mathew must have thought the same thing since he ended up picking Julie as his girlfriend for that week and never really spoke to Veronica again.

Luckily for her, Veronica would go on to have many more first kisses. And they were much more memorable than Mathew's had been.

But her first kiss with Tomás Ortega had blown all of those out of the water.

It was tender until it wasn't. And it had lingered long after she'd crawled into bed last night. And as much as she had tried to get some sleep, she could barely keep her eyes closed. Because she wasn't just replaying the kiss in her head all night. She was creating scenarios that involved Tomás showing up outside her door and them doing more than just kissing.

So, even though she was dead-tired that morning, all of her senses and nerves came alive once she walked into the stable after her training session with Charles and saw Tomás waiting for her.

"Good morning," he said and tipped his hat in her direction.

She couldn't help but smile in response to the huge grin he wore. "Good morning to you too."

"How was your session?" he said once she was only a couple of feet away.

Veronica shrugged. "Fine, I guess. I just do what he tells me to do now. Even though his exercises are basic and don't challenge me or Takuache." She noticed his grin disappeared.

"What's wrong?" she quickly asked.

Tomás shoved his hands into his pockets. "I'm not sure my exercises will either. Sorry."

Ugh. Why did she say that? Hadn't she promised Tomás that she would be open to his methods? "I'm sure what you have planned is going to be way more impactful than what I just went through with Charles. Please don't think you need to impress me. Ever."

He seemed to believe her. Although she still sensed some uneasiness from him.

"What else is wrong?"

"Nothing is wrong. I, uh, I was just wondering how you were feeling about how things went last night. You know, with Mia, and with …"

Veronica's chest tightened. She figured he'd want to talk about their kiss. She just hadn't expected he'd want to discuss it first thing.

"You mean that kiss?" Might as well rip off the Band-Aid.

"Yeah. I wanted to make sure you weren't regretting it or feeling upset about it. That's all."

"No," she rushed. "I'm not upset. Not in the least."

"Really?" he said, the tension visibly erased from his expression. "I'm glad."

Veronica took a deep breath and asked her own question. "What about you? Are you regretting it or anything else we did last night?"

He shook his head vigorously. "No. Not at all."

"Good," she said.

"Good," Tomás said back.

They stared at each other for a few more awkward seconds before Veronica finally said, "Well, should we get started?"

"Yep," he said. "I'll meet you and Takuache outside the corral. I'm going to get Peanut."

Veronica couldn't help but be surprised. "Peanut?"

"We're all going to be training today," he replied with a wink.

And that's when she realized how different this session was going to be already.

She couldn't wait.

⚘

The four of them made their way just beyond the stables to a nearby dirt path. Once they reached a clearing underneath some trees, Tomás told Veronica to dismount Takuache.

"Why aren't we in the corral again?" she asked after doing what he instructed.

"I think you two need a change of scenery. You've already been exercising there all morning. This will help put you both in a different frame of mind."

"If you say so," she said with a teasing tone.

He rolled his eyes at her, then walked over to Takuache. "I want you to lay your hand against his side and feel how he's breathing, okay?"

Veronica raised her right hand and gently laid her palm just below her saddle.

Tomás stepped closer. "Tell me what you feel," he said softly.

She closed her eyes and concentrated on the rise and fall of Takuache's side. "His breathing is quick."

"Good. It shouldn't be since he was only moving for a few minutes. Now go and feel Peanut's side."

Tomás followed her to his horse and watched as she placed her palm against Peanut. This time, though, he covered her hand with his. "What do you feel?" he asked.

"It's slower than Takuache's," she replied, trying to not react to the feel of his skin against hers. Despite his palm being a little rough, his touch was warm and comforting.

"That's right. And his breaths are more drawn out. Watch our hands—see how they rise after a few seconds?"

She studied how his hand practically engulfed hers. He was cradling it almost. The gentleness took her breath away. And then a pang of disappointment hit when he finally removed his palm.

Veronica let her own hand slide off Peanut and she cleared her throat, as if that would also clear the tingling sensation that lingered.

"So why is Peanut's breathing slower than Takuache's when they both traveled the same distance?" she asked. The question was a distraction, but she also honestly wanted to know.

"Well, for one, Takuache has been exercising all morning. So his starting levels would be more elevated anyway. But it's also because Peanut is more relaxed than him. I'm sure Takuache is wondering what we're doing out here—just like you are. I'm not saying he's totally anxious, but he has his guard up. And that takes energy, which results in quicker breathing."

She looked over at Takuache. "And that's a bad thing?"

"Not necessarily. I just wanted to show you how you can sense how he's feeling based on his breathing and by your touch. That way, before you even take him out of his stall in the morning, you will have a better idea of how he might perform."

Veronica nodded in understanding. It did make sense—even if it was something she hadn't really considered.

Tomás took a step closer. "You know, you can do the same thing to yourself."

"What do you mean?"

He took her right hand and placed it over her heart. "You also should be aware of any anxiety you're bringing to Takuache. It's just a way to stop and take a moment to get out of your head."

Although he'd stopped talking, Veronica noticed his hand hadn't left hers. And that only made her heartbeat quicken so much that she was worried he could feel it too. So before he could ask why her heart was beating so fast, she took a slight step backward to break the contact.

"Maybe I should be skipping that second shot of espresso from now on," Veronica said, hoping the joke would distract her from the emotions bubbling up inside her.

Tomás chuckled and nodded. "Maybe."

They spent the next hour riding down the dirt path. Tomás explained he wanted Takuache to get more comfortable with the property. To trust that he was safe there. To enjoy himself.

"And what about you, Veronica?" he asked as they rode side by side.

"What about me?"

"Are you enjoying this?"

She didn't even have to hesitate. "I am."

"Can I ask you something else?"

"Go ahead."

Peanut stopped in his tracks—or rather Tomás guided him to a stop. So she did the same with Takuache.

He met her eyes. His gaze was soft but serious. "Are you wanting to compete again because it truly makes you happy, or are you trying to prove something?"

This time she had to think about her answer. "I, um, actually, I'm not really sure." Veronica was surprised by her own candor. She had never admitted that to anyone—not even herself. "When I was a little girl, all I ever wanted to do was ride and compete. Then something changed."

"Your accident?"

She shrugged. "I don't know. I mean, that would be obvious. But even before then, I was feeling tired of it all. It had become something I had to do—it was a job. Of course I wanted to be the best, so that fueled my drive to win. But that high only lasts a little bit. And then I'd sink into this funk until it was time to train again for the next trophy. It was a vicious cycle until my accident. The time away gave me what I needed—a break."

"So that's why you wanted to compete again? Because you were able to take a much-needed break and realized competing was what you wanted to do?"

Veronica laughed. "Not exactly. But I had to do something. I couldn't hide away in my family's home until eternity. I knew I was good at equestrian jumping. And I decided to go back to what I knew."

Tomás didn't say anything else. Instead, he clicked

his tongue to get Peanut moving again. But Veronica didn't follow right away.

His questions had raised one big one of her own. A question she'd been trying to ignore for some time now: Did competing still make her happy?

Veronica decided she wasn't ready for the answer.

Chapter Twenty-Six

They're back."

Tomás turned around to see Cruz standing at the entrance to the stable. His expression was serious. Even somber.

He nodded in understanding and followed his brother to go see their parents at the house. They were back from meeting with their dad's oncologist. They'd left while Tomás had been out doing his morning chores.

Although Tomás didn't want to think the worst, he sensed the news wasn't what they were hoping for. Part of him wanted to go find Veronica, get the horses and ride as far away as possible so he didn't have to hear it. Although yesterday's outing had technically been a training session, Tomás had enjoyed their time talking. He couldn't deny that he was growing closer to Veronica. Or that his feelings toward her were changing into something he hadn't experienced in a long time.

When he and Cruz entered the house, everyone was already sitting in the family room. Cruz sat down in an armchair, while Tomás took a seat next to Nico on the love seat. Abuelita, Gabe, and Nora were on the couch, while Daniel sat in the room's other armchair. His parents were seated on two chairs that had been brought over from the dining room.

His dad cleared his throat. "Well, I'm just going to get right to it. My doctor says that surgery is no longer an option because the cancer has spread from my prostate to my bones. He wants to try—um—what did he say?" his dad asked his mom.

"Hormone therapy or immunotherapy," she answered quietly.

Tomás's chest tightened with dread. He forced himself to keep breathing.

"And what if those don't work?" Nico asked.

"Then ya es todo. That's it, Mijo. There is nothing else they can do for me," their dad said.

Tomás choked on emotion as others began raising their voices in protest.

Finally, his mom silenced everyone with a clap.

"That's not true, boys. The doctor said he could qualify for a clinical trial after they've tried all the other treatments."

His dad threw up his hands. "For what?" he scoffed. "So I can be a guinea pig? I'm not leaving this earth with a body full of poison or a mind that doesn't work anymore. If I die, then I die on my terms and here on my beloved Rancho Lindo."

Gabe shot out of his seat and pointed at his dad. "Why are you so damn stubborn? You would put Mom—you would put all of us—through something like that just because you refuse to believe that doctors know what's best for you? I can't believe you right now!"

Tomás's heart sank as he watched Gabe's face crumple with emotion before he rushed out of the house. Nora let out a small whimper but quickly regained her composure. "I'll go see if he's okay," she said softly to his mom.

His mom nodded and wiped her eyes with the tissue she'd been clutching in one hand.

"What's next, Mom?" This time it was Cruz who spoke up.

"He needs to do more scans and lab work tomorrow and then we go back to see the oncologist on Friday to find out which treatment he can start and when."

Abuelita stood up. "I'm going to my room."

"Mamá, you haven't eaten lunch yet," his mom said.

She waved her off. "I had a big breakfast."

No one else argued because they all knew the real reason she was going to her bedroom. Abuelita was going to go pray.

His dad announced that he was going to look for something in the office. That meant the family meeting was officially over.

Tomás sat on the couch as the rest of his siblings walked out to go do whatever they needed to do in order to digest what they'd all been told. Eventually, it was just him and his mom. He walked over to her and sat in the chair his dad been on.

He put his arm around her and told her that everything would be okay.

She lowered her head onto his shoulder and, although he couldn't see her face, he felt her body shudder with emotion and heard her sniffles. His mom had rarely cried in front of him and his brothers when they were growing up. She was usually the one comforting everyone else. She had to be strong for all of them. If his mom was fine, then he knew he would be fine too.

Lately, though, even though she did her best to hide them, her tears were a common occurrence.

So he held her until her sobs subsided and she blew her nose into the tissue.

After a few minutes of silence, she grabbed his hand. "It's good that Gabe has Nora to talk to about this. And now you have Veronica."

"Mom, we're not Gabe and Nora. We're...uh..." He couldn't find the words.

"New," she answered for him. "I know. I know. You two have only known each other for a little while, but I can see the way you look at her, Mijo. I see the way she looks at you."

That took him by surprise. "How does she look at me?"

"Like she trusts you. Like she knows you—the real you. Trust me, a woman can tell these things."

"You and Abuelita sure seem to think you know a lot about this type of stuff."

His mom patted his hand. "That's because we've lived a long time and experienced many things. That's why I'm telling you not to push Veronica away now, Tomás. I know you trust her as much as she trusts you. I see you opening up when you're around her. So don't close off now. You need to get out whatever you're feeling about Dad. Otherwise it will eat you up inside."

His heart sank. He hated that he was still lying to her. He had planned on talking to his mom about Veronica over lunch, but he knew there was no way he was going to confess his deception now. But he also didn't want her to be disappointed when things ended between them. Because they were going to end eventually.

"I like Veronica, I do. But like you said, this is all new. Plus, she's leaving soon and going back to her life in equestrian jumping and probably Mexico. I just want to be realistic."

"I know. I know. And I'm sorry, I don't mean to give you any more pressure like I did with Mia."

Tomás studied her face and saw shame. "What do you mean, Mom?"

She sighed and leaned her head against his shoulder. "I know I was a little pushy when you two broke up. But that was because I hated to see you hurting."

He sighed. "Mom, stop. Yes, it was hard, but I think it was for the best, right?"

"Yes, I see that. I have to tell you how happy I am to see you opening your heart again. It's true we don't know what's going to happen with Veronica. But at least, for now anyway, I can be happy that you're happy. This is a hard time for our family. And I need to hang on to the good things for as long as possible, okay?"

"Okay, Mom." Tomás tried to take comfort in knowing that at least he was one less person she had to worry about today.

They sat together for a few minutes before his mom told him she was going upstairs to lie down for a bit. She let him know there was deli meat in the fridge for sandwiches since she hadn't had a chance to cook anything for everyone. He told her not to worry and that he and his brothers would manage.

Instead of a sandwich, though, Tomás decided he was in the mood for something else. He grabbed the keys to the SUV and headed outside.

"There you are." He raised his head to see Veronica walking toward him.

"Hey," he said with a nod.

"I thought we were meeting at eleven to start our training sessions. I was waiting for you at the stable and tried texting you, but never got an answer."

"Oh. Sorry. It's been kind of a hectic morning."

She nodded, but didn't seem convinced. "So are we still training?"

It was the last thing he wanted to do. He wasn't in a good headspace; the horses would sense it, and it would just be a frustrating session.

"Sorry. Um, something unexpected came up and I have to leave."

He had expected for her to accept his dumb excuse. He should've known better.

"Are you serious?" she scoffed. "The competition is less than a month away. I need to take advantage of every day I have left to train. You promised me."

"Well, not everything is about you, Veronica!"

Tomás hadn't meant to raise his voice. But the tornado of emotions he was feeling in that moment just ripped off whatever filter he usually had. He expected her to storm away or tell him off. So it was a surprise when she did neither.

Veronica stepped closer and seemed to study his face. "What's wrong?"

He flinched at her question only because he wasn't quite ready to answer it. Instead he said, "I'm going to go eat some ramen. Do you want to come?"

"This is really good," Veronica said after taking her first slurp.

"I told you. See, I don't just eat steak and potatoes," Tomás teased.

They were at his favorite Japanese restaurant in Santa Barbara. He and Nico had discovered it last year and they usually stopped by whenever they were in town. But sometimes Tomás came by himself. It was his go-to place whenever he just needed to get away from everything.

And now he'd brought Veronica to it.

He wasn't quite sure what had made him invite her. In fact, he wasn't quite sure how he wasn't burning with embarrassment. He'd had another racy dream about her last night. Tomás was sure it was his subconscious response to their supposed fake kiss. It had taken him completely by surprise. He had fully intended to only briefly tap her lips when Veronica had ordered him to kiss her in front of Mia—but as soon as he'd had a taste of her, he couldn't get enough.

Tomás glanced up from his bowl and watched Veronica as she brought the spoon to her mouth. It took everything he had not to ask if he could kiss her again right then and there.

As if she could sense what he was thinking, she met his eyes. Hers were bright and wide, almost sparkling. They seemed to be looking right into his heart.

"I thought you were hungry?" she asked.

He took a moment to translate her words in his brain and make sure he hadn't heard her ask if he was hungry for *her*. Because he was.

"I am," Tomás told her and scooped noodles into his mouth.

"So, do you come here a lot?" she asked.

"Not a lot. But it's where I go when I'm craving comfort food."

She nodded. "There's this little bistro a few blocks away from our house and they have the best French toast I've ever tasted. That's my comfort-food place. Even just thinking about it makes my mouth water."

He could hear the wistfulness in her voice. "You must be missing it. I'm sure you're missing lots of things."

"I am." Veronica nodded. Her eyes seemed sad and he wished he could fix the ache he knew she must be feeling in her heart. "I miss my room and my bed. I miss being able to walk downtown and stop to pick up my favorite muffins or get a pedicure. I miss the kids I worked with at the equestrian center. But I think I miss my sister most of all."

"I thought you talk to her every day?"

"I do. But it's not the same. I miss having what you have."

He arched his eyebrows in surprise. Veronica's homesickness—although difficult—was temporary. Based on what he already knew about her, it seemed like she had a good life back home. What on earth could he have that she didn't? "Oh, and what's that?"

."Your family all under the same roof. You're very lucky."

His throat tightened. Veronica didn't need to remind him of how lucky he was to have his family so close. "I guess I am. I mean my brothers are pains in the ass, but it's been nice to have all of us back in the house again. Gabe was gone for so long while he was in the army, I had almost forgotten what that had felt like."

She set down her spoon. "And you have your parents and your abuelita too. Sometimes I try to remember what it was like when my mom was still alive and the four of us would eat breakfast together on the weekends. Sometimes we'd stay in our pajamas all day. My mom said pajama days were family days and no one was allowed to go anywhere—even my dad. I remember I really loved pajama days."

Tomás tried to smile even though his heart was breaking. But Veronica must have seen right through his attempt. "Okay, that's it. Talk to me, Tomás. I know something's wrong. Please tell me."

She reached across the small table and covered his hand with hers. Her expression was soft, and he could tell how worried she was about him. That was enough.

Although his family had agreed to keep his dad's health issues among themselves, his mom had basically encouraged him to tell Veronica. Because his mom knew what Tomás was just realizing. He felt safe with Veronica.

"My dad...he has prostate cancer and we found out this morning that it's spreading," he said in a low voice.

"Oh my gosh, Tomás. I'm so so sorry." Her hand was squeezing his as if she was trying to pull out the sadness from him. If only it were that easy.

He cleared his throat. "We'll know more later this week. But for now, I'm just kind of struggling with how to feel. I don't want to think that this is the beginning of the end, but at the same time I don't want to pretend that the worst-case scenario can't actually happen. I feel like I need to prepare myself, but then that would be admitting there's no hope."

When he met her eyes again, he could see a shine of tears. "I'm sorry," he said quickly. "I didn't mean to be such a downer and I definitely didn't mean to make you sad either. It was insensitive of me to bring this up to you."

She let go of his hand to pick up her napkin and dab her eyes. "It's fine, Tomás. I'm glad you felt like you could talk to me about this."

"Thank you for listening," he said. "Can I ask you a question?"

Veronica nodded.

"How did you and your sister get through it?"

He didn't need to explain. She knew exactly what he meant. "Losing our mom?"

"Yeah," he said and lowered his head. "I can't even comprehend my dad not being here one day. How on earth can I prepare for that?"

Veronica sat back in her chair and folded her arms across her chest. "You can't," she told him gently. "All you can do is take it minute by minute, day by day, year by year. But your dad is still here, Tomás. Don't focus all of your energy on what-if. You need to keep living your life and focus on what's right in front of you before you miss it."

He knew she was talking metaphorically, of course. Yet he couldn't shake the feeling that the universe was being more direct.

These past few days he'd been so focused on what Mia thought about him that he hadn't seen Veronica. Like, really seen her.

There was a reason that pretend kiss had turned into a real one.

Today, he couldn't deny that his pretend feelings were turning into a truth of their own.

Chapter Twenty-Seven

When Veronica had agreed to be Tomás's fake girl-friend, she thought she was signing up for a one-night commitment of pretend.

Yet it had somehow turned into a weeks-long arrangement that had her questioning her own mind and heart.

After Tomás had told her about his dad and how much his mom seemed to find some joy in their not-real relationship, they had decided to keep up with the charade until Veronica left Rancho Lindo. Then it would be easier to explain why the relationship didn't work out. She had grown quite fond of Señora Ortega and would never want to hurt her on purpose. This way, it would be a soft disappointment and Veronica would be thousands of miles away when it happened.

In the meantime, she would play Tomás's girlfriend, and that meant having dinner with the Ortegas every night—sometimes even lunch.

For instance, on this particular day, Tomás's abue-lita, Doña Alma, had invited both of them to help her make albondigas soup. It was a rainy spring afternoon, and training sessions with both Charles and Tomás had been canceled.

Doña Alma already had all of the ingredients for the traditional Mexican meatball-and-vegetable soup set up on the kitchen island when Tomás and Veronica walked through the back door at eleven on the dot.

The older woman didn't even say hello—she just put them straight to work. "Okay, go wash your hands and put on the aprons I leave for you on the stools," she ordered.

"Don't say I didn't warn you," he whispered as they stood next to each other at the sink.

It was true that he had. The previous night, during dinner with the family, Margarita—Tomás's mom— had asked Veronica what she liked to eat when she was cold. The rain had already started by then and everyone was talking about how the weather was perfect for soup.

That's when she had shared that she loved eating her father's albondigas soup but that he hadn't made it in several years. "Doña Alma, yours is probably the closest to his that I've ever had," Veronica said genuinely.

"Then I teach you mine," Doña Alma had announced.

"Oh, that's not necessary, Doña Alma," she'd protested. "I know it's a lot of work and I don't want to trouble you."

The elderly woman waved her hand. "No trouble. You and Tomás come tomorrow. We start at eleven."

"Hold on," Tomás had said. "How did I get roped into this? Besides, we have to train tomorrow."

That's when his mom spoke up. "It's going to rain

all day. I think you both will have time to cook with Abuelita."

When the conversation changed, Veronica had leaned over to apologize for dragging him into the cooking lesson. But he'd just smiled and said, "It's fine. Just be ready. Because Abuelita does not play when it comes to her cooking."

Despite his best attempts to tease her, Veronica was determined to learn a few things from Doña Alma. She enjoyed cooking for herself and for her sister and her dad when she could. But it was true that it had been a long time since they'd had a family meal. Her father's business kept him out of the country most weeks and when he was home, he was always on the phone or in Zoom meetings. Their cook handled most of their meals, especially since her dad ate at random times. And Valeria preferred eating out with her friends. That meant Veronica was eating lunches and dinners mostly on her own. It was the reason she'd jumped at Tomás's suggestion for her to join his family for their dinners.

She was enjoying being a part of their animated conversations. She was definitely going to miss these times.

Veronica shook off the wave of unexpected sadness and concentrated on washing her hands.

"Your abuelita is not that bad," she told Tomás as she watched him take his turn at the sink.

He shrugged without looking at her. "The fact that she wanted to teach you how to make the soup means she likes you—but that doesn't mean she's not going to be a drill sergeant and tell you everything you're doing wrong."

Veronica leaned her body over to bump his side. "Thanks for making me nervous now."

Tomás bent his head down and moved his lips close to her ear. "Don't worry. I'll protect you."

His warm breath tickled her skin and his words ignited waves of desire deep in her belly. He'd whispered them so Veronica knew it hadn't been for Doña Alma's benefit. Tomás had meant what he'd said, and that thrilled her in ways she hadn't felt in a very long time.

For the next half hour, she did her best to dismiss her feelings about Tomás and concentrate on Doña Alma's instructions.

While Tomás cleaned and chopped a variety of herbs and vegetables like carrots, chayote, zucchini, potatoes, and cabbage, Veronica was responsible for making the meatballs. Doña Alma told her to start mixing the ground meat in a large mixing bowl with different spices and uncooked rice.

"When they are mixed very good, add the eggs. That will make sure the bollitos don't break apart once they're cooking in the broth."

"Do you have food prep gloves?" Veronica asked, raising her bare hands over the bowl.

Doña Alma scoffed. "Que gloves? Use los manos. You have to be able to feel the meat so you know if you need to add more egg."

She nodded in understanding and grabbed a handful of meat and began forming little balls. After a few tries, Doña Alma finally approved the correct size and gave Veronica permission to continue.

"Is this pork or beef?" she asked as she placed her next meatball onto a nearby tray covered with parchment paper.

"Both," Doña Alma said. "I think they are more flavorful together."

"My dad once tried to make his albondigas with turkey, and Mom could taste the difference right away," she told them. "She made him promise never to do it again."

Veronica laughed at the memory. It was one she hadn't thought of in a long time.

"I always thought it was funny that my dad was the cook of our family," she continued. "My mom always used to say that she didn't even know how to make a salad until she started dating my dad."

"Really?" Tomás asked from across the kitchen island.

"Oh yeah," Veronica said. "My grandparents had a personal chef and I guess they figured there was no reason for my mom to learn. So my dad was the one who had to teach her."

"My husband taught me a few things, too, because he wanted me to cook like his mother," Doña Alma added. "But after a few years he told me that he liked my cooking much more."

They all laughed at that and continued with their tasks until Tomás asked, "Do you still see your grandparents?"

A heaviness sat on Veronica's chest, and she had to sigh to relieve some of the pressure. "No. After my mom died, they sort of drifted away. They never liked my dad, so I guess they figured they didn't need to tolerate him anymore and stopped visiting. They would call once a year and ask for me and my sister to go spend a month with them over the summer or during Christmas, but we never wanted to leave my dad so we never went. After a while, they didn't even ask."

Veronica's dad had worked for her mom's family. That was how they had met in the first place. It was an understatement to say that her grandparents didn't like him. They thought he didn't deserve her and tried many times to keep them apart, even going so far as to send her away to a boarding school. Her mom had told her that all that did was make them want to be together even more. So once she was eighteen, they ran away and eloped in secret. She didn't see her parents again until Veronica was a few months old.

Veronica could feel the pity emanating from Tomás, and she refused to meet his eyes. "And, well, my dad's mom passed away when I was just a baby and I never met my abuelo. So really my family is just me, my sister, and my dad. Not even close to how big yours is."

He cleared his throat, so she looked up. But instead of pity, Tomás only gave her a smile.

"Trust me. Having a big family isn't as fun as you might think. When I was little I used to dream that I was really an only child and my real parents were going to come for me one day."

Doña Alma reached over and slapped Tomás on the arm. "Desgraciado! You shouldn't think such things."

Tomás laughed. "Abuelita, I don't think that now."

The weight of the conversation about her grandparents lifted, and she wondered if Tomás had done that on purpose.

She looked over in his direction and caught him staring at her. The heat of his gaze warmed her up all over again. Especially when he didn't even try to look away.

"Mija, is it too warm in here for you? Your cheeks are turning red," Doña Alma said.

Veronica stilled in embarrassment. "Um, yeah, it's a little warm," she said, not adding the real reason her body temperature had risen.

"Tomás, open the window over the sink a little. Let's let in some fresh air," she said.

Grateful that Tomás's attention was redirected to something else, Veronica exhaled and finished forming the meatballs.

A few minutes later, she was at the stove with Doña Alma, watching as she put all of the ingredients into one large pot.

"I didn't realize there was so much that goes into this soup," Veronica admitted.

"Sí. It is why there is so much flavor. If you take one thing out, it will change it all. When it comes to cooking—and love—there is no such thing as too much."

It took everything Veronica had not to look in Tomás's direction at that moment. Why, oh why, was she acting like a lovestruck teenager today? She had to shake it off somehow. They were pretend-dating, not really dating. Veronica couldn't afford for Tomás to get the wrong idea. It would be horrible—beyond horrible—if he thought she wanted more. Especially since he had given her no reason to think that he wanted the same.

"Abuelita, you need to teach Veronica how you make your chiles rellenos." Tomás's voice startled her. She had completely forgotten that she was having this internal debate with herself all while he was standing only a few feet away. "I know! Let's have them for dinner this weekend."

Doña Alma nodded with a smile. "Sí, that's a good idea. But we have to do it Sunday since we won't be here Saturday."

"Why? What's happening on Saturday?" Tomás asked.

"Pues, the engagement party," his abuelita answered.

Doña Alma had to be talking about Mia and Brian. Veronica watched Tomás's reaction carefully. But the news didn't seem to faze him. "Oh, it's this Saturday? I thought it was next weekend."

Tomás looked over at her. "I was going to tell you about it, but it slipped my mind since I thought it wasn't for a while. It's just going to be a few of the Riveras' friends. Not at all as big as their vow renewal reception here. You don't have to go if you don't want to."

She hoped the disappointment that twisted her insides didn't make an appearance on her face. Did Tomás not want her to go?

"Um, I don't mind. Do you want me to go?" she said softly, trying not to sound too affected by his comment.

He smiled. "Of course I want you to go."

A rush of happiness instantly heated her cheeks, and she couldn't help but notice that Tomás seemed equally thrilled. Even his abuelita clapped with delight and hugged Veronica. She was caught off guard by the gesture, but she didn't mind it. She hugged Doña Alma back.

After letting her go, Doña Alma patted her cheek gently and gave her a huge smile. "Bueno! We all go then. It will be a good time. Very good."

Veronica glanced over again at Tomás and grinned.

Suddenly she was very excited to go celebrate his ex-girlfriend's engagement.

A few days later, Veronica and Tomás were on their way to Mia's engagement barbecue with Gabe and Nora. The rest of the Ortegas had gone in another car.

Her heart hadn't stopped racing since she'd woken up that morning. She wasn't exactly sure why. She'd been spending enough time with Tomás and his family and was comfortable around them—even though she was still pretending to be his girlfriend. And she had no reason to be nervous around Mia. By now the woman had to believe Veronica and Tomás were a couple. Plus, she would be leaving Esperanza after today and it didn't really matter what she thought after that.

And that's when it hit her.

Mia leaving was also a reminder that soon Veronica would do the same.

"Are you ready?" Tomás asked, breaking through her troubling thoughts.

Veronica had been so immersed in them that she hadn't realized they'd already arrived at their destination.

"Always," she replied.

"Well, I'm ready too," Gabe announced from the back seat of the SUV. "Ready for some barbecue."

"We know," Tomás and Veronica groaned in unison, along with Nora.

The small group piled out of the cramped vehicle and walked together to the open gate on the side of Mia's parents' home.

They had only been there ten minutes when Mia and Brian approached them.

"We're so happy you all were able to make it," she said. Brian nodded happily at her side. "Please help yourself to drinks. The food is almost ready."

Veronica surveyed the modest home's backyard and saw that Tomás's parents and abuelita were already seated at a table in the corner. They had left about twenty minutes before the younger group since they planned on leaving before it got even colder. His dad had gotten news the day before that his immuno-therapy appointments were going to start the follow-ing week and his mom didn't want to risk him coming down with a cold, which might make the doctor decide to postpone the treatment.

She hated that Tomás and his family were having to go through something so difficult. But they were close and strong. As long as they helped one another through this time, they would survive. Just as she, her sister, and their dad had.

And as if his ears were burning at the thought of him, Veronica's phone buzzed with the notification that her father was calling. She showed Tomás the caller ID. "I'll be right back," she said before walking over to an empty square of the backyard.

"Hola, Apa," she said.

"Vero?" his dad asked. "I can barely hear you. Where are you?"

"I'm...I'm at a restaurant. Let me go outside." Veronica didn't like lying to her dad, but she figured it was easier than explaining the truth. She walked out of the backyard and onto the sidewalk in front of the house. "There. Can you hear me now?"

"Yes, much better. I'll let you get back to your meal. I just wanted to check in to let you know everything has been secured for the photo shoot. Since we'll be transporting Takuache directly to arena, the photog-rapher and I decided that you'll do a few shots here at the estate and then he'll take more once you and Takuache are together in Kentucky."

"That sounds fine to me," she said.

"Good. How are you doing? Are you getting excited?"

"Yes. And also a little nervous."

Her dad scoffed into the phone. "You have no reason to be nervous, Mijita. Charles says you have improved so much. He really thinks you've got a shot to make the team."

It grated her nerves that Charles was probably taking credit for Tomás's work. She could feel her confidence growing every time they trained. And Takuache was basically a different horse than when he'd first arrived at Rancho Lindo. Veronica truly believed that Tomás had a gift for this kind of work. She had already decided that she would tell her dad about who was really responsible for her improvements when she flew back to Mexico for the publicity campaign before the competition. Tomás deserved the recognition. In fact, she was going to make it her mission to send more riders to him.

She wasn't blind or ignorant. Veronica had come to the realization that the Ortegas were in need of new business and new customers. She knew Tomás was too proud to ask for referrals. That's why she planned to go to Cruz with her idea very soon.

But this wasn't the day or the place to have that conversation with her dad. She needed to get back to the barbecue and Tomás.

"Okay, Apa. I've gotta go. I'll call you tomorrow, okay?"

He agreed and then told her that he loved her and that he was proud of her.

Veronica ignored the familiar pang of guilt. It was getting stronger every time she talked to him. The antidote was always her sister. She glanced at the backyard gate just in case Tomás had come looking for her. When she didn't see him, she figured she had a few more minutes and clicked on her sister's contact name.

"Tell me I'm not a bad person," Veronica blurted as soon as Valeria answered.

"Hello and you're not a bad person."

"Then why do I feel like it?"

"Let me guess. You're having another existential crisis about this fake-dating arrangement with Tomás because you finally realized you're starting to have real feelings for the man?"

Valeria had decided this was true a few days ago after Veronica mistakenly told her about the hot kiss they'd shared on the dance floor.

"No. Actually, it's because I just talked to Apa. I don't like lying. Especially because I just found out that apparently Charles has been telling him how improved my jumps are. I wanted so bad to tell him that it's because of Tomás."

"So why didn't you?" she asked.

"Because I have a feeling that's going to be a big conversation and I'd rather do it in person when I'm home for the publicity shoot."

"Oh yeah. Dad has been talking about that for days now. He's so excited. Speaking of, when were you going to tell me that Charles was going to be a part of the photo shoot too?"

Veronica stopped pacing. "Charles?"

"Dad says he's never been to Mexico and he's never been interviewed by *Equestrian Today*. Dad wants the photo shoot with you two to go perfectly, so he even offered to buy Charles a whole new outfit just for the occasion."

"Hold up," Veronica said. "Charles is part of the photo shoot?"

"That's what Dad told me. Did he not tell you? And Charles hasn't breathed a word of it either?"

Irritation burned the back of her neck, her cheeks, and her forehead. "I can't believe this. I can't let Charles be a part of the photo shoot and then take credit for Tomás's work. It isn't right."

"I'm sorry, Vero. I really thought you knew about this. Apa has been so busy these days, he probably thought he told you."

Veronica didn't tell her sister that she doubted that. Did her dad forget that she had asked him to fire Charles?

Out of the corner of her eye, she spotted Tomás waiting for her at the gate. She would have to figure things out after the barbecue.

"Let's talk tomorrow," she told her sister. "I need to come up with a plan."

She said goodbye to Valeria and walked up to Tomás.

"Everything okay with your dad?"

"Yeah, everything is good. He's just excited about me coming home soon."

Something she couldn't decipher crossed his face. "I'm sure he is. Uh, the food is ready if you want to eat?"

She nodded and he reached out his hand. Veronica expected him to explain that Mia was watching or had said something else to him. But he didn't.

She took it anyway.

Although Veronica was still pretty pissed about the whole photo-shoot-with-Charles dilemma, she had tried to enjoy the barbecue. The food had been outstanding and the company had been even better. Tomás was the ever-attentive fake boyfriend, making sure she had enough to drink and eat. And then gave her his jacket to wear over her shoulders once the temperature began to drop.

"Are you having a good time?" he asked after he brought her a piece of cake.

"I am," she said honestly. "It's a nice party. Are you okay?"

He squinted at her. "Me? Yeah, totally. Why wouldn't I be?"

"Because this is your ex-girlfriend's engagement party, that's why."

"Hmm. I guess I kind of forgot that was why we're here. I was just enjoying the festivities. I haven't even really thought about Mia. In fact, I don't think I've talked to her since when we first arrived."

Veronica had to think about that for a second. It was true. She'd been at Tomás's side all night, except for the phone calls with her dad and sister, and Mia had stayed away. She found it odd, though. Before tonight, she had thought that Mia had been overly friendly with both of them. She had even told Valeria that she thought maybe Mia was trying too hard in order to hide the fact that she was jealous.

"Maybe Brian is her fake fiancé and this was her way of getting Tomás back," Valeria had said.

"You read too many romance novels," she'd told her at the time. "I highly doubt that she has any interest in getting back together with Tomás."

The fact that Mia was now staying away from them seemed weird to Veronica, but she eventually chalked it up to the fact that she was the guest of honor and lots of people wanted her attention.

Veronica glanced up when Gabe and Nora, who had been sitting at the same table, got to their feet. Gabe motioned to his watch.

Tomás laughed. "I think he's done for the night," he said. "Are you ready to go?"

"I'm ready if you are. Although I do want to run to the bathroom before we leave."

"Sure. I'll gather my other brothers and we can say our goodbyes."

"Oh, that's right. They're leaving tomorrow. Do you want me to go with you?"

Tomás seemed to consider her offer for a few seconds. "Nah. It's okay. It's going to be quick and clean. I'll meet you out here when you're done."

She smiled and tried not get offended that he didn't need her around when he said goodbye to Mia.

A few minutes later, Veronica was back in the backyard, but she didn't see Tomás. However, after walking around a little, she did find everyone else.

"Where's Tomás?" she asked Nico.

"I think he's still inside talking to Mia. He told us to wait out here for him."

"Oh. Well, I'll go find him and let him know we're all ready to go. Why don't you guys wait in the car so you can warm up."

Nora, who had been blowing into her hands, nodded furiously. The rest of the group agreed and headed to the gate.

Veronica walked back inside the house. She checked

the kitchen and the living room, but he wasn't there. She decided to stop at the bathroom again, but it was empty. Veronica tried not to feel annoyed that Tomás had disappeared on her. But the more she looked, the more her irritation grew. Finally, she walked back into the living room and noticed an arched doorway off to the side. As she got closer, she heard voices. And one of them she recognized as Tomás's.

She turned the corner and saw them. His back was toward her as he leaned in to give Mia a hug. Mia wrapped her arms around his back and gave him a kiss on his cheek. When she pulled away, she met Veronica's eyes and gave her a curious look that she couldn't decipher. Instead, Mia whispered something in Tomás's ear and then disappeared farther into the room.

Tomás stood there for several more seconds. When it looked like he was about to turn around, Veronica took a step backward and pretended like she had just walked into the area.

He smiled at her in a way he never had before. Why did it look like a guilty smile?

"There you are," she said, trying not show any emotion. "Everyone is waiting for us in the car."

Tomás nodded. "Great. Let's go then."

When he was at her side, he tried to put his arm around her back. She maneuvered her body out of reach, though, and said, "She's not looking anymore."

The ride back to Rancho Lindo was quiet. She could feel Tomás's eyes on her, but she refused to look his way. He was driving the SUV this time since Gabe wanted to be dropped off at Nora's cottage. The group had left the front passenger seat open for her and she'd spent the time looking out at the nothingness through the window. Veronica hated that she was mad about what she had seen. She had no right to be.

After dropping off Gabe and Nora, Tomás drove to the house to let his brothers out. She had hoped he would stop at her cottage first instead. Veronica knew he knew something was wrong and that meant he probably wanted to get her alone so they could talk.

But she was in no mood.

So when he put the SUV in park, she told him good night and practically ran to her cottage and rushed inside.

As soon as she shut the door behind her, there was a knock.

"Veronica, please talk to me."

Tomás's voice on the other side of the door was urgent, but soft.

She let out a long breath and opened it. "I'm tired, Tomás. We can talk tomorrow."

"Judging by the glare you're giving me right now, it seems like you never want to talk to me again."

Realistically, that would be impossible since she still had a few more weeks of training left. But she could admit that it really wasn't what she wanted anyway.

Instead of telling him that, though, Veronica left the door open and walked to the kitchen to pour herself a glass of water from the ceramic pitcher she kept on the counter.

From behind her, she heard the door close, followed by footsteps.

"So what's going on with you?"

Veronica set the pitcher down and turned around

to face him. "I don't like being embarrassed, Tomás."
Even now she could feel heat burn her cheeks.

"Of course not. No one does."

"Then why would you do that to me?"

Tomás closed the distance between them and took
her hands. "Veronica, I honestly don't know what
you're talking about. I swear I would never go out of
my way to hurt you."

The sincerity of his tone made her waver for a
second. But she knew what she'd seen back at the
barbecue.

She pulled her hands from his grip. "Look, I know
this whole pretending-to-date thing wasn't your idea
and I basically had to convince you to go through with
it. And I realize that Mia is leaving tomorrow. But I
thought we were going to make it seem as real as possible until I left for your mom's sake."

His eyebrows arched and his eyes searched hers.
"And we are. Why? Do you want to stop now?"

Veronica could see his earnestness. She wanted to
believe she had been wrong. But she couldn't yet trust
her own feelings. Not until she heard it from him.

"No," she told him with a shrug. "I guess I'm wondering if you do, though. I saw you and Mia hugging inside
the house tonight and God knows who else saw it too.
By tomorrow, all of Esperanza is going to think I'm the
biggest fool in the world for believing you were over her."

His grip tightened. "I am over her. I swear. What
you saw was us finally having our closure. I told her I
was happy for her and Brian, and I meant it."

She wanted to believe him. And why did she care if
Frances and the rest of the town thought he was cheat-
ing on her? This was all for pretend.

Wasn't it?

"Then why did she give me that look?"

"What look?"

"Mia saw me when she hugged you and she had this weird expression on her face. Almost like she knew something I didn't."

That's when Tomás let go and stuck his hands into the front pockets of his jeans and sighed. "Because I told her the truth. About us."

Veronica gasped. "But why? Why would you tell her after everything? She's leaving tomorrow. She believed we were a couple. Why ruin the plan?"

"Because it was a dumb plan. And because I'm ready to stop pretending."

Hurt slammed into her chest so hard that Veronica's knees nearly buckled from the impact. Of course he was ready to stop pretending. He wanted to get back to the way things were before he had to try to make believe that he had romantic feelings for her.

"I see," she said softly. "And what did Mia say? Because from where I stood, she didn't look mad. In fact, she kinda looked happy."

Maybe Mia was happy to hear their relationship had been fake because that meant Tomás was really single. Veronica's heart fell at that thought.

"She was annoyed at first that I had lied to her. But I guess in a way she was a little pleased."

"Why on earth would she be pleased?" Veronica asked in surprise.

Tomás shook his head. "Because she's happy with Brian and she's happy for me too. I guess she doesn't have to feel guilty anymore about breaking my heart because she knows I met someone who put it back together."

Emotional chaos then rendered her completely frozen as Tomás took another step closer and leaned in until his face was only inches away from hers. "I'm done pretending, Veronica, because I want to do this for real."

She recognized the longing in his eyes and it made her breath hitch in anticipation. She'd meant to be stoic—to prove to him and to herself that she didn't want the same damn thing. But she was also tired of pretending. She leaned into him ever so slightly.

He took her mouth in a crushing kiss. Then he moved his lips to her ear. "I can't take it anymore. I'm dying for you, Veronica."

She took great pleasure in knowing how much Tomás needed her. Because she needed him just as badly.

Chapter Twenty-Eight

Tomás rolled over onto his side and put his arm out expecting to touch bare skin. He only got a handful of the comforter. He opened his eyes. The other side of the bed was empty.

Veronica was gone.

He sat up and looked around the room. There was no sight of her or the dress that he remembered being on the floor next to the bed. Then he caught a whiff of freshly brewed coffee, which woke him even more, and he smiled. After pulling on his pants, he made his way to the kitchen, hoping to find her in only a towel or sheet. Something he could easily pull off so he could properly tell her good morning.

But the kitchen was empty and so were the living room and bathroom. There was no sign of her anywhere. He rubbed his eyes and headed for the coffeemaker. The pot was full and a single mug sat next to it. Inside was a curled-up piece of paper.

Tomás pulled it out and read the note: *Your mom texted that she made chilaquiles for breakfast, so I'm going to the house to get some for us. Oh, and she also said that if I*

see you at the stable to tell you to go eat. Apparently she's
been texting you and you haven't been answering.

He laughed at the little smiley face she'd drawn at
the end of the note.

Tomás still couldn't believe that last night hadn't
been just another dream. He had really told her how
he'd felt and how much he'd wanted to be with her for
real. And—to his amazement—she hadn't gone running out the door. It was still way too early to talk
about what last night had meant or what, if anything,
would change.

For now, Tomás just wanted to focus on having
breakfast with Veronica, just the two of them. He
wouldn't have to worry about his mom or brothers
interrupting them.

Then an idea popped into his head. While Veronica was taking care of their breakfast, he was going to
start planning lunch.

"Where on earth are we going, Tomás?" Veronica
asked as they stepped out of the truck and into a field.

"I told you it's a surprise. So let me surprise you."

Tomás laughed at Veronica's obvious annoyance.
He knew how hard it was for her to let someone take
control. But he knew her short irritation would be
worth her reaction once she saw what he had done.

He held her hand as they walked toward the creek
he and his brothers used to swim in when they were
kids. The water was still too cold to do that, but he
had other things in mind once they made it to the spot
he wanted to show her.

They walked past several bushes until they came upon an enormous oak tree that sat just a few feet away from the roaring creek. The tree's bare branches allowed the afternoon sun to spray them with some warmth as Tomás laid out the flannel blanket on the ground and began to set up the picnic he'd packed all on his own.

"This is the surprise?" she asked.

His heart dipped. Was she disappointed?

"It is. What do you think?" he asked with slight hesitation.

She put her hands on her hips and turned in a full circle. "I think it's perfect."

"Well, you did say you wanted to see it. Although don't you dare go for a swim. It's still way too cold."

"I won't. But now it's definitely on my bucket list. I guess I'll just have to be here during the summer so I can finally do it."

The reference to Veronica being in Esperanza over the summer nearly drifted over his head. He liked the thought and decided to hold on to it.

After Tomás set out the sandwiches and fruit he'd brought, they began to eat and take in the scenery.

"If Nora was here she'd be pointing to every bush and flower and tree and telling you its name. She's such a nerd when it comes to plants," Tomás explained with a laugh.

Veronica pushed his shoulder playfully. "She's not a nerd; she's a horticulturist. You love horses; she loves plants. Same thing."

"I guess," he said and popped a grape into his mouth. "I always thought she'd grow up to be a librarian because she always had a book in her face."

"Maybe one day she'll write about a book about plants. I like to think we don't have to limit ourselves when it comes to our talents," she said.

"Does that mean there's something else you'd like to do if you can't ride anymore?" He asked the question, but Tomás couldn't imagine Veronica doing anything else really.

She arched her eyebrows. "If? More like when. I'm hoping I can retire within the next five years. That is, if I get to the Olympics. If I don't, then I would gladly retire as soon as this competition is done."

"Really?" he asked. Veronica was so committed to her sport that it surprised him she wanted to give it up so soon. "But why? You're young. I bet you could rack up a ton more trophies."

"Maybe. But trophies aren't important to me. Remember I told you about my mom's glass case? The trophies I've won could fill up two of those. Competing for so long has made riding and jumping more like a job. Actually, technically, it is my job. Prize purses are my main income, along with some endorsement deals. I'm getting tired, though. Some days I think I would be okay if I never rode a horse again."

Tomás nodded in understanding. When he was a kid, the stable was his playground. He loved being there among the horses and could spend all afternoon riding around Rancho Lindo's property. But now, with the pressure to bring in more business, the idea of that playground was long gone. The stable was work. Lots of work.

"I feel like that sometimes. I guess the trick is to find the time to find your joy again. What would make you happy then if you weren't competing?"

She seemed to think about her answer for a little. Then she met his eyes and smiled. "I think I want to be a trainer one day. I really enjoy teaching kids."

"I can see you doing that," he told her.

"Really?"

"Definitely. You love horses, and anyone who loves horses loves sharing them with others. I think you'd be an amazing trainer."

"First a picnic, and then a compliment? Who would've thought that Tomás Ortega would be so nice to me."

He laughed. "What are you talking about? I'm always nice."

"Um, am I the only one who remembers how mean you were to me when I first got here?"

"Mean," he scoffed. "I think your recollection is a little hazy. Let me fix that for you."

Tomás lifted his butt off the blanket and softly tackled Veronica and then rolled her on top of him.

She squealed with laughter but got quiet when their eyes met.

He loved how they fit together perfectly. He brought his head up near her ear and inhaled the sweet, fruity scent of her perfume. They didn't talk for a few seconds and he let himself enjoy the feel and smell of her.

"This is nice," she said after a few more quiet moments ticked by.

"Mmmhmmm," he answered.

"Can I ask you a question?"

He was tempted to say no, wanting to savor this moment between them for as long as possible. But he also wanted her to feel like she could talk to him about anything. So he nodded.

"When did you decide that you wanted to stop pretending?"

Tomás couldn't help but laugh. He should've known better than to think she wouldn't bring up his admission from last night. "I don't think there was an exact day or time. I think it was different moments added all together."

She was quiet for a few seconds. He felt her take a deep breath before she asked, "And did you know that I felt the same?"

"Not in the slightest," he admitted with a chuckle. "But maybe that was because I was afraid to hope that you did."

"Okay, I have another question."

"How about you save all your questions for the ride home. Right now I just want to enjoy holding you this close."

Her body pressed deeper into his and he couldn't control his response.

"I like being on top of you," she said. The rasp in her voice thrilled him. He wondered how much more he could take before he gave in to his desires.

Tomás raised his head to look into her eyes. The want reflected in them nearly took his breath away.

And for the first time since he'd admitted his own feelings, Tomás knew exactly what Veronica wanted from him.

After their picnic, they stopped in town to pick up a few things for dinner. Veronica had told him since he'd made their lunch, she wanted to cook for him.

"Why do you look so shocked?" Veronica exclaimed as they made their way through Esperanza's only grocery store. "I used to cook for me and my sister all the time. My dad had a lot of dinner meetings and once I was old enough to watch my sister on my own, I had to make her food since our cook usually went back to her home in the evening."

"Sandwiches don't count," he teased.

"I'll have you know that our cook taught me everything she knew. I was serious about getting some of your abuelita's recipes, because I want to make them myself."

"Fine. I will trust in your culinary skills. What masterpiece will you be making tonight?"

Veronica gave him a bright smile. "Spaghetti."

That made him laugh for a lot longer than was necessary. "I can make spaghetti, Veronica."

She waved a hand in front of his face. "Not like I can. Now I'm going to go find pasta. You go over there and get me some tomatoes, garlic, and an onion."

Before she left him, though, Tomás grabbed her hand and pulled her in for a quick kiss.

"What was that for?" she asked.

"That was an I'm-sorry-for-teasing-you kiss," he said.

"Oh. I like that kind of kiss," she said with a huge grin.

"Good. I'll make sure to give you more of them."

She looked into his eyes and smiled. "Promise?"

"Promise."

Tomás smiled too and was tempted to go in for another kiss when he spotted an older man by the cereal aisle, watching them. Deciding it was better not to give grocery store customers a show, he released Veronica and told her he'd meet her at the register in a few minutes.

He walked over to the limited produce section and

began searching for the perfect tomatoes for Veronica's spaghetti. He took a few minutes before finally selecting three perfectly plump and red ones. As he put them inside the clear produce bag, he looked up and spotted Veronica talking to the man who had been staring at them earlier. He seemed familiar, but Tomás couldn't place him. He dismissed it and went back to examining the tomatoes. But when he looked up again, he noticed that Veronica didn't seem too happy with whatever the man was telling her.

Tomás dropped the bag he'd been holding and stormed over to where they were.

"Everything okay here?" he asked, pulling her close to him.

"Yes, it's fine," she told him. But he knew by her stiff posture that it wasn't.

"Who are you?" Tomás asked. He didn't care if he sounded annoyed.

"I'm Eduardo," the man said matter-of-factly. "I'm a friend of Lina's and a friend of Señor del Valle."

The mention of Veronica's father's name stilled Tomás. "Oh. I see. I apologize for my questioning then."

Eduardo waved his hand at him. "No need for apologies. I was just telling Veronica that I'm actually going to see her father in a few days and I asked if there was anything she wanted me to tell him."

Veronica folded her arms across her chest. "And I told him that I talk to my father almost every day so there was no need."

Alarm bells went off in Tomás's head. He didn't like her terse tone. Something else was going on between them.

"Well, it was good to meet you. We really need to be going now as my family is expecting us for dinner."

He grabbed Veronica's hand to pull her away, but she didn't budge.

"It was nice to see you again, Eduardo. I truly hope you didn't really mean what you said, though."

"What did he say?" Tomás asked Veronica.

"He said that he knows a reporter at ESPN Mexico and he wants me to let him negotiate an exclusive interview for me. But when I explained that my exclusive was already arranged with a magazine, he mentioned that the reporter might be interested in knowing where I've been all these months instead then."

The threat was obvious, and Tomás couldn't help but feel enraged.

He let go of Veronica's hand and pointed a finger in Eduardo's face.

"I don't care if you are friends with Lina. If you leak Veronica's whereabouts, I'll make sure you pay for it one way or another."

Veronica reached up to pull his hand down. "Let's go, Tomás. He's not worth it."

"Maybe not, but I want to make sure we have an understanding."

Eduardo shrugged. "I suppose. I would never do anything to make Señor del Valle's daughter upset. So if she doesn't want me to tell a reporter where she is or what she's been doing, then I won't."

He couldn't quite put his finger on it, but Eduardo's words seemed insincere. But there wasn't anything they could do about it in the middle of the grocery store.

Tomás let Veronica pull him away and they forgot

about the groceries they'd already picked up and left the store. She didn't say a word on the short trip back to her cottage. It wasn't until they were inside that she finally spoke.

"What on earth was that back there?" she asked.

"What do you mean?" Tomás couldn't help but be surprised by the annoyance in her voice. "I was supporting you. I wanted to make sure that jerk knew he couldn't get away with what he was threatening."

"That jerk does business with my father, Tomás. I was handling it. I didn't need you to rescue me."

He immediately realized she was right. He could've made things a lot worse.

"I'm sorry," Tomás said. "You're right. That was a dumb thing to do."

Her shoulders visibly eased in relief. "What were you thinking, Tomás?"

"I wasn't," he said. "That's the problem. When it comes to you, it's like my mind turns into Jell-O." He moved closer. Her chest heaved, and he wondered if her breath was labored from their arguing or from him.

"What do you mean?"

"It means I won't stand by and let anyone threaten or hurt you."

"I can take care of myself," she said and put her hands on her hips.

"I know you can," he said and stepped closer. "But I want you to know that you don't have to do anything on your own if you don't want to. I'm here for you, okay?"

He pulled her into his arms and held her tight. Knowing what she had endured the past few years only made him want to keep her close and keep her safe. Of course he knew she'd be leaving soon, and then it would be impossible. Until then, though, he was going to stay at her side.

"I'm sorry," he whispered into her hair. "Please don't be mad anymore."

He felt her body sag against him. "How can I be mad when you make me feel like this?" she whispered back.

Longing ignited deep within him. The ugliness of the evening disappeared, and all he could think about was being with her again like he had been last night.

He guided her backward until she was against the front door and then moved his hand to her chest and traced the outline of her cleavage. She took a deep breath and whispered, "What do you want, Tomás?"

"This," he rasped just before their lips crashed together in one hard, demanding kiss. Her tongue sought his and he groaned into her mouth. He cupped her butt and lifted her up so she could wrap her long, lean legs around his hips.

He couldn't believe that she wanted him just as much as he wanted her.

"Don't let go," she whispered.

"Never."

Veronica held on to him tightly. They devoured each other as if their next kiss would be their last.

Tomás didn't know what this thing with Veronica was becoming. All he knew or cared about at the moment was that she was in his arms.

And for now, that was enough.

Chapter Twenty-Nine

Mija, did you hear me?"

Veronica stopped doodling her fifth heart on the back of an envelope. "Sorry, Apa. I didn't. What did you say?"

He sighed long and hard on the other end of the phone. "What's wrong with you today? You seem distracted."

"No, I'm just tired, that's all," she said, leaving out the fact that she and Tomás had been up almost all night watching movies on the couch before moving their date night to the bedroom.

"Well, after we finish talking, you should go take a nap. If you're tired then your immune system isn't as strong as it should be, and you can't afford to get sick right now."

"I know, Apa. I'll make sure I take it easy for the rest of the day."

Veronica was actually being truthful. Tomás had left less than hour ago for a trip with his brother Gabe. He wouldn't be back until later that night, which gave her time to enjoy a long, hot bath and even longer nap.

"Good. Well, what I was saying was that I've set up some meetings for possible sponsorships next year. I think after the competition, though, we'll have more prospects to choose from."

"Unless I totally bomb it, like last time."

Veronica snapped her mouth shut. It had been a while since either of them had brought up what had happened three years ago. She braced for her dad's reaction.

"Don't say things like that, Mijita."

"Why? Because it's true?"

"Of course it's not true. You are going to the Olympics. I know it in my heart."

Frustration exploded inside her. "Stop!"

"Que? Stop what?"

Tears welled up in her eyes and then spilled onto her cheeks. "Stop telling me things like that, Apa. I'm already under so much pressure—I can't take it anymore. Because what if I don't make it? I can't stand the thought of disappointing you . . . or Mamá."

"Your mother? What does she have to do with this?"

All of her emotions about the upcoming competition bubbled up to the surface. She couldn't contain the flood of the feelings she'd tried to dismiss for weeks. It all came pouring out.

Now Veronica was sobbing. "I've only ever wanted to make you both proud. I promised her that I would never give up, but now I don't know if I want to keep doing this."

"Oh, Mijita. I'm so sorry you're feeling like this. You always make me proud, okay? You're just nervous about the competition. You'll feel better once you come home. We both know you don't want to quit... not now."

Veronica took a long breath. "Actually, I've been thinking about becoming an equestrian jumping trainer."

"I think that would be wonderful."

"You do?" she said tearfully.

"Of course. It's good to have a plan for when you retire in ten years. And once you're an Olympic champion, you'll have your pick of athletes—only the crème de la crème."

"Actually, I was thinking of training children. You know, like when I volunteered at the center back home."

Her dad scoffed. "Vero, that was charity work. You can do that when you have time. But I'm talking about having your own Olympic-standard training business. Don't you want that kind of success?"

She didn't answer right away, and eventually she was saved by her dad's next meeting.

"We'll talk more later, Mija. I need to take another call."

Later, as she relaxed in the bathtub with a glass of wine, Veronica tried to imagine herself working at an award-winning equestrian center training Olympic hopefuls. But the picture wouldn't come into focus, even when she rested her head on the back of the tub and closed her eyes.

Because that wasn't what she wanted for her life. As usual, it was what her dad wanted.

He was a shrewd businessman who measured success by either the number of deals you brokered or the number of people clamoring for your next deal. Her dad couldn't see the value in spending your time or your energy on something that wasn't going to result in a big payday eventually. He wanted a return on his investment every single time.

Even when it came to his daughter.

Veronica wondered if she would ever get up the nerve to tell him no. Although she was grateful to him for a million things, it bothered her that he basically controlled her present life. And if she didn't put her foot down soon, he'd also control her future.

That was probably why she hadn't mentioned that she and Tomás were seeing each other. It was nice having a part of her life that was hers only. She had told her sister, of course. But Valeria was also keeping her boyfriend on a need-to-know basis and had decided that their dad did not.

So until something changed, Veronica had no plans to share her news either.

Chapter Thirty

Time moved excruciatingly slowly when you were waiting for a shoe to drop.

Tomás checked his watch again. It was only two minutes since the last time he'd looked.

He sat at a table in the corner of Lina's Diner and watched the front door. Veronica's dad was supposed to walk through it any second now and Tomás was doing everything he could not to change his mind and leave before Señor del Valle spotted him.

The man had called him out of the blue early that morning, introduced himself, and told him he would be arriving in Esperanza about ten in the morning. He asked if there was somewhere they could meet away from the ranch and away from Veronica.

Tomás's first instinct was to say no. He didn't want to sneak behind Veronica's back. Not when things between them were going so well. They trained in the afternoon, then they usually had dinner together either on their own or with his family. And they'd spent every night together in her cottage for the past week. He couldn't believe how much their relationship had changed in the past three months. Although they were both ignoring the fact that she would be leaving for Mexico next week for the publicity shoot and then heading to Kentucky for the competition. His brothers and Nora kept asking what was going to happen after that and he couldn't answer. It was obvious to all of them now that their fake relationship had turned into a real one. So, like him, everyone wanted to know what was going to happen next.

That's why he first told Señor del Valle that he wasn't comfortable meeting him without Veronica.

"I would consider this a personal favor, Tomás. It's important to me that I'm able to speak freely and I have a feeling that having Veronica there might not be efficient. I promise it won't take long and since you would be doing me a favor then, of course, I would owe you one in return. You know I have lots of friends in many businesses out on the West Coast—friends who trust my recommendations and referrals."

Tomás heard the subtle hint loud and clear. He also heard Cruz's voice in his ear. His brother would have a meltdown if he ever found out that Tomás had thrown away the chance to bring in more business to the ranch. And although Veronica might be upset at first, he knew that she would understand he'd done it for Rancho Lindo. So he agreed to meet Señor del Valle and had already decided he'd call Veronica immediately after.

The bell over the diner's door rang to announce the arrival of a new visitor. Tomás looked up and instantly knew the man walking inside was Veronica's dad. He was a big man with broad shoulders. He wore a coffee-colored fedora and matching long coat.

The man caught his eye and recognition crossed his face. It seemed that they both spotted each other.

As he worked his way to Tomás through the restaurant's maze of tables and chairs, his imposing figure made it seem as if the furniture belonged in a dollhouse. He bumped into a few unoccupied chairs, while the handful of patrons he passed had to scoot around to let him go by.

When he finally arrived at the table, Tomás stood up and held out his hand.

"Hola, Señor del Valle. It's good to meet you in person."

The older man nodded and shook Tomás's hand. "Mucho gusto," he said. After removing his hat and coat, he took a seat across from Tomás.

"Would you like something to drink or eat?" Tomás asked. "I can call over the waitress."

He shook his head. "No, I'm fine. Thank you."

Tomás nodded. It was obvious the man hadn't traveled all the way to Esperanza for diner food. He clasped his hands on the table in front of him and took a long breath. "What did you want to discuss with me?" Tomás asked.

"I want to know how long you've been dating my daughter."

If he'd been eating, Tomás would've choked. "I... who told you that?" He knew with absolute certainty that it hadn't been Veronica. She had told him the other day that she hadn't said a word to her dad about their training—and other—activities.

"My old friend Eduardo. You met him last weekend, I believe. I had suspected that something was going on with Veronica. She's been distracted and distant lately. Still, it was a surprise to learn my daughter found herself a boyfriend here in Esperanza." Señor del Valle seemed to study Tomás, perhaps waiting to see if Tomás would lie. He knew he was better off admitting both.

"I did meet him. And I regret that I lost my temper with him. However, I was only protecting your daughter."

Señor del Valle sat up straighter. "How so?"

"He was trying to blackmail Veronica into letting him arrange some type of exclusive interview with his friend at ESPN. When she declined, he threatened to tell that friend where Veronica was staying."

The older man's eye twitched. Tomás had figured that Eduardo hadn't shared that part of their conversation.

Señor del Valle confirmed it. "I see. I guess I owe you a thank-you."

"You don't owe me anything, sir. Like I said, I did it to protect Veronica."

"I appreciate you saying that," Señor del Valle offered. "And I think then you'll understand why I wanted to meet you."

Tomás nodded. "I do. Your daughter is very important to me and I'll do anything to make sure she finishes out her training at Rancho Lindo without any disruptions."

"Aren't you a disruption?" Señor del Valle said.

"How so?" Tomás bristled at the accusation.

"Do you know what happened to Veronica three years ago?"

"I do. I know everything."

Señor del Valle's head nearly fell back in surprise. "Really? She told you about Sebastian?"

"She did," Tomás said. "She wanted me to understand how important this upcoming competition was
to her. And I get it. That's why I'm trying to help…"
He stopped before saying anything about their training. That wasn't something he wanted to share before
Veronica had the chance to tell him herself. "That's
why I want to help make sure that she remains focused
on her goal."

Veronica's dad leaned forward. "But how can she
stay focused when she has a new relationship to worry
about? I'm assuming she cares about you very much
because she's kept you a secret from me. So naturally
I'm worried about what's going to happen when she
leaves next Friday. Is this thing between you going
to continue? What about when she makes the Olympic team and has to train in another state or another
country? What then?"

Tomás didn't know, but he didn't want to say that
to Señor del Valle. "We'll figure it out. Like I said,
right now my only concern is doing what I can to help
her perform well in Kentucky."

"If you're really concerned then you'll step aside."

Tomás's heart fell into his stomach. "What?"

"That's why I'm here, Tomás. I want you to stop
seeing my daughter so she can concentrate on getting
ready for the competition. I'm confident that she's
going to make the Olympic team. Do you know the
amount of focus and drive it takes to compete at the
Olympics? Her life is going to be equestrian jumping
twenty-four seven for the next year. She'll have no time
for anyone. Not me, not her sister, not you. But her
sister and I are used to this, and it doesn't hurt our
feelings. We know we can't make her feel guilty for

canceling on things. Do you really think you'll be able to have a relationship like that?"

As much as he tried not to show Señor del Valle that he was making valid points, Tomás felt his resolve weaken. Of course he had hopes that Veronica wanted what he wanted—to find a way to keep seeing each other.

But was he just being naïve and setting himself up for another Mia situation? Tomás's life would always be on Rancho Lindo. Veronica's life, especially if she did as well as he expected her to in the competition, would be about getting ready for the Olympics. He knew that and he was willing to be at her side—whether it was back on the ranch to continue training or from a distance if she decided to go back home to Mexico. The real question was: Would she still want him there after going back to her life before him?

Maybe she would realize, like Mia, that Tomás had no place in her new world. He didn't want Veronica to ever resent him or see him as a burden—someone she was obligated to stay with because he had been convenient. They'd only known each other three months. Maybe the fake-dating had tricked them into thinking they had real feelings for each other.

Señor del Valle stood up and grabbed his things. "I can see by the look on your face that you know I'm right. You're a smart man, Tomás. And I will always do business with a smart man. I'll have my assistant set up a call with you and your brother after the competition. Let's talk about how I can help you and your family's ranch. Have a good day."

Tomás knew that was going to be impossible now. He pulled out his phone and texted Veronica that he was coming over to see her so he could talk to her about something.

Then he texted Nora and asked her to be on standby. Because if Veronica didn't need a shoulder to cry on after their talk, then he would.

Veronica was waiting for him on the porch.

He knew she probably didn't appreciate his cryptic text, but he didn't want to start the conversation on the phone. He needed for this to be in person.

"Tomás Ortega, you better tell me what's going on right now," she blurted out, pointing her finger at him.

"Let's go inside first," he said.

She folded her arms against her chest in defiance. "No. Tell me."

He took off his cowboy hat and ran his fingers through his hair. Then he met her eyes.

"Your dad is in Esperanza. I just met him at Lina's Diner."

Her eyes widened in shock and her mouth dropped open. Then she turned on her heel and stomped inside swearing in Spanish. "Where are you going?" he called after her.

"To get my phone so I can call my dad and give him a piece of my mind."

Tomás reached out and grabbed her hand before she could go any further. "Wait. Let's sit down and talk first. Then you can say whatever you want to him."

He guided her to the couch and sat next to her, holding her hand. She regarded him with questioning eyes. "Tell me what he said," she whispered.

"He knows we're together . . . that we're dating."

Her head dropped and she sighed. "It was Eduardo, wasn't it? I figured it was only going to be a matter of time before he said something."

"It was, but don't worry. The old man shot himself in the foot. I let your dad know exactly what Eduardo had threatened you with. Something tells me that friendship and whatever business relationship they had is over."

Veronica nodded in relief. "Good. Okay, what else?"

Tomás scooted closer to her, still holding on so she would know that he didn't want to let her go.

"He wants to make sure that you're focused on the competition. That you're keeping your eyes on your dream to be in the Olympics."

"I am," Veronica said. "I don't understand why he had to come all the way to Esperanza to tell you that. Which brings me to my biggest question—why did you go meet him without me?"

"I wanted to tell you. In fact, I refused at first to go without you. But he hinted that it wouldn't be in Rancho Lindo's best interest if I didn't do what he asked."

Veronica closed her eyes, and Tomás watched as her cheeks turned a dark pink. "I'm so sorry, Tomás. My dad thinks everything in life can be negotiated with leverage. He once made me sign a contract that I'd get at least a B in math one semester or else I couldn't participate in our town's Christmas parade with my riding team. I know how persuasive he can be. I hate that he put you in that position and I promise you, he's about to get an earful from me."

She stood up, but he wouldn't let go of her hand.

"That's not all, Veronica. I need to tell you something else."

Veronica looked down at him with her big, beautiful eyes. He hated that he now saw worry reflected in them. She dropped back onto the couch.

"You're scaring me, Tomás," she told him, her voice low and soft.

"I don't mean to, I promise. But I think we need to finally have the discussion we've both been avoiding. What's the plan when you leave Rancho Lindo?"

"You know the plan. I'm going to Mexico for a week and then on to Kentucky. If—*when*—I make the team, then I start training for the Olympics."

Tomás smiled. "Exactly. You've got an amazing road ahead of you. You're going after your dreams, Veronica. I'm so proud of you. I hope you know that."

"I do," she replied, her eyebrows arched in apparent suspicion. "What I don't know is where this conversation is going."

"I...I don't think this is the best time for you to be starting a relationship."

Veronica leaned back as if his words had pushed her away physically. "Hold up. This is my dad talking. I know him. I know this is him."

The urgency in her voice was almost enough to change his mind. But he knew he had to go through with it. He told himself he was doing this for her.

"It was. But the more I thought about it, the more I agree with him. Although this is the last thing I want, I think we should put a hold on things...on us. You have too much to worry about right now. I don't want to hold you back."

Isn't that what he'd done with Mia? She'd made it

clear that his commitment to Rancho Lindo would prevent her from moving on to bigger and better things. He couldn't bear the thought of Veronica ever regretting their time together.

Her eyes glistened with unshed tears, and it nearly broke him. "If you don't want it, then why are you saying it? I know we haven't talked about where this thing between us is headed, but I feel like there's something here, Tomás. I'm not ready to give it up yet. Are you?"

His answer was no—a million times no. If he told her that, though, then she wouldn't let him let her go.

"All I want to do is remove any kind of pressure for you to commit to something you have no idea you'll still want a month from now. Absence doesn't always make the heart grow fonder, Veronica. I've done a long-distance relationship and it's hard. And neither of us was training to become an Olympic champion."

Veronica pulled her hand out of his grasp and stood up. She walked across the room as if she couldn't stand to be so close to him. His heart sank. But he had to be strong for both of them. He hated this, but he knew he was making the right decision.

"I know why you're doing this and it has nothing to do with my dad. You're just using him as an excuse because you're afraid."

Tomás stood and went over to her. "Afraid of what?"

"Afraid of what you've been avoiding for eight years—getting your heart broken again. Lots of people have successful long-distance relationships. Just because the first one you had didn't work out doesn't mean this wouldn't. But you're too scared to even try, aren't you?"

Was he scared? Maybe. But he was more terrified by the way Veronica was looking at him. He had hurt her and he desperately wished he could take it all back.

"Veronica," he said and attempted to hold her hand again. But she stepped out of his reach.

It was too late.

He'd already let go.

Chapter Thirty-One

There you are, Mija."

Veronica entered the stable on Takuache and saw her father and Charles standing together. Her gut twisted and she willed herself not to cry. Although she'd be surprised if she had any tears left after the hour-long ride she'd just had where she'd let them fall freely.

As soon as Tomás left the cottage, Veronica had changed and practically run to the stable to take Takuache out. She'd wanted to be alone, but also just to be free. Because if she couldn't convince Tomás that she wanted to be with him even after the competition, then she didn't know what to do next.

She dismounted her horse, grabbed his reins, and walked toward them. "Oh. So now you want to talk to me?"

Her dad rolled his eyes. "Mija, I know you're upset, but you'll get over it and you'll get over him. You're so close to getting everything you ever wanted. I did what I had to do to remove the distraction."

"Well, good job then. Because you got what you wanted. So why are you still here?"

Sabrina Sol

He ignored her biting tone and motioned to Charles. "Since I'm here, I thought the three of us could sit down and go over the publicity shoot. Cruz said we can use the office inside the house. The photographer has some ideas and I wanted to run them by you. I always prefer in-person meetings. I feel they're more productive."

The anger Veronica had just spent the past hour trying to shake off came rushing back. He knew what he'd done and how upset she would be. But instead of telling her everything would be okay or apologizing for barreling into her life and tossing it upside down, he was all business.

Suddenly, something finally broke inside her. And she let it all out.

"I'm not coming to Mexico."

"Veronica," her dad began. "Don't be a child."

"Then don't treat me like one. How dare you come here without telling me and meddle in my life."

"I did what I did to protect you and your dreams, Mija. You will thank me later."

She shook her head. "I won't. Not this time. You crossed a line today, Apa."

Charles cleared his throat. "I'll just let you two talk—you know, father-to-daughter. I don't need to be here."

Veronica folded her arms against her chest. "You're right. You don't need to be here. In fact, I think it's time you go back to England. You're fired."

"Excuse me?" he said.

Her dad waved his hand at her. "Veronica, you know I'm the only one who can fire Charles. I pay his salary."

"Fine," she said with a shrug. "Then pay him to do something else. He's no longer my trainer."

Charles opened his mouth again, but her dad held up his hand again to stop him. "Charles, why don't you go back to your condo. We'll talk later."

"You see now what I've been dealing with for the past three months," Charles complained.

His dad furrowed his eyebrows in response. "I said we'll talk later."

When Charles left, her dad turned his glare on her. "You're being impossible, Veronica. You're not showing up to the competition without a trainer."

"Fine. Then I'll take Tomás with me."

"Be reasonable, Mija."

"I am. I'll take Tomás not because I have feelings for him, but because he's the best trainer I've ever had since Mom. He's the reason I've improved my jumps— not Charles."

"Tomás runs this stable," her father said. "He's no Olympic equestrian jumping trainer."

"You're right. He's not. But Tomás is a horse expert. He knows what they want and how to get them to trust him. And I've learned how to do that with Takuache and that has made me a better rider. I finally figured out what my problem has been this whole time. It wasn't all those trainers I had you fire—it was me. You should've fired me."

Her dad shook his head. "No entiendo, Mija. I don't understand why you think these things. You didn't get to Kentucky the first time or this time because of Tomás. You got there because of you."

"I got there in spite of me, Apa. Not because I forgot how to perform, but because I had forgotten that I enjoyed it. My heart hasn't been into competing, truly into it, because I was there for all the wrong reasons.

Making the Olympic team was never my dream. I only
wanted it for Mom—for her memory."

"What are you saying, Mija? Are you quitting?"

Tears wet her eyes and she had to wipe them away
in order to see her dad. She could only hope that he
finally saw her.

"Not yet. I guess I'll decide after the competition. I
just know that I want to love riding again."

And she wanted Tomás to let her love him too.

Chapter Thirty-Two

Tomás opened the refrigerator and then promptly forgot what he was supposed to get from it.

"Is there milk or not?"

Nico's question answered his own and he pulled out the gallon of milk for their cereal.

"What's up with you?" his brother asked several minutes later, after Tomás took only his second spoonful.

"Nothing. I'm just tired. I didn't sleep very well."

"Of course you didn't. You're an idiot."

Tomás set down his spoon. "What's that supposed to mean?"

"Cruz told me that Veronica is heading to Kentucky earlier than expected. I'm assuming it's because of you."

He shrugged. The last thing he needed after a crappy night was an inquisition by Nico of all people. "She wants to get there now so she can have enough time to get situated."

"And because of you."

Tomás let out a long sigh. "If you have something to say, Nico, just say it."

His brother dropped his spoon onto the counter. "Fine. I will. You are an idiot for letting Veronica go."

"What are you talking about? She was always going to leave, remember?"

Nico shook his head. "Not like this. She didn't even pack up the cottage—she told Cruz someone would come get the rest of her things later. Something happened between the two of you, so tell me what you did so I can tell you how to fix it."

Suddenly, Tomás wasn't hungry anymore. He picked up his bowl, walked over to the sink, and threw everything down the drain. He stood there for a few seconds.

Without turning around, he told Nico, "There's nothing to fix. All I did was tell her that I thought she should focus on the competition. I don't want to get in her way."

"Bullshit," Nico said behind him.

Tomás spun around and folded his arms against his chest. "It's the truth. Veronica has a chance to go to the Olympics. Her career is about to take off and her world is going to change in ways I can't even imagine. And sooner or later she was going to realize that I don't belong in that world. It sucks. But it's better this way."

His brother sighed. "Again. Bullshit."

"Whatever," Tomás said and turned back around to rinse out his bowl and spoon and stick them in the dishwasher.

"You're just telling yourself that because you don't want to admit the truth."

Tomás dried his hands and looked over at his brother again. "And what's the truth, Mr. Know-It-All?"

"That you're scared. You'd rather hide out with the horses than risk having your heart broken again.

You love that woman, but you're too afraid to admit it. And now she's going to leave and you're going to be miserable. Again."

"You don't know what you're talking about."

Nico got up and walked over to him. "She isn't Mia."

"I know she's not."

"Then why are you acting like her going to Kentucky was going to be the end of you two? It's not like she was going to a competition in outer space. She probably would've come back if you had asked and not pushed her away."

Tomás couldn't contain his annoyance. His brother didn't understand. None of them did.

When his mom had asked him last night why Veronica hadn't come for dinner, he wasn't sure what to tell her. So he'd said she was busy packing for Kentucky—which was the partial truth. Somehow she knew something was wrong and simply told him to fix it.

If only it were that easy.

"I'll admit that I have feelings for Veronica, feelings that actually started after we started pretending," he told Nico. "So yeah, it was nice to spend these past few weeks with her and pretend for a little while that she wasn't going to leave me behind to go follow her dreams. The only thing that changed was the timeline."

"Bullshit number three."

"Excuse me?"

"Look, I don't know if this thing between you two is the real deal. All I know is that you can't be afraid to find out. So maybe it's time to stop pretending."

"Stop pretending what?"

"That you're *not* crazy about her, that she doesn't mean more to you than Mia ever did. You may have a sixth sense when it comes to horses, but I know *you*. And Veronica does something to you when she's around."

Tomás's stomach dropped. His brother was right. Veronica did do something to him. She made him want to feel love again. And that scared the crap out of him. All these years, he'd told his family that he'd gotten over Mia—and that was the truth. What he hadn't gotten over was the way she'd made him feel. He and Rancho Lindo hadn't been good enough for her, and that had broken his heart in a million pieces.

She isn't Mia.

She isn't Mia.

She isn't Mia.

Nico's words repeated over and over again in his thoughts.

Of course she wasn't. But the differences between the two of them were more than he had ever realized.

Although Mia had grown up in Esperanza, she'd always told him that she dreamed about leaving it one day. She longed for life in a big city because she loved the hustle and bustle of it all. Veronica had grown up in a big city but preferred the seclusion of her family's estate. And like Tomás, she loved horses and riding. Just like that night at dinner when he told the story about missing his prom, Veronica could relate because she understood his commitment to his animals and his family.

No, Veronica wasn't Mia, because she knew him— the real him.

And somehow he knew her too. Whatever he'd been feeling toward her, she'd been feeling the same. He could see that now. And what did he do? He threw it away just to protect his own heart.

"God." Tomás groaned, sat back on the stool, and put his head in his hands. "I'm such an idiot."

Then a realization hit him. His head snapped back up. "Wait a second. I thought you were interested in Veronica. Why are you all of a sudden 'Team Tomás'?"

"It's not all of a sudden," Nico explained. "You're my brother. I want you to be happy. And I'm also not stupid. I know when a woman is into me and I know when she's not. Veronica has always had a soft spot for you. You were just too stupid to see it."

Nico also sat back down and folded his arms across his chest. "Don't you think she deserves to know that you've finally come to your senses?"

Tomás let out a long sigh of regret. "I think it's too late."

Later that afternoon, Tomás considered going back to bed. He had never felt so disconnected.

The horses could feel it too. Not one of them wanted to follow instructions or even just settle down.

He was antsy, so they were antsy as well.

"Fine," he announced while standing in the middle of the stable. "You all win. I'll leave you alone today."

"I guess I'm not the only one having a bad day."

Tomás whipped around to see Señor del Valle standing at the entrance. He nodded at him as the older man walked over.

"What are you doing here? Veronica left this morning."

"Yes, your brother just told me. I had hoped I could get here before she left."

"Didn't you tell her you were on your way?"

He shrugged. "I tried to. But she's not answering my calls or texts. Her sister was the one who told me that she was leaving today instead of on Friday like we had planned. Apparently, she is going straight to Kentucky and not back to Mexico for the big publicity photo shoot I had planned. I guess she's mad at both of us now."

Tomás stilled at the statement. He wasn't sure how much to tell Veronica's dad. Although he knew he really couldn't blame the man for his own actions, Tomás didn't feel like giving him the satisfaction of knowing that, yes, Veronica was very angry at him too. "She just decided it would be best to go a few days early and get Takuache situated herself."

Tomás walked over to Peanut's stall and began gathering his grooming equipment.

"I see. So you weren't the one who sent her away?"

He stopped and faced Señor del Valle fully. "I just told her that I wanted what you wanted."

"And what's that?"

Tomás shrugged. "To do her best. She needs to focus on the competition now and I don't want to be a distraction." Even now as he said it, he could hear the shallowness of his words. He wasn't even trying to make her dad believe them at this point. But it was still easier than confessing the truth about how he'd hurt Veronica for no reason other than being a coward.

"And is that really how you feel?" As expected, Señor del Valle didn't believe his lie.

"What do you mean?" Tomás asked.

"Do you really see yourself as a distraction?"

"Isn't that what you told me?" he said bitterly.

"I know what I thought. Now I want to hear if you think the same thing. The truth."

"Your daughter is one of the best riders I've ever seen. She's got what it takes to become an Olympic champion. She doesn't need me in her life anymore." It hurt Tomás to admit that last part.

"She told me that you're a pretty good rider yourself. In fact, she says you're one of the best trainers she's ever had."

Tomás winced in surprise. He couldn't believe that Veronica had really told her dad that.

He cleared his throat and began to pack up his grooming equipment. "I'm no trainer. I'm just a stable manager."

He heard a loud sigh. Tomás looked up and saw that Señor del Valle was standing only about a foot away from him now.

"Do you use natural or synthetic brushes?" the older man asked and pointed to Tomás's open groom box.

The question came out of the blue, so it took him a few seconds to respond. "Natural," he eventually replied.

Señor del Valle reached into the box and pulled out the large brush that Tomás had just placed inside. He ran his hand over the bristles and seemed to nod in approval. "When I worked in the stables, I always preferred the natural brushes. But I'd use synthetic if I was brushing a show horse. Carlotta—Veronica's mother—had a show horse and wanted me to use one of her own hairbrushes when I groomed him. Eventually I convinced her that synthetic was best, especially right before her competitions."

Tomás wasn't exactly sure if he had understood what Señor del Valle had just told him. "Wait. You used to work in a stable?"

He set down the brush he'd been holding. "Yes, when I was a teenager. It was my first job."

"You were a stable boy when you met Veronica's mother?"

"Sí. I was her stable boy. Well, her family's."

The realization swept over him in a wave of surprise. Señor del Valle's reputation as one of Mexico's most successful businessmen had never included such humble beginnings.

"I had no idea," Tomás said.

"It's not something I talk about that much anymore," he said. "Not because I'm ashamed. But because it's painful to think about now. It just makes me miss Carlotta even more."

"Is that when you two started dating?" Tomas knew he had no right to ask the question. He wouldn't be surprised if Veronica's father told him exactly that.

Instead, a wistful smile spread across the older man's face. "I was seventeen and she was sixteen. It took me almost a year to work up the courage to ask her out on a date."

Tomás couldn't imagine the towering and intimidating man in front of him being afraid of anything. "Why?"

"Because she was Carlotta Bermudez. Her family owned almost every business in our village. To me, she might as well have been a princess. And I was a nobody."

"So what made you decide to finally tell her how you felt?" Tomás didn't care anymore about what he should or shouldn't ask. His curiosity was too strong for him to worry about coming off as nosy.

"I guess I just got tired of talking to the horses. I thought she would never go out with me because I was a stable boy. But eventually I realized if she could see me outside of the stable, then I would just be a boy. A boy she might even like. So I asked, and the rest, as they say, is history."

Tomás tried to tamp down the roil of emotion swirling around his gut. This was not a conversation he was prepared to have with Veronica's father. He didn't trust himself to speak, so he didn't.

"Carlotta once told me that she used to think I preferred horses over people. That was one of the reasons she was afraid to show her true feelings for me. It turned out she'd had a crush on me for almost as long as I'd had one on her. Sometimes I still kick myself for not being man enough to say something earlier. I could've had almost another year with her."

Touched by the regret he saw on Señor del Valle's face, Tomás finally spoke up. "Veronica showed me a photo of your wife. She was very beautiful."

"She was," he said, his eyes shining with deep emotion. "She was also very kindhearted and smart. In fact, I only asked her out after she made a particular comment to me. It was her way, I guess, of letting me know she had been waiting for me to finally speak up."

"What did she say?"

"She had asked me if I was planning to see the new movie that had just come out at the theater and I told her I didn't think so because I had to work. She told me I worked too much and I told her that the horses needed me. That's when she said, 'Relationships with people are just as important, especially with the ones you love.' "

Tomás laughed. "She said that?"

"She did and then she walked away. It only took me about two minutes to realize what she was really saying. I ran after her and asked her if I could take her to go see the movie."

He nodded and grinned, but his smile faltered when he realized Señor del Valle wasn't. "I'm so sorry you lost her," Tomás said. "It sounds like you two were very much in love."

The older man cleared his throat. "We were. But as hard as it's been to live without her, I would do it all over again. Besides, I still can hear her in my ear sometimes. Especially when I've been such a fool."

"How do you mean?"

The older man looked at the ground. "I should've never come here. I should've trusted Veronica more. I've spent so many years trying to protect her that sometimes I forget she's not a little girl anymore."

"You only want what's best for her," he said. He could see now that Señor del Valle only had good intentions when it came to his daughter and her career.

"Yes, I do. But I also have to trust that she knows what's best for herself," he said. "I wish she would've shared with me that you were helping her."

Tomás shrugged. "Maybe she didn't think it was that important."

"Tomás, she didn't fail to tell me that you were training her because you weren't important to her. She failed to tell me because you *were* that important to her."

Tomás couldn't help but be shocked. "I . . . I . . ." He couldn't get the words out.

Señor del Valle shrugged. "It's obvious that my daughter is in love with you, young man. And the fact that you sent her away because you didn't want to stand in the way of her dream tells me that you're in love with her, too."

He opened his mouth to argue or protest. But he knew that Señor del Valle was a smart man—just like he'd described to Tomás. He would see right through Tomás's feeble attempt to hide his feelings.

So he admitted his feelings for the first time out loud.

"I love her very much, Señor del Valle."

"Then go after her, Tomás. Take Carlotta's advice."

He hesitated. "I don't want to be a distraction. I don't want to be the reason she doesn't get everything she's ever wanted."

"But what if what she wants is you?"

Chapter Thirty-Three

Athletes and their rituals.

Some baseball players wore the same smelly socks every day of a tournament. Some hockey players refused to cut their beards in the middle of playoffs.

Veronica's ritual the day before a competition was to get pampered.

Manicure, pedicure, massage, and stone facial. All of them helped to release her stress and clear her mind if only for a couple of hours.

But by the time she arrived back in her hotel room, Veronica could feel the balls of anxiety start to tighten her muscles all over again. So, when her dad texted that he'd just checked into the room next to hers, she nearly convulsed into an anxiety-ridden pretzel.

She knew better than to think his unanswered texts and missed phone calls would be enough to keep him away. Her sister Valeria had even tried to convince Veronica to reach out.

"He's really sorry, Vero. I've never seen him like this," Val had told her just the night before.

Guilt had kept her up most of the night. Her dad

had crossed a line, but she knew some of her anger was misdirected. After all, Tomás didn't have to listen to him. He could've told Veronica that no matter what her dad had said, he wanted to be with her.

She had found out from Valeria that their dad had stayed in her cottage at Rancho Lindo for a few days after she'd left. They couldn't come up with one logical reason why. Part of her had wanted to text Nora to ask. But then she knew she'd also want to ask about Tomás. And she wasn't ready to know.

A few minutes after the text from her dad, there was a knock on her door.

She considered ignoring him and whatever attempt at an apology he was going to give her. But it was exhausting being angry all the time. She couldn't waste energy on this anymore.

Veronica opened the door, but it wasn't her dad standing there.

For the millionth time in the past three months, Tomás Ortega had surprised her.

What was he thinking, showing up the day before she was going to compete?

She folded her arms over her chest. "What are you doing here?"

The tightness in her throat warned her that tears were on their way. She didn't want to cry in front of Tomás. It would show him what a freaking emotional wreck she'd been the last few days, trying to forget the way he'd touched her or made her feel like she could do anything she ever wanted because he was at her side. It was the day of that horrible video all over again.

Veronica decided she couldn't let him know that she'd fallen for him during all of their pretending. But she knew it would be that much more difficult to pretend she didn't care.

So she needed to put an end to whatever it was he was doing by showing up here.

"You should leave," she told him.

Tomás nodded. "I will. But just give me five minutes."

Chapter Thirty-Four

I almost didn't come," he admitted. "It took me a good hour to even let your dad text you that we'd arrived."

"*We?*" she said, her eyes wide with surprise.

"Yeah. He's the one who brought me. He says to tell you that I'm his apology."

If someone would've told Tomás that he'd get on a private plane with Veronica's dad so he could confess his love, he would've laughed in that person's face.

Señor del Valle, or Enrique, had apparently somehow become one of Tomás's biggest fans. Once they mended fences, the older man had asked if he could stay in the same cottage as Veronica until it was time for him to travel to Kentucky. He'd wanted to observe Tomás working with the horses on the ranch. Apparently, it only took three days to convince Enrique that Tomás had a gift. And it only took one more day to convince Tomás to come to Kentucky and try to win Veronica back.

"Since when are you and my dad buddies?"

Tomás held up his hand. "Whoa. I wouldn't go that far. But I think we do understand each other more. It was his idea for me to come. And he eventually talked me into it."

"Why did he have to convince you?" she asked softly. She dipped her chin and then she lowered her eyes. "Because you didn't want to see me again?"

"No. God, no."

Tomás stepped closer. "Tomorrow is a big day for you. I didn't want to distract you." When she looked up again, he made sure to meet her eyes so she could see he was being genuine. "I still don't."

Veronica held his gaze for a few seconds but then looked away. His stomach fell as he recognized the hurt in her expression.

"Then why are you here? You're the one who told me to leave. Why come all this way to see me now?"

He let out a long sigh. She had every reason to be so confused. Hell, he'd been confused too. That's why he hadn't begged her to stay.

"I shouldn't have said that. I was stupid. I was scared."

"Scared of what?"

"Scared of the feelings I had for you. I had forgotten what romantic love felt like. Part of me thought it would be easier if I was the one who told you to leave instead of hearing you tell me that you were leaving. Or worse, telling me months or a year from now that you couldn't see a future with me."

Like Mia had.

He knew now that was the reason he'd been holding back. He had been afraid of accepting his feelings for Veronica because he'd been afraid of getting hurt again. Because he knew what he felt for her was different from anything he'd ever felt for Mia. He hadn't been able to trust that a future on Rancho Lindo would ever be enough for Veronica.

He couldn't trust that he would be enough.

But he would never know unless he asked the question.

When she didn't say anything, Tomás continued talking. "But your dad helped me realize that I would be missing out on something amazing if I continued hiding away in the stable."

She raised her eyebrows. "My dad?"

"He told me the story about how he had been afraid to ask your mom out because he was only a stable boy when they met," he said.

Veronica smiled. "And she was afraid to tell him that she liked him because she thought he hated her."

"But then one day he decided to be bold."

"And she decided to be brave."

"So he asked her to go to the movies with him and she said . . ."

"Yes," Veronica said with a breath. "Why did you push me away, Tomás?"

"Because I was scared—again," he said, his voice thick with emotion. "I'd never felt so alive or free or satisfied and it terrified me to think it hadn't been real. But when you left, that made me realize that there's only one thing in this world to be afraid of now."

"And what's that?" she asked in a small, unsteady voice.

He moved closer and finally cupped her face with his hands. "A life where you don't wake up in my arms every day. I love you, Veronica."

"How can I trust what you're saying?" she asked, her eyes wet and sad. "You hurt me."

"I know I did and I promise I'm going to spend the rest of my life making it up to you. Starting now." He rubbed the tear away with his thumb and then leaned down for a kiss. He hesitated, though, until she nodded and gave him permission to find her lips.

Tomás closed the distance between them and wrapped his hand around the back of her neck to bring her lips to his. When he did, she melted against him.

His hands still cradled her face, letting him control the tempo of the kiss while their tongues did their own tango, tasting each other back and forth. Any doubt, hurt, or hesitation fell away.

"Te amo. Te amo. Te amo," he whispered against her temple.

"I love you, Tomás," she replied.

Their lips met again.

After a few seconds, he reluctantly pulled away. "As much as I would love to take you to the bedroom right now, I promised your dad we'd go hang out at the pool."

She playfully punched his arm. "I don't know if I can handle this bromance. Fine, but only because I have to get ready for this dumb party later tonight for the riders and their trainers. How about we pick this up when I get back? Do you promise to stay here?"

"I can't."

Veronica stilled. "What? You're going back to Esperanza now?"

He chuckled. "Oh no, ma'am. I'm going to this dumb party later tonight for the riders and their trainers." The look on her face was priceless.

"Wait. Does this mean—"

He couldn't stop grinning even if he tried. "Your

dad made some calls, filled out some forms, and voilà. I'm officially your trainer here at the competition. I get a little badge and everything."

Veronica jumped into his arms. "I can't believe this," she whispered, her voice cracking.

"Believe it. I'm going to be there at every one of your competitions. Starting tomorrow. If I'm not your trainer, then I'll just be your boyfriend cheering you on from the stands."

"Even it's in another state or another country?"

"Por supuesto. If you're riding, then I'm cheering. In fact, I already started saving up for a trip to the Olympics."

"And what happens if I don't qualify?"

"Of course you're going to qualify. But if for some reason you don't, then we'll just watch it on TV and you can tell me all the gossip about the riders."

"Sounds like a plan," she whispered before sealing their promise with a kiss.

U

Tomás finally remembered to breathe.

He exhaled and clasped his hands over his head. "I don't know how you two are able to stay so calm," Tomás said. "My heart feels like it's about to explode. That's how freaking nervous I am."

Veronica and her father looked at each other and chuckled.

"Believe me, we're just as nervous as you are," Veronica whispered after leaning closer to him. "But we've had years of experience of learning how to hide it. Especially when there are tons of cameras watching."

The three of them stood close to Takuache as they awaited the last rider's final scores. According to Señor del Valle, Veronica's shot at the Olympics was going to be determined in these last few seconds. If her total score was higher than the last rider's, then she was in.

Tomás dropped his hands and tried to look more relaxed. Takuache took a couple of steps toward him and snorted. Even the horse was telling him to calm down.

"They're coming," Señor del Valle yelled and pointed to the large monitor hanging near the judges' tables.

Random numbers flashed on the screen. First the technical scores. Tomás had no idea what he was looking at, but he did know that the rider had received at least one score higher than Veronica. Within seconds, the screen changed and the artistic scores flashed.

Señor del Valle chanted, "Eso! Eso! Eso!"

Veronica gasped and brought her hands to cover her face. She was shaking and he immediately enveloped her with his arms.

"Does this mean—" he asked.

She nodded and looked up at him with a tear-streaked but smiling face. "It means I'm going to the Olympics."

Tomás hugged her hard as he fought back tears of his own. His throat tightened with all sorts of emotion: pride, joy, relief. But mostly love. So much love.

He pulled away to meet her eyes. "You did it," he said.

"We did it," she told him.

With a full heart, he leaned down, eager to taste her

again. But before finding her mouth, he looked around and noticed they were quickly being surrounded by members of the media.

"The cameras..." he whispered, just inches away from her face. "This could go viral, you know."

"It could," she whispered back and shrugged. "But I don't care."

He smiled before lowering his head closer and then pressed his lips against hers. They kissed, long and deep. Tomás's hands slid down her back and he moved to pull her tighter against him. He couldn't get enough and he told her that.

The sounds of the crowd and the clicking of the cameras eventually drifted away. It was just Veronica and him. Tomás knew in that moment that he would do whatever it took to always be this close to her.

Because he wasn't afraid anymore to let Veronica know what she meant to him. He trusted her. He felt safe with her.

His heart had finally been healed.

Acknowledgments

I hope you enjoyed reading *The Cowboy Whisperer*.

Like I mentioned in the dedication, this book is about trying again after not succeeding in something the first time. Whether it's pursuing a dream or risking it all for love, it takes courage, fortitude, and true determination to not give up.

And it also helps when you have a team of people cheering you on from the sidelines.

So now I want to thank all the special people who make up my team.

First, a huge thank-you to my agent, Sarah Younger. The Cowboys of Rancho Lindo would not exist if it weren't for her belief and trust in me that I could write books about a family of Mexican-American cowboys.

Next, I want to thank my editor, Junessa Viloria. Not just for her expertise and guidance, but also for her patience and kindness. And special thanks to everyone at Forever for their hard work and support.

In case you didn't already know, it's easy to doubt yourself when you're writing a book. And it doesn't matter how many times you've done it before. Every word can be a struggle. So when that happens, it's good to have a group of people you can turn to for encouragement, advice, and inspiration. I'm so lucky to have author friends who know exactly what I need and when I need it. Thank you to Marie, Nikki, Alexis, Natalie, Adriana, Zoraida, Liana, Angelina, Diana, Priscilla, and Mia.

Finally, I want to say a special thank-you to my biggest fans and my biggest supporters—my family. I love you all.

About the Author

Sabrina Sol is the chica who loves love. She writes sexy romance stories featuring strong and smart Latina heroines in search of their Happily Ever Afters. Sabrina and her books have been featured in *Entertainment Weekly*, *Book Riot*, and *POPSUGAR*, and her Delicious Desires series has made The Latina Book Club's annual Books of the Year lists. Sabrina's common themes of food, family, and love are woven into intricate plots that all connect for a powerful read that lingers in the hearts of readers. She is proud of her Mexican American heritage, culture, and traditions—all of which can be found within the pages of her books. Sabrina is a native of Southern California, where she currently lives with her husband, three children, and four dogs.

You can learn more at:
SabrinaSol.com
Twitter @TheRomanceChica
Facebook.com/TheRomanceChica
Instagram @Sabrina_TheRomanceChica
TikTok @Sabrina_TheRomanceChica

all day. I think you both will have time to cook with Abuelita."

When the conversation changed, Veronica had leaned over to apologize for dragging him into the cooking lesson. But he'd just smiled and said, "It's fine. Just be ready. Because Abuelita does not play when it comes to her cooking."

Despite his best attempts to tease her, Veronica was determined to learn a few things from Doña Alma. She enjoyed cooking for herself and for her sister and her dad when she could. But it was true that it had been a long time since they'd had a family meal. Her father's business kept him out of the country most weeks and when he was home, he was always on the phone or in Zoom meetings. Their cook handled most of their meals, especially since her dad ate at random times. And Valeria preferred eating out with her friends. That meant Veronica was eating lunches and dinners mostly on her own. It was the reason she'd jumped at Tomás's suggestion for her to join his family for their dinners.

She was enjoying being a part of their animated conversations. She was definitely going to miss these times.

Veronica shook off the wave of unexpected sadness and concentrated on washing her hands.

"Your abuelita is not that bad," she told Tomás as she watched him take his turn at the sink.

He shrugged without looking at her. "The fact that she wanted to teach you how to make the soup means she likes you—but that doesn't mean she's not going to be a drill sergeant and tell you everything you're doing wrong."

Veronica leaned her body over to bump his side. "Thanks for making me nervous now."

Tomás bent his head down and moved his lips close to her ear. "Don't worry. I'll protect you."

His warm breath tickled her skin and his words ignited waves of desire deep in her belly. He'd whispered them so Veronica knew it hadn't been for Doña Alma's benefit. Tomás had meant what he'd said, and that thrilled her in ways she hadn't felt in a very long time.

For the next half hour, she did her best to dismiss her feelings about Tomás and concentrate on Doña Alma's instructions.

While Tomás cleaned and chopped a variety of herbs and vegetables like carrots, chayote, zucchini, potatoes, and cabbage, Veronica was responsible for making the meatballs. Doña Alma told her to start mixing the ground meat in a large mixing bowl with different spices and uncooked rice.

"When they are mixed very good, add the eggs. That will make sure the bollitos don't break apart once they're cooking in the broth."

"Do you have food prep gloves?" Veronica asked, raising her bare hands over the bowl.

Doña Alma scoffed. "Que gloves? Use los manos. You have to be able to feel the meat so you know if you need to add more egg."

She nodded in understanding and grabbed a handful of meat and began forming little balls. After a few tries, Doña Alma finally approved the correct size and gave Veronica permission to continue.

"Is this pork or beef?" she asked as she placed her next meatball onto a nearby tray covered with parchment paper.